THE UNMADE BED

THE UNMADE BED

Françoise Sagan

*Translated from the French
by Abigail Israel*

A STAR BOOK
published by
the Paperback Division of
W. H. ALLEN & CO. PLC

A Star Book
Published in 1985
by the Paperback Division of
W. H. Allen & Co. PLC
44 Hill Street, London W1X 8LB

First published in France by
Libraire Ernest Flammarion, Paris
under the title *Le Lit Défait* 1977

First published in the United Kingdom by
Aidan Ellis Publishing Ltd 1978

Copyright © Flammarion 1977
English translation copyright ©
Aidan Ellis/Dell Publishing Co., Inc. 1978

Printed and bound in Great Britain by
Anchor Brendon Ltd, Tiptree, Essex

ISBN 0 352 31690 X

To Isabelle Held

'Face aux rideaux apprêtés
Le lit défait vivant et nu
Redoutable oriflamme
Son vol tranchant
Eteint les jours franchit les nuits
Redoutable oriflamme
Contrée presque déserte
Presque
Car taillée de toutes pièces pour le sommeil et l'amour
Tu es debout auprès du lit'

PAUL ÉLUARD

I

'It's funny,' Béatrice's voice was saying – higher up, much higher up on the bed than he was, it seemed to him – 'it's funny that you still remember me after five years ...'

He said nothing. He listened to his heart beating, tried to regain the breath sucked out of him by their lovemaking and rubbed the sweat from his forehead against that thigh at once so familiar and long-lost. There was nothing to say except that, thanks to her rejection, he had been out of step with himself for the past five years, out of step with both body and soul, had wandered like a vagabond, at the same time unconscious and conscious of what had befallen him. No, there was nothing to say except that, only now, his head abandoned to her shoulder, did he recognize where he belonged.

Béatrice was intrigued by his silence. Several years before, she had met the young man in question, then an insurance broker, at the home of mutual friends. At the time, he'd struck her as pathetic more than anything else but, since he'd reminded her of a young goat, she'd admitted him to her stable for six months; had even made him her favourite. He was charming and tender, with brown hair and eyes but, she'd thought, a little bland. Whereas she, Béatrice, knew how dark she was, and beautiful, with high cheekbones, full lips, and (as both critics and lovers repeatedly pointed out) a manner at once savage and vulnerable. Béatrice had made a brilliant career for herself in films as well as in the theatre – a theatre considered light and facile but which hadn't been so light and facile at the time. And now it seemed that the young Édouard, the lost kid with the long, too long, legs, was well on his way to becoming one of the better playwrights of the 'other theatre', the one known as esoteric. The distinction, of course, was only the hair-splitting of intellectual snobs. People either laughed, cried, or were bored by the same shows, and (government subsidies apart) only success – in other words, money – assured the survival of the thespians in both tents.

Three years earlier, Édouard Maligrasse, long since abandoned by the Béatrice who had loved him when he was unknown, had dared to venture a small and, in his opinion, insignificant offering. For her, actually. Strangely this small offering, considered ingenious by the boyfriend of a girl friend, had then been performed in public and immediately discovered by ten serious and nine hundred society critics. And although he had finally understood that Paris might yet in a certain way belong to him, Édouard, the son of retired parents, the sad, lost, and lovelorn young man, still had never dreamed that there might one day be a correlation between this stroke of luck, literary and Parisian, and the recovery of the object of his love, warmth, sensuality – in short, of all he had stood to gain or lose since his arrival in Paris, namely, Béatrice.

They lay stretched out in the darkness, his body angled across hers as if in readiness for some sort of crucifixion. Through Béatrice's dark hair, he gazed at the beige rug and the mauve tulips now awake and trembling on the windowsill. Five years ago, he had watched these same tulips and this same window, it seemed to him, and this same dusky-rose skin in the foreground, and he had felt at the time, or rather believed he had felt, an imperishable happiness. He had never stopped dreaming of it since, but it was only now that he became fully aware of it, the moment this woman uttered those words, words so falsely modest and as if suspended in the blackness : 'It's funny that you still remember me after five years ...' Now she was tugging at his hair, laughing softly; and furious, he half missed what she'd said but understood that it called for a reply. And already he wanted to, had to, keep quiet, and forced himself to do so.

And what have I done during these five years? he asked himself, his head still buried in her naked shoulder. *What have I done besides try to forget her in becoming a celebrity, as they say, putting up with polite conversations and the asinine inter-*

views of slick superficial journalists, dreaming about what I'd written and what I wanted to write and what I could perhaps write? What have I done, except want to return here? Five years spent trying to forget her like some romantic hero out of de Musset and, as a crowning absurdity, I didn't even know it was she – my tormentor, my spouse, my sister – she alone that I wanted to forget.

Then, since she went on tugging at his hair and worrying in a mocking tone over his sudden lapse of consciousness, he too began to laugh, raised his head, placed his lips at the corner of hers and, smiling, said off-handedly – or at least in a voice he meant to sound off-handed – that he had never stopped loving her but that just the same he'd like a drink. She got up immediately and went off towards the pantry. And he, who had only the vaguest notion about himself and his true nature, to say nothing of his future, suddenly felt himself the object of some inexorable destiny. The feeling was as obvious as it was baroque, and was confirmed by the voice of Béatrice herself who had returned to the bedroom with two glasses.

'I'd forgotten,' she said, 'I'd forgotten you made love so well.'

He was already raising his head to answer: 'That's because you didn't love me then,' but thinking better of it, sank back into the unmade bed and pronounced clearly, over the protests of his heart:

'I've learned since then ... What did you expect?'

2

The following day, he offered to take her out for lunch, remembering only too well, almost with masochism in fact, her
appetite for self-display, the same appetite, he thought, that had
prompted her to replace him five years before with a more pre-
sentable lover. He himself was, by nature, altogether indifferent
to gossip, echoes, rumours, in short to all the damp fireworks
of success. But that morning, knowing she cared about such
things, he'd decided to hide her desires in the guise of his own
initiatives. And already fearing, above all, that he would find
himself alone once again – in the street, on a bed, no matter
where – alone, deprived of her scent and the sound of her
voice, he would willingly have summoned, had she expressed
even the slightest wish, all the regulars in every fashionable bar
and restaurant to an official luncheon celebrating their reunion.
The rhythm of his heartbeat and the trembling of his hands
made him realize to what extent he had been deprived of
blood, oxygen, and nerves these past five years. Yet he made
no attempt to understand why he had been so in love with
this woman nor how he had ever hoped to forget her, nor even
why he was remembering it all so violently now. He bowed before her as before the Holy Sacrament. He no longer guided his
footsteps but resigned himself to following where they led.

To his great surprise, Béatrice refused the lunch. She preferred, she said, to stay alone with him, and ordered sandwiches, white wine, fruit, and coffee to be brought to their
room. With a kind of hostile playfulness, she drew cabbalis-
tic signs on his chest; she touched his neck, his shoulder, his
foot, his groin. She seemed to be retaking possession of something that had always belonged to her without her knowing it,
and for a moment he wondered if she too might not be a victim

of the same phenomenon, if that same theatrical impression of possession and fatality hadn't struck her as much as him. But he had lived in Paris for a long time, knew its rhythms and detours to be far more everyday than Stendhalian, and so he declined to ask her. At the same time, he smothered another secret voice, the same sinister and jealous voice of five years ago that stubbornly asked why she didn't want to be seen with him, why she didn't want to show him off triumphantly in that particular restaurant where every lunch was a public confession and where he, Édouard, would make a very suitable accomplice. Did she still want to hide him? Yet he knew the secrecy that might have existed between them during her ascendancy was no longer necessary: he was known, she was known, they had the right to share an order of Baltic herring at two in the afternoon in that artificially homely *brasserie* where such an act was tantamount to declaring: 'We've just got out of bed, we pleased each other, now we're hungry.'

'Are you ashamed of me?' he said.

She looked at him, caressed his hair as if she were currying him, felt the texture of his skin, smiled as she watched him, ironic, pensive, and tender – intelligent perhaps? In any case, she looked as he had dreamed of her during those long years when she'd left him and when he had, or so he'd believed, forgotten her.

'*Ashamed* of you?' she replied. 'No. You're handsome, you know. But why do you want to go out? All that daylight and sunshine annoy me.'

She swooped down on him, sought the vein in his neck.

'Right now, I'm going to brand you, my little boy,' she declared. Coldly, albeit with a hint of savagery. 'You're going to be stamped in indelible ink, right there, for two weeks, and your women won't be able to do anything about it.'

She sank her teeth into him, sucked the blood from his throat, his own private vampire.

'Do you really want to be alone with me?' he asked, tangled up in his ideas, in his memories, and in the sheets, which had wrapped themselves around both of them and now seemed to billow as if lifted by the wind.

She did not answer and indeed, there seemed to be no questions left to ask.

At four o'clock they were seated at a table in the *brasserie*, pale, dishevelled, and triumphant. To the regulars, the shadows under their eyes would have been so many honours and laurels. At four o'clock, with languid gestures and too-clear eyes, they exchanged herring, potatoes, and vows. All of it perishable, of course, but none the less remarked upon, watched over, and duly noted by those indefatigable voyeurs, those ferrets, those arbiters of good and evil, sometimes called the *Tout-Paris*, sometimes dear friends – in short, the others. One of them was doubtless saying: 'Yes, yes, don't you remember, five years ago, they had a fling together ...' And the other replying, indignant: 'Really, it's incredible; after all, she's never done anything more than light comedy, but his work, now that's really something else, isn't it?' And the first concluding: 'Yes, well I've got nothing against experimental theatre, but she's disgustingly gorgeous, isn't she?' And all those delighted and curious looks seemed so many hostile or friendly stagelights sweeping over them, bringing them together and separating them in a kind of perpetual unreal film.

'You don't eat enough, Édouard,' Béatrice was saying. 'Do you love me?'

And he, listlessly helping himself to potatoes he had no desire for: 'I love you, I've never loved anyone but you. On the other hand, I don't think I give a damn about this herring.'

Whereupon, sovereign, she raised her hand and the *maître d'hôtel*, who had been their accomplice from the instant he'd seen them come in, hurried over and the herring vanished. And so, behind the glassed-in terrace at four in the afternoon, in broad daylight – broad shadow, actually, although one could sense the sun shining busily outside – they ordered two strong drinks like the Fitzgerald characters which – fatigue, desire, and alcohol contributing – they felt themselves becoming. And no one could see or hear them any more, for that day Édouard and Béatrice were together at the very peak of happiness.

For years and years, Béatrice had kept a diary. It was a red leather notebook with vellum paper and a vague sort of 1930s lock that didn't work. She had acquired the habit – deliciously childish and old-fashioned, she thought – of hiding it among her nightgowns. Having left Édouard that day with her customary abruptness, she took up her pen and wrote the following sentences:

'Found Édouard again. Still as charming as ever. Still that starved look that made me fall in love with him? years ago.' (Here she stopped, the question mark more plaintive than cynical. Given her inability to remember with any precision her all-too-numerous lovers, Béatrice had begun to deplore her lack of what she amiably referred to as a memory for dates. A faculty which would in any case have led if not to remorse, then at least to total confusion.)

'His talent apart,' she continued, 'one feels in him such a need for warmth, there's such a yearning in his gold-brown eyes' – the hyphen placed with great care and delectation – 'that I've decided to make a clean break, to wipe out everything of my life before now. Tomorrow I'll break off with B ...' (The ellipsis, however, would have held no mystery for anyone, as the whole of Paris knew she was having an affair with the producer Bruno Kane.) 'And then I'll tell Édouard I'm his.'

Having thus concluded this virtuoso performance of punctuation and bad faith – its last sentence seeming to her definitive, at least for the moment – Béatrice closed the notebook with the gothic key and put it back among her nightgowns. (Like so many highly sensual libertines, she felt she was exonerated by the mere fact of announcing or writing down her decisions, no matter how cruel they might be.) Then she combed her hair, redid her face, and settled herself, knees pulled up modestly under her chin, on a garnet-red *chaise longue* obviously conceived for such a posture. She tried to find a book that would seduce Édouard when he walked in. (Béatrice was no illiterate. She'd read a great deal, and thus hesitated a long time over her choice.) A detective story risks making her frivolous, a Proust pretentious, a Valéry, she thought, mysterious. She chose the last.

During this time, Édouard wandered around Paris like a madman, asking himself every other second whether he had a chance, a small chance, any chance at all, of seeing Béatrice again. She had left him so abruptly in front of the *Brasserie Lipp* ... He bought flowers, records, books, all the things he loved, and all of it for her, with the frail hope that her *concierge* wouldn't kick him out into the street with all his presents. He was mad, he was weak, and he'd been rash; he ought to have felt his way forward gingerly, he ought to have said: 'When can we see each other again? And where?' There was no reason to assume they had any specific plans just because Béatrice had said 'I love you'. He really ought to have remembered that, even when someone says I love you, that person is only referring to the immediate moment of his desire – *his* desire, never yours. And given the enormity and the permanence of his, Édouard's, love, any rendezvous would only be a delay, any date an affront.

Admittedly, he had spent the night in her arms and she had convinced him of her love, and admittedly he could always telephone. But she'd gone off so quickly after lunch and had said good-bye so gaily that now he didn't know what to think. He mistrusted his senses, his memory, his luck; in short, he wasn't sure of anything about himself. In his bewilderment, he collided with several strangers who must have taken him for a maniac, one of those who thinks it's Christmas in September, which was precisely the case. And so, resigned to the worst, he finally arrived at her block of flats.

It was already seven o'clock and, out of sheer boredom, Béatrice had begun to doubt her famous power of seduction. Nothing had happened since her casual good-bye in front of the restaurant: not a telephone call, not a flower, not a single sign. So she began to hate herself again for, oddly enough, when things didn't go as she wanted, Béatrice thought no more of protest than of introspection. She simply hated herself, as she hated failure of any kind. But then, suddenly, the doorbell rang, she heard the garbled explanations of Guillaume, the *concierge* who doubled as valet-cook, in the entrance, but strangely, not even for an instant did she sense it might be Édouard. And when she saw him standing before her, his arms overflowing with packages and flowers in spite of Guillaume's help, when she saw both men, each as awe-struck as the other, as terrified, apparently, by her sheer presence, Nefertiti, Queen of the Realm, she felt a veritable surge of love for Édouard. He'd come back, he was hers, he justified her entire existence, he was the answer to the great question: 'Do I please?', that awful question which had haunted her since childhood. In fact, there must have been such an expression of relief on her face that for once, Édouard the distracted, the dreamer, noticed. He dropped his packages, took her in his arms and – as Guillaume slipped out with a long-practiced alacrity – said with exaggerated self-assurance, given the hell he'd just been through: 'So you missed me, did you?'

He wasn't surprised when she nodded or when, lifting her head, she kissed him slowly at the corner of the mouth, or when she opened first his coat, then his jacket, or when still not looking at him, she unfastened his belt. They were both still standing in the brightly lit hallway, perhaps even observed. But apparently she didn't care and he, feeling the blood coursing once again through his veins, forced himself not to move. The corner of his mouth still against her lips, he told himself, reminded himself, that love was a thing sublime. Now she slipped her hand between his shirt and his skin, his, Édouard's, the unloved, she was coming to him; and there, in this absurdly bright hallway, she pressed him to her, sighing, repeating his name 'Édouard, Édouard,' in an odd little voice. His lips hurt now, he was breathing rapidly, he told himself it was mad, all this, extravagant, that the blue bedroom was only two steps away. So what were they doing there, tangled up in their clothes, staggering back and forth in each other's arms like two exhausted wrestlers? In some obscure way, however, he sensed she was right, that they didn't have time for steps and that the imploring hand at his back, like the exacting one urging him on in front, contained as much wisdom as it did madness and maniacal precision. Moving his head slightly to one side, he ran full tilt into her lips and immediately stopped struggling, drew aside her scarlet bathrobe, not in the least astonished to find her naked, waiting for him, whereas an hour earlier he would have committed suicide for what was now being offered to him. And so, bracing himself against the nearest wall, between two heedless green plants, he took her; her mouth opened under his; she pulled the demanding hand away and tried to link hands behind him, began beating him gently about the ribs, nibbled at his face, mumbled incomprehensible sounds. Then — but here he was so happy, so close to the edge, that he had to clench his fists against the wall so tightly that it hurt — she pulled herself up against him and began groaning softly, while her two hands settled definitively against his now rigid back. And her voice (now lower, foreign, superb) ordered 'Come' in such a tone that he immediately abandoned himself to her while she sank her teeth into the lapel of his jacket in an ultimate and belated effort at decorum.

She was rigid against him now. They remained standing, haggard and exhausted, their eyes open under the pale lights of the chandelier, so pale after their pleasure and the dazzling short-circuits exploding under their eyelids. Then slowly, without looking at him, Béatrice pulled away, kissed him on the mouth, pensively it seemed, and he let her, immobile, drenched with sweat, with fear, with happiness, who knows?

'What's in those parcels?' she asked.

He raised his head and looked at her. She loved him, he could feel it, that very moment she loved him and whatever happened afterwards, now at least she loved him.

'I don't know,' he said. 'Presents for you.'

'I don't want presents from you,' she said softly. 'It's you I want, just you.'

She walked away. He remained in the hall a moment, then guided by the light, made his way to the blue bedroom and the tulips. Béatrice lay across the bed, a hand against her lips. He looked at her, then lay down on top of her. And at that moment, when she began to call to him, then to beg him, then to insult him, he knew he would never get over her, that, in short, he was made for fidelity.

3

'It's incredible!' declared Tony d'Albret (born Marcelle Lagnon, in the town of Provins) in her loud brassy voice. 'Only you could get away with something like that . . .'

There was a hint of admiration mixed with the reproach that thrilled Béatrice. She had been one of Tony's clients for seven years and, together with a dozen other actors, had every reason to congratulate herself on her agent. Short, compact, and cunning (she referred to herself with satisfaction as quick-silver), Tony d'Albret combined the soul of a slave with an avidity, a keen nose for business, and an unscrupulousness that made her one of the best agents in Paris. Depending on their threshold of sensitivity, people who knew her spoke of her as either a tonic or a terror, but all of them recognized that it was better to have this particular public menace on their side. Tony, of course, adored this definition of herself.

'I haven't heard from you all week,' she went on. 'What have you been indulging in all this time? Besides romance, that is,' she added with a short gurgle of laughter meant to sound conspiratorial.

Besides being an agent, Tony also played the rôle of friend and confidante; that is to say, mother. In fact, for these unfortunate children-turned-actors, she played all conceivable parts. She also wagered on everything: on their greed, their courage, their vanity, and their vices, if they had any. There was no terrain on which she didn't try to win. And if she was a guide in every sense of the word, she none the less always made sure her hold was well secured before making her next move.

A victim, yet not really a dupe, Béatrice watched her through her long eyelashes. True to form, Tony was badly dressed and too obviously made-up, and as usual, Béatrice, who had no idea that this was deliberate, felt both condescension and amusement.

'Apart from romance, I've done nothing else whatsoever,' she confessed.

'And might one ask with whom?'

Tony's impatience was feigned. Ten witnesses had seen Béatrice lunching *tête-à-tête* with the young playwright Édouard Maligrasse, but no one had heard anything further of them for the past week. Tony had done some investigating on her own, however, and was sure of her information.

'You don't know him,' Béatrice replied dreamily.

Really, she must think I was born yesterday, Tony thought. Édouard's second play was being performed at that very moment in Paris; in fact, both of his plays had been very successful. Admittedly they were intellectual theatre, the kind that bored everyone who wasn't a snob, and certainly simple straightforward people like herself. But they had had great critical success none the less, and Édouard's face had appeared on the pages of at least a dozen magazines. Tony was more than willing to go on asking questions out of politeness, but she didn't want to be taken for a fool either.

'You probably know his name, of course,' Béatrice said, still dreamily. 'But you don't know *him*. Nobody knows him. Nobody *really* knows him, I mean.'

Terrific, she thinks she's in love again, Tony thought. She was used to Béatrice's passing fancies, knowing she cultivated two kinds in particular: the first, utterly classical and without sentiment, and the second – much more trying to her entourage, but a lot rarer, thank God – with sentiment. She sighed, then for once voiced a sincere opinion.

'He's got talent, certainly, but it's not really our sort of theatre, is it?'

'Don't confuse the issue,' Béatrice said severely.

With her back to the morning light, Béatrice really was extremely pretty, Tony had to admit. She certainly didn't look the thirty-five years she readily confessed to being.

'May I remind you that you leave on tour in a week, my dear,' she said.

Béatrice nodded, this time with genuine melancholy.

'He's going to take that very badly,' she replied. 'He's very sensitive.'

A joyful and virile voice singing an old opera tune came from the direction of the bathroom. The door flew open suddenly and the sensitive man in question appeared in a bathrobe, his hair uncombed, and, or so it seemed to Tony, extremely young. He stopped short and started to excuse himself. With a languid expression on her face, as if this were the most classical of situations, Béatrice introduced him.

'Édouard Maligrasse,' she said, 'Tony d'Albret, my guardian angel and pimp.'

She burst out laughing while the two shook hands and Édouard blushed. Tony, on the other hand, was visibly delighted.

'Tony's come to remind me cruelly that I have to go on tour in a few days,' she went on.

For the past week – a flamboyant and tender week, a week coloured red and pearly-grey – Édouard had forgotten about life, or rather what people referred to as life, and this compact, dark, and determined woman sitting squarely in her armchair terrified him. She was the very picture of fatality. This small ordinary woman, whose true character he had immediately divined in spite of his natural tendency to be indulgent, reflected the spirit of his age, of his environment, and of a mentality he had always despised and that he now considered the worst enemy of his happiness. Béatrice, he felt – had always known – sometimes indulged in that mentality and often took pleasure in doing so.

'We start up north, in Amiens,' Destiny's messenger declared. 'Then we move back towards Paris before going on down to the Midi. I was very fond of your latest play, Monsieur Maligrasse, *l'Orage Immobile*.'

She had paused after the 'Monsieur', thinking he would immediately say 'Call me Édouard', but it obviously hadn't occurred to him. She was annoyed. After all, these intellectuals were as much a part of the communications game as she was, she said to herself. They were all in the same boat really ...

Béatrice saw her wince slightly and was amused. More out of habit than necessity – for she was now a well-known actress – Béatrice needed Tony, but she took great pleasure in putting her in her place. Yet she was also very sensitive to the aura of raw and often vulgar energy that emanated from the woman. Thus she laughed with her, hugged her, cajoled her, but by a kind of animal reflex – the way one avoids a rodent or a freak – was careful to keep her at a distance. With Béatrice, instinct often, and fortunately, replaced reflection.

'But if you leave,' Édouard was saying with the utmost openness and naturalness, 'what will become of *me*?'

Tony started. He seemed so vulnerable, so sincere. *Either he's stupid*, she thought, *or he knows precious little about women. About Béatrice, in any case. He's obviously heading for trouble* ... But something seemed to melt, to dilate, in Béatrice's clear eyes, and the smile she gave him contained a glimmer of something Tony had never seen before, something that seemed remarkably close to tenderness. With her unerring flair, Tony d'Albret decided that this episode deserved to be followed more closely. Inventing an appointment, she left to do some more research on the young Maligrasse.

After her departure, Béatrice smiled at Édouard.

'What do you think of her?'

'I don't think of her,' replied Édouard.

And, in fact, he had no opinion whatsoever about Tony d'Albret. All he knew was that she had opened the door to the closed, insulated, and disorderly room in which he'd been living for the past ten days, and that the gusts of Paris, of the outside world, of the others, had blown in with her. He lay down on the bed in his bathrobe, his head turned towards Béatrice.

As usual, she thought, *it certainly didn't take long* ...

In fact, this look of his had not left her once during the last ten days, ten days during which all she'd seen of herself was this passionate reflection. It seemed to her she was losing herself in it; she even reached the point where she sometimes brought her hand up automatically to shield her eyes. She lay down next to him, breathed in once again his odour mixed with hers on the sheets, the faint, stubborn, and violent odour of physical love. She sighed. The landscape had remained unchanged during all these days and nights: the rivers of carpet, the hills of sheets, the suns of sensuality; and even though her taste for pleasure had met its match, it seemed to her as if she'd been participating in a retreat as pious as it was luxurious. She was astonished. For a long time, her ambitions and her concern for her career had divided her time into a sequence of precise and practical events that were almost disdainful of love. But her surprise also contained a certain element of satisfaction. For, where her body was so uncomplicated, so animallike, her mind was not, and thus she sometimes felt a sort of discomfort in herself, like a strange hiatus. She had reached the point where she found it almost original to have been able to spend ten such identical days and nights without being bored, and she congratulated herself on her temperament. Just as she would have congratulated Édouard – of whom her memories were rather confused – for the violence, the insatiability, and the virtuosity of his desire.

She didn't know, however, that this technique she was so ready to congratulate him for was the kind that often inspired fear. She didn't know that each cry he wrung from her reassured him even before it excited him. She didn't know that he had become greedy and scientific, that he hoarded paroxysms, vows, words, gestures, that he tried, at the most blinding moments, to seize a detail, a landmark, a milestone to which his memory might return at some later date for its delectation or its suffering. She didn't know that each instant of these ten days had been a stolen instant for Édouard, a reprieve, a stay of execution.

Nor, finally, did she know that it was precisely the most instinctive part of herself that gave her her charm. Once in her bed, one became her property, her toy, her torturer or her slave, according to her moods. She proclaimed herself proprietor not only of her own body, but of her partner's, and this in a language that went from the lyrical to the crude, with gestures from the humble to the despotic, all of which made her a kind of implacable baroque idol before whom Édouard, like the noble but starving savage, could not help but kneel. These ten days had indeed been a truce with time, but life, real life, was outside and it was time for her to return to it. For Édouard, on the other hand, real life was right there, at that very instant, an observation she made confusedly but that had already begun to annoy her.

'Are you really going to leave?' he asked.

'Of course. You come and join us wherever you like.'

Already she was saying 'us', an 'us' which meant her fellow actors on tour, her agent, the technicians, hotel managers, friends, in short all those who already drove him to distraction. He must have shown as much, for she began to laugh and tousle his hair.

'Now that's really beautiful,' she said, 'that tuft of hair sticking up. Just what you need when you're received into the *Académie française*.'

'Don't talk like that,' Édouard replied weakly.

'Why not? You'd be very handsome. Your eyes are a little green, you know, right there . . .'

And she leaned towards him, pushed up his lip with her fingers, inspected his teeth, pulled back the skin on his cheek to erase the shadow under his eye, weighed, measured, amused herself.

'I feel as if I'm playing Colette's *Chéri*,' she said. 'Why are you making such a face? We can't really spend our whole life in this room, you know!'

Édouard raised his head and looked at her. There was something in his look, a warning, a plea, perhaps a kind of resignation – Béatrice couldn't say just what – that troubled her and made her lower her eyes.

'And why not?' he asked sadly.

4

They sat side by side in the dark in a large theatre on the Champs-Élysées, and Édouard tried to interest himself in the film. It was their first time out together, a film première, and their arrival had provoked a foreseeable number of raised eyebrows, murmured remarks, semi-congratulations, and faked expressions of surprise. They had been escorted to their seats by photographers and popping flashbulbs, and Béatrice had done her panther act: there was a way she had of holding his arm, of giving him her coat, of leaning towards him, as if she were wholly indifferent to everything else – in fact, as if they were alone – and it both unnerved and delighted him. He felt at once bewildered, awkward, envied, and misunderstood. Yet there was a grain of triumph in his embarrassment. This woman who smiled at him, whom other men greeted with a flicker of remembrance in their eyes or voices, this woman who made him the envy of so many others – for on this occasion she was particularly beautiful and arrogant – this woman whom he had thought irretrievable and who had been recovered so miraculously, this was now *his* woman. The stares were proof of it. They may have come from people he didn't know or instinctively feared, but they were none the less proof: she belonged to him. Out of the corner of his eye he studied the distinctive cheekbones, the slanted eyes, the straight full mouth, the face that had crumpled at his will and that he'd even brought to tears during their recent and interminable nights together, and he felt the absurd and delicious pride of ownership. Yes, he, Édouard, who scorned more than anything else the idea of property and who, in his private morality as well as his writings, attributed to it all the evils of the world.

Béatrice felt his eyes on her and smiled. She knew she was

on form this evening; the stares of the women as well as of the men had made that clear. And she knew that the delicate, the sensitive, the modest Édouard was purring with pride beside her, as had all his predecessors. In fact, he too was beautiful, with his long stride, his finely-chiselled features, his nonchalance, and his big awkward hands. That too she had read in *their* looks. With an intense feeling of contentment, she turned and smiled at him in the dark.

'What would you say to getting out of here?' he whispered, 'I'm bored stiff.'

She shrugged. He was so childish. You didn't leave a première just like that if you didn't want to fall out afterwards with the producers, the director, and the other actors. She would really have to educate him, something she hadn't had the time for five years ago when he'd been only a passing fancy. But now that he'd become someone himself, now that they could share equitably not only their private but their public lives, their affair would have to develop within the conventions. Even if Édouard dreamed only of being alone with her in bed – a flattering idea – it was no less essential for him to remain quietly in his orchestra seat, then at a table in a restaurant, then perhaps in a chic night-club. Public approval was of the essence in these kinds of liaisons. (Like all those who rely solely on their own minds, or rather instincts, Béatrice had a great and permanent thirst for respectability, that is to say, for approval; and this particularly at major social events.)

The film was over at last and Tony, dressed to the nines, was pumping their hands heartily as if they'd just got married. She seemed, by her enthusiasm, to be ratifying their union, and to be showing the *Tout-Paris* – evidently speechless with surprise – that it was true: Édouard Maligrasse, young author newly famous, and Béatrice Valmont, beautiful actress, were sleeping together.

Up to this point, Édouard had been entirely passive, but suddenly he roused himself and waved. Kurt van Erck, the so-called avant-garde director, was walking towards them. A short red-haired man with piercing eyes and a crisp voice, he had directed Édouard's first two plays, and was generally feared for his abrupt judgements, his terseness and his professed scorn for all theatre that was not 'committed'. Pleased to find a familiar face, Édouard introduced him to Béatrice who flashed him a ravishing smile. In vain, however. As far as Kurt was concerned, she was only a second-rate, light-comedy actress. He found it most unfortunate that Édouard Maligrasse should be wasting an appreciable amount of his valuable time in her bed. None of this was said, of course, only hinted at in the way he greeted Béatrice and nodded at Tony. But Béatrice registered it, and just as immediately detested him.

'You two don't know each other?' Édouard inquired naïvely. 'It's odd, but I'm so rarely at events like this.' He motioned vaguely at the rest of the audience. 'I thought everyone in the theatre knew everyone else.'

'Just one big happy family?' Kurt replied with a sneer.

'Of course. We're all more or less in the same business,' Tony said obligingly.

'You think so?'

Kurt's question was tinged with insolence and, despite his distractedness, the tone made Édouard uncomfortable.

'*I* don't think so,' Béatrice replied amiably. 'I'd even go so far as to say: Thank God we're not.'

Addressing a warm smile at Kurt as a gesture of farewell, she turned to Édouard.

'Édouard, angel,' she said. 'I'm dying of thirst.'

The look she gave him was so tender, so filled with happiness, that Édouard instantly forgot about Kurt and their discussions of old times and future projects and, leaving the director standing there, cleared a path to the bar for his two women.

'Have you known him for a long time?' asked Béatrice, once settled at the bar.

Old friends and former acquaintances paraded in front of them, intrigued or titillated by the new liaison in their midst. But Béatrice seemed to have eyes only for Édouard.

'For years,' he replied. 'He's my best friend.'

Béatrice let out a short and just slightly dubious laugh, which was loyally echoed by Tony.

'My poor darling,' Béatrice said, shrugging her shoulders.

Then, in a different tone of voice: 'Personally, I prefer Nicolas.'

Édouard turned to the crowd as Béatrice gestured with her chin towards the still handsome Nicolas Sainclair who was heading their way. They fell into each other's arms. There was something irresistibly attractive about Nicolas, partly because he seemed so irresistibly attracted to others. Which in fact he was, even at forty-five and despite the widespread and immoderate use he'd made of his seductiveness. Failed actor, bad father, hopeless husband, deplorable screenwriter, scrupulous gigolo and penniless patron of the arts, Nicolas still continued to exude love for his neighbour. He'd been the lover of innumerable women in Paris and every one of them had carried away charming memories at the end of the affair. What was even more curious was the fact that men were never angry with him. (Having never really been successful in other areas, Nicolas hardly ran the risk of being hated.) Always broke, a parasite who never held a grudge, and at present more than a little drunk, Nicolas lived on nothing at all; he could be seen everywhere, ever faithful – to the point of caricature – to the image people had made of him. An atmosphere of obligatory frivolity reminiscent of Feydeau followed him everywhere like a royal train and reduced all situations, no matter how dramatic, to the dimension of the *déjà-vu*. And since he had neither a critical frame of mind nor any capacity for mockery, he always managed to defuse even the most difficult situations, a talent appreciated by no small number of wives.

Behind the image, however, a small, sensitive, fearful, and dyspeptic boy suffered in silence, for despite the thousand rôles and beds of his frenetic life, Nicolas had never found the so-called milk of human kindness. But he did seem genuinely pleased to see his two friends reunited; he'd once spent a long season in Béatrice's arms, and as for Édouard, he'd been sponging off him for the past two years.

'I didn't know about you two,' he said, flinging his arms around their shoulders.

Both immediately felt guilty for not having telephoned him the day after their first embrace. Béatrice leaned up against him, as all women did when they found themselves next to Nicolas, and Édouard put his arm around his shoulder. In his own way,

Nicolas was the godfather of all Paris liaisons. When he finally disengaged himself to greet another of the evening's celebrities, Édouard and Béatrice looked at each other fondly.

'I spent a whole spring with him,' said Béatrice dreamily.

'Oh?' said Édouard, surprised. 'I didn't know that.'

'Of course I did!' Béatrice exclaimed with a certain severity. 'After all, he was so good-looking!'

Her tone of voice suggested that it would have been vulgar, even indecent, not to have succumbed to such good looks. Indeed, the same tone could be heard in the voices of all Nicolas's former women; and like all their men, Édouard silently accepted the fact that Béatrice had had little choice in the matter. But then the awful thought came to him that there must have been others beside Nicolas, and he cast a curious and furtive look around, trying to imagine on whose lips, among all those faces, bearded or clean-shaven, witty or stupid, Béatrice might have placed hers. Inevitably, and angrily, he came up with a good fifteen candidates.

'And that one?' he said, jerking his chin towards an unhappy but rather seductive young man who was waving in their direction.

'Don't be ridiculous!' Béatrice laughed. 'That excuse for a man? ... Anyway,' she added with conviction. 'I hate actors.'

It was true. Béatrice did feel a secret scorn for her colleagues. As an actress accustomed to using all the tricks, the little lies, and all the various other feminine arts, it had become impossible for her to separate her femininity from her trade. As far as she was concerned, and despite several experiences to the contrary, any actor worthy of the name concealed either impotency or homosexuality. This was another thing she would have to explain to Édouard who now appeared to have added jealousy to his perpetual naïvety. And so she hesitated: should she portray herself as a vamp with a troubled past or don the more serious disguise of the actress in love above everything else with her art? She wasn't sure yet which of the two rôles she preferred. And of course it never occurred to her to worry about what truths Édouard might eventually unearth, or what inevitable contradictions he might turn up in either version. After all, she was the only one who knew the truth about her own life and, as far as that went, it was difficult not to admire her good faith even when she was obviously lying. For Béatrice had convinced herself so thoroughly about certain aspects of her past that when she mentioned them, the few witnesses she invoked, trapped between contradicting her or denying their own memories, invariably chose to remain silent.

And so she vacillated between two desires. She could dazzle Édouard, terrify him, perplex him by a series of allusions, memories, ambiguities. Or – a more maternal rôle – she could reassure him, allow him to believe in her essential stability, even in the possibility of a future. And why not? Yet it had been a very long time, she realized, since she'd envisioned a future as far as a man was concerned. For more than fifteen years, she'd lived only in terms of the week to come. Yes, she would have to ..., a vague phrase she often used instead of a decision.

Nicolas had surfaced again and was asking where they wanted to go, as if it were inevitable that they all go somewhere together. Even Édouard, who dreamed only of being alone with her again, had to bow before such resolution. And so, framed by her two men, escorted by beauty, love, and talent, a delighted Béatrice sailed through an exit as successful as her entrance.

They got home at dawn, and the blue room seemed to Édouard like a long-lost paradise. While Béatrice collapsed fully-dressed on to the bed, he disappeared into the bathroom. By tacit agreement, he always dressed or undressed before she did, as if it were taken for granted that she would always be the one waited for. He smiled at his reflection in the mirror – that of a comely young man, clean-shaven and reassuring, whose face was sufficiently pleasant for the door of the blue room to admit him and for his desires, as immoderate as they were dangerous, to accompany him surreptitiously inside. *Poor Béatrice*, he thought, *poor gullible Béatrice*. Here she believed she was harbouring a man who pleased her, whereas in fact she was harbouring one who loved her. Édouard smiled at his deception and, more tenderly, at certain little things picked up here and there during the evening from his conversations

28

with Nicolas and the other hangers-on. There was one in particular that had moved him to tears; the fact that Béatrice lied about her age. Nicolas had burst out laughing when she'd alluded to her thirty-five years, and when he realized what he'd done it was already too late. Édouard had felt a wave of tenderness wash over him at the idea that Béatrice, who was so beautiful and so unchangeable in his eyes, should so childishly cut a few years off her vital statistics. It had seemed to him an unhoped-for crack in the impenetrable armour of this exquisite woman. *So she's afraid of something,* he thought. *She's afraid of getting old.* Not for a moment did he consider the threat such a fear might one day pose for him, for people afraid always need reassurance. They have to have proof. And for Béatrice, the men she seduced had always fulfilled this function. *Men,* that is, not one man.

In addition, Édouard had been astonished to learn that in her long-ago affair with Nicolas, the ardour of the male had been the first to pale. Not that Nicolas had said as much of course, for malice was not his strong point. But he had let slip an 'If I'd only known', that seemed to suggest a certain regret at not having foreseen the brilliant future of his young mistress. The idea that someone could actually leave Béatrice surpassed Édouard's understanding – not only instinctively, not only because he loved her and because he would have been incapable of leaving her himself, but also because such a thing simply failed to match her personality. His *femme-fatale* image of Béatrice was at once stylized, intransigent, and naïve, but more important perhaps, it had never been challenged. Now, however, in just one evening, he had learned that this woman had lived through ruptures and withstood wrinkles, that the statue on the pedestal had cracks in it, unknown fissures. Far from diminishing his love, however, this discovery intensified it. For, in keeping with the classical lover's phenomenon, whatever he found to be dissembled or contradictory in his mistress appeared as so much evidence of her essential humanity. (What he didn't know, of course, was that one's partner's 'weaknesses' tend to seem touching before revealing their more fatal aspects. One is hurt less by a flaw than by the absence of a quality. And Édouard would not suffer half as much later on from

Béatrice's deceiving him as from her failure to be faithful to him.)

As he came back into the bedroom, he found her still lying on the bed, make-up and clothes untouched, her eyes closed. He laughed and pulled away the sheet; she hadn't even taken her shoes off.

'Are you planning to sleep like that?' he asked.

She opened her eyes and stared at him.

'I'm not planning to sleep. Planning to think.'

She was serious and Édouard sat down sheepishly at the foot of the bed. Sitting there in his bathrobe in the presence of a woman wrapped in black ostrich feathers against a backdrop of white sheet, he felt altogether bare and insignificant.

'Think about what?' he asked. 'The sun's coming up, you know. It's no time for thinking.'

'There's no fixed time for thinking,' she replied, casting a scornful look at him.

He remembered then that she'd drunk a great deal and from the very beginning of the evening. She'd taken up one glass after the other, hesitantly at first, weighing them, and then, as if she'd thought it over very carefully, downing the contents at one go. She'd seemed to be drinking in order to get drunk and, apparently, she'd succeeded. Édouard, who became gay and tender when under the influence, suddenly felt enchanted. Here he was at five in the morning with bare feet and transparent expression at the bedside of a beautiful woman dressed in black whose eyes seemed to burn through the fresh sheets.

'We must look like some lascivious engraving from the *Belle Époque*,' he said. 'Except that usually it's the man who's in evening dress and the woman undressed, isn't it?'

She didn't answer, only beckoned him closer with her forefinger until his face was next to hers. He breathed slowly and gently, saw the red lips so close to his own, revelled in the pale odour of alcohol, tobacco, and perfume emanating from the body that offered itself to him. His temples throbbed with fatigue and happiness.

'Going to tell you a secret,' she murmured. 'A big one.'

He couldn't help a momentary twitch of fear lest all of it –

the room, the woman, the bed, the evening, the happiness —
shatter and become once again what he still feared it really
was: a dream.

'In the final analysis,' she went on confidentially, 'I hate
them all.'

He laughed with relief. 'Them all' excluded him.

'But you didn't want to go home,' he replied. 'You didn't
look at all as if you were bored, not at all . . .'

Béatrice drunk, detested irony as much as when she was
sober, and cast a severe look at her attentive young suitor.
As attentive now as he was five years ago, she thought. *And so
vulnerable.* Then she closed her eyes.

'My poor Édouard,' she said finally, while her face composed itself into what she hoped was an expression of bitter
resignation. 'My poor Édouard, that is only my mask. How
little you know me. Even you. If you only realized . . .'

But he was not to realize more, at least not that evening,
for a moment later Béatrice fell asleep as violently as she
might have taken her pleasure. And in the golden halo dif-
fused by the lamp in the big bedroom on the rue Chambiges,
the lascivious engraving gave way to a young man leaning
forward awkwardly, cautiously pulling the covers over the
abandoned strangely-plumed body of a beautiful siren washed
up by the sea.

5

The Magritte painting depicted a rather attractive middle-class home drawn against a sky of an indefinable blue – a dawn blue, violent, pale, raw and sombre – a house with a streetlamp next to it in the foreground, a house Édouard knew. He was sure he had spent his childhood there, or rather one of his childhoods. Similarly, he was sure that he would have liked to live in that house for ever, and Béatrice with him, and that he could enter the painting, go up the porch stairs, climb the dark stairway inside and find Béatrice waiting for him in an old-fashioned armchair behind the lighted window on the right, beside herself with worry over his lateness.

The museum guard coughed politely and Édouard hurried back down the stairs, closed the door of the house behind him, left the painting, then the Jeu de Paume Museum itself. In reality, Béatrice *was* waiting for him, but in Amiens, in an anonymous hotel and certainly not, alas, beside herself with worry. During the past week while she'd been away on tour, their phone conversations had consisted of nothing but the vaguest, most nerve-wracking and distracted exchanges. He would ask, 'How can you stand it?' – 'it' being their inhuman separation – and she would reply that 'it' was indeed unbearable, but that it was after all a question of her career. 'Do you miss me?' Édouard would ask into the horrible, damp, cold ebony receiver that was their lifeline. 'Of course I do,' Béatrice would reply. 'Of course I miss you.' While Édouard wanted to shout at her, 'Of course? Why? Why "of course"? You lived long enough without me. Are you so sure you're really suffering when I'm not there? How can I be sure you're suffering?' But all he said was, 'You're not too tired, are you? You're not unhappy? Is your room quiet enough?'

When she'd left, she'd said, 'See you Saturday', and this

Saturday had immediately become the only real day of the week for him, but he had the feeling she might just as well have said, 'See you Tuesday' or 'Monday'. He had stopped at the Jeu de Paume so as not to get to her too early or to have to kill time on the road. He didn't want to have to drive slowly, which for him meant carelessly, but he'd none the less gone through the exhibition at a gallop. All those master-pieces, those slices of painted canvas filled with the sweat, blood, nerves, and souls of other men had been but ob-stacles, ridiculous little hurdles, between him and the entrance to the Autoroute du Nord. Only the Magritte had really made him stop, and this one long moment before he'd brought Béatrice into the house had inflicted an almost sensual happi-ness on him, the sort of proud pleasure sometimes inspired by certain works of art.

Now, however, he was on his way. Night was already falling on to the road and Édouard suddenly realized it was autumn. For some time now, there had been no seasons in his life, no streets, and no dates, except for this Saturday underlined in red and black or squared off in a childish little box on all his calendars. As if there were any possibility whatsoever of his forgetting it. During the past week, each time he'd opened his diary to make an appointment he cared nothing about, this underlined red Saturday had leapt out at him like a kind of indecent promise. Behind those eight flat letters lay Béatrice's burning body, her demands, her words of love, and Édouard had hurriedly closed the diary as if he'd accidentally stumbled on some prurient message addressed to him alone.

Amiens ... the banal and dismal city of Amiens had become a sort of Capua in his imagination. And of course he arrived much too early, then felt an obligation to lose his way. He couldn't forget the ridiculous lines Béatrice had had to speak in a play, at the time of their first meeting five years before. They were lines he had listened to every night when, crazed with suffering after her rejection, he would spend his last few francs on a seat in the theatre where she was performing. She had played the maid, the smallest rôle in the play, and she was supposed to say, 'You must understand one thing, sir. For a woman, there is no such thing as the right moment. After the moment, it may still sometimes be the moment. But before the moment, it never is!' That was the extent of it and although they were hopeless platitudes, the lines had never failed to wring his heart for they had made him think that his own moment had passed and that it would never come again. Doubtless, an intelligent and sensible formula about the passage of time and its ravages would have struck him less forcibly, or at least less cruelly and viciously, than that particular piece of nonsense.

Édouard did realize, however, that for Béatrice to have become what she was – a consecrated actress, a star – she had had to want it desperately, to struggle mightily, to endure a great deal. But to picture Béatrice wanting something without getting it immediately, to picture Béatrice waiting, Béatrice begging, Béatrice suffering snubs was impossible for him. It disturbed his fairy tale image of her. In any case, he was sure now that as long as he lived, such things would never happen again. Teeth clenched at the wheel of his Peugeot 504, Édouard Maligrasse, like a belated adolescent, vowed to give his mistress a charmed life paved with love and triumphs (only the latter in the plural, of course). In fact, this was one of Édouard's greatest charms, not to say virtues: he couldn't, and didn't, imagine Béatrice defeated and disarmed, calling for help, nor (except where passion was concerned) Béatrice in need of him. He had never imagined such things. Even during the worst moments of their separation, he had always wanted her to be desired, happy, and applauded. It should be recognized, however, that this wish was prompted not only by his natural goodness but also, and particularly, because, although he was not aware of it, his sensuality was more excited by the image of a Béatrice triumphant. And as he was above all else a writer, he instinctively and rigorously avoided modifying the course of his reveries. In real life, on the other hand, he rejected anything that didn't conform to them. Thus, unconsciously, Édouard was constructing his love as he constructed his plays. He didn't know that in so doing, in making himself both object and subject of his passion, he was running the risk of becoming a slave twice over. For the moment, however, he had managed to recover his Béatrice and it never crossed his mind to fear the worst. And so, as both aging youth and young swain, he cheerfully asked each pedestrian he came across the shortest way to the Hôtel de l'Univers.

Béatrice laughed out aloud. The hotel dining-room was empty and in the little corner which had been left lit as a special favour for their late supper, she and Édouard whispered together like two old boarders. From the moment he had arrived, he'd been sucked up into the usual whirlwind of suitcases, hasty kisses, taxis, and introductions. Afterwards he'd watched the play as if in a dream, but now at last they were alone together, albeit in a most lugubrious place. He was with her again after an interminable week, but the reunion he'd imagined in shades of purple and gold – like royalty actually – had taken place between beige walls looming up from a dark-brown imitation leather floor in front of a waiter grey with fatigue. *And it's always been like this*, he thought. Later, however, they would merely have to turn off the light for the anonymous hotel room, shabby and timeworn, insignificant and banal, to cast its spell and become, thanks to the darkness, the closed field of their finest encounter. There would be the white lightning of Béatrice's arms; there would be the black of her hair, blacker than the darkness itself; there would be the almost visible red of the blood in her throat as he led her to pleasure. There would be all these pale and violent colours he'd been severed from during seven interminable nights without her.

'And what's more, I can't stand him!' Béatrice was concluding. 'I can't stand that sort of person; I feel utterly hostile towards him. I feel all of a piece, as some people like to put it.'

The last expression was not, in fact, entirely unjustified. If Béatrice was never all of a piece, if on the contrary she was composed of a thousand closely related yet contradictory pieces, she was none the less always and in all circumstances wholly each and every one of those pieces. And as she never felt divided, never at a distance from herself, she could be completely hard or completely tender in succession, completely idiotic or completely lucid. Indeed, perhaps the reason she could never share her feelings with anyone else was that she had never been able to admit the ambiguities in them. On the other hand, this counterfeit façade – an armour so shabby and patched that no mediaeval knight would have dared to put it on – had sheltered her from countless blows, to say nothing of hard knocks. She had never let herself slip into comfortable friendships or reassuring confidences. In fact, she had never slipped into anything that could be called a habit. Her entourage, including all friends, male and female, as well as her lovers, had always been alternately subject to savage ill-treatment or equally savage adoration, and none of those who approached her ever had the right to trust her. Yet if they could expect anything and everything from her, they could also take a certain comfort in her unpredictability. They could be sure, absolutely sure, that she was as capable of holding out her hand to pull them from the water as of stepping on their heads while they drowned. And they could also be sure she would do both with the same absence of calculation and the same clear conscience.

In fact, in an age that was so filled with moralistic sermonizing and was so conformist in its self-styled nonconformity, Béatrice was one of those rare women, among all the catechized numskulls and sheep bleating to the wolf, who prided herself as much on her bad as on her good deeds. Only her failures caused her to doubt what she thought of as her divine immunity (something that others might consider merely her good fortune); her failures and also, of course, her illnesses, since for Béatrice a bad case of 'flu was as humiliating as a bad review. In neither case, however, did she ever give in to expressions of resentment. Instead of accusing either virus or critic of incompetence, she merely tossed her head and fell back on Destiny. Thus, everything that went wrong in her life was diverted on to a mysterious, astrological, and malefic plane. On the other hand, everything that went well she considered hers by divine right. More than a few men had had the door slammed in their faces, and their nerves and sometimes their hearts broken by their efforts to prove to her that she had at least some responsibility for her own existence.

'He really upsets you?' asked Édouard with a hint of facetiousness in his voice. 'I'll beat him to a pulp in the morning if you like.'

Béatrice laughed, but her eyes sparkled. She would love to have people fighting over her. For a moment, she had a vision of Édouard – bloody, dishevelled, lying at the feet of a piece of period furniture – and herself, on her knees, reaching into his dark-brown hair sticky with bright red blood and raising the warm head, herself, greedy but gentle, on the rug, violating a half-conscious man ... An odd vision, for when you thought about it, it was strange that she didn't imagine Édouard haughty and upright, prodding with his foot some boor he'd just knocked out. (After all, that was usually how she imagined her men.)

On the other hand, it was no less odd to imagine this desperate lover and so well-brought-up boy, writing plays, and these plays being considered successful by the most cynical critics in a city that was already cynical enough. When she looked very closely at him, when she saw how obviously and how passionately in love he was, Béatrice wondered in what secret corner of his mind under that soft childlike hair lay hidden the bizarre and perhaps unhealthy force that she none the less instinctively respected: his ability to write. In his desire, Édouard's look was so pure and his face so open. What was behind this apparent innocence? Where was the background, that notorious background? Where did the inviolable begin in someone who had already been violated and who asked only to be violated again and always, in both body and heart? The day would surely come when she'd have to find out. Meanwhile, however, an unfamiliar desire was sparked in her, a mixture of curiosity and the will for power. Suddenly, she wanted to know everything. She didn't know why, but she didn't want anything about him to escape her. *And yet*, she thought, confused, *I'm not in love with him. At least not really. I always knew he'd be here today and the wait didn't seem particularly long* ... So why this confusion, this insatiable hunger without real appetite?

She shook herself, then smiled wearily at him. He called the grey-faced waiter who brought along a crimson autograph book with the bill. Béatrice signed the book carefully, smiling with exasperation and resignation. Then she handed it to Édouard who lowered his eyes, embarrassed, and signed in turn.

They had a performance in Lille the next day and Édouard, who had imagined a melancholy and poetic trip in a northern landscape of black slagheaps and a pale-blue sun, had to drive for three hours instead in the pouring rain, three hours to the rhythm of the windscreen wipers and the intermittent comments of Béatrice who had woken up in a bad mood. She'd announced the fact straight away. 'I feel bad-tempered this morning,' she'd said, with a kind of fatalistic objectivity, as if she were saying 'It's raining'. Obviously, she considered her moods natural phenomena, as unpredictable and as independent of her will as meteorological disturbances. Then, having set the tone for the day, she worked at intensifying her aggravation, her complaints, her boredom, until, completely exasperated, she arrived in Lille at a hotel that was almost identical to the one in Amiens.

Worn out and depressed, his arms hanging down at his sides, Édouard watched her open cupboards and suitcases and, when she asked him with a short bitter laugh if she just might have a few hours of peace and quiet in order to project herself into her rôle, he turned tail and ran for cover to the deserted hotel lobby. He read the *Journal du Nord* three times, not understanding a word of it, ventured a few steps out into the rain, got as far as a bookshop and found nothing but two detective novels he thought he might have read before. In desperation, he bought *Madame Bovary* for the tenth time, in paperback; then, to assure himself a cosy end to the afternoon, he ordered five o'clock tea. Afterwards, not daring to go up to the room yet, he waited downstairs for another two hours.

But Édouard did feel a certain pleasure in the desolate lobby. It was a sinister day in a sinister place, but he knew that nothing in the world could tear him away from it. *It's one of love's greatest charms*, he thought, *not to have to wonder any more what I'm doing here, but to find myself asking how I can manage to stay ...*

Meanwhile, Béatrice had very quickly become bored. She missed Édouard, or rather her bad temper missed him, so she finally came downstairs ready to pick a quarrel. First, she said that he looked like one of those pathetic heroes in a Simenon novel, then that his apathy, his obvious lack of curiosity about the lovely city of Lille, was more than a little revealing. In a vague way, she hoped he'd answer her with the truth : that he was there for her alone, that he was happy enough being her chauffeur, and that he was in no way responsible for the fact that the tour was so rainsoaked and deadly. But Édouard was neither a complainer nor a squabbler, so Béatrice, frustrated with the whole scene, advised him to go on back to Paris the following morning. Or even that very evening, if he preferred; an ultimatum designed expressly to poison his evening, to depress or anger him, to put a little spice into their reunion after the performance. For if the truth be known, Béatrice was rather fond of complications of this sort. As far as she was concerned, affairs of the heart should be filled with tension, especially when the general *décor* was so lifeless.

Édouard lingered in the lobby for another hour, worried and unhappy, but without even thinking of gallantly slipping away. The tone of Béatrice's voice had seemed to suggest that no matter what happened, she was sure to find him there when she got back, a tone that left no doubts about where his duty lay. For Édouard, Béatrice's vision of their relationship was accurate, and he wasn't at all interested in modifying it. He didn't want to shock her; he just wanted to tame her, and for that he had to make himself indispensable, a habit that would become second nature to her. Consequently, despite the fact that he was passionate, young, and in love, he used the tactics of an older suitor. The hotel manager felt sorry for him, though, and suggested his trying a nearby cinema. He went. He would much rather have stayed in the room and stared at the ceiling, but he knew that when Béatrice got back, she'd ask him what he'd done and if he answered, 'Nothing', he'd feel guilty. He'd like at least to be able to tell her the plot of the film.

*

Of course, what he really and desperately wanted was to talk to her about their first affair, about why they'd split up, about the years of separation, about their present happiness. But she'd made it perfectly clear that morning that she was not in a good mood, and Béatrice's bad moods excluded any and all introspection. It was only when she was happy – or rather, pleased with herself – that she agreed to gambol down the verdant and sinuous paths of psychology. This was something Édouard remembered full well, even though it seemed to him the woman he'd loved five years ago had had an entirely different kind of ferocity.

The film was about a Boeing, lost and off-course, and for a while he watched a frantic stewardess desperately trying to comfort her passengers. An hour later, he got up, thoroughly exasperated. Like many highly-strung people, he could stand being bored when he was on his own, but not being forced into it by some outside element. He walked back to the hotel with determination, kicked off his shoes, and lay down on the bed. It was half-past ten. Béatrice would be back in a little over an hour. All he had to do was lie there and wait. Wait, with the certainty of her return as delicious as the slightest doubt would have been unbearable.

In a way, he found himself in a situation similar to Frédéric's. For some time now, he had almost forgotten the hero of his new play, although he occasionally thought of him timidly, with a sort of tenderness and remorse, the way one might think of a close friend depressed by the sudden and brutal departure of his wife. Of course he'd never spoken of either his play or his hero to Béatrice. In the first place, the mere mention of his work would have seemed to him the height of immodesty, and in the second place, he'd thought up Frédéric, the character of Frédéric, long before he'd recovered Béatrice. It seemed improper now to confess the presence in his life of any other figure, even if that figure were imaginary, or rather invented. The trouble was that Frédéric had, in fact, been conceived in his own mind, and thus tended to reappear quite frequently, and with far more insistence than any former mistress. He'd even come up with a new idea for the second act while driving to

Amiens. He now knew perfectly well what he wanted to say; it was just that he hadn't been able to work out how to put it on the stage. Getting up mechanically, he opened a drawer, drew a brisk black line through the engraved Hôtel de la Poste letterhead, and began to write. It would only take a few minutes and he'd be that much further along.

Two hours later, he was surrounded by sheets of paper covered with scribbling, no longer in Lille but in a city in Louisiana. He was whistling a few bars of a song over and over again under his breath when someone opened the door behind him and an unfamiliar voice spoke his name. He jumped. It was Béatrice, back late from having dinner with some local journalists, armed with vague excuses and already annoyed at having to make them. But, instead of an anguished young lover nervously pacing back and forth in an hotel room, she found a perfectly satisfied young man. And, although he leaped to his feet, radiant, the moment he saw her, she realized for a second – a very short but very alarming second – that she'd disturbed him.

Later, as she brushed her hair thoughtfully in front of the bathroom mirror, gaily relating all the vicissitudes of the evening's performance, Édouard's answering laughter came like an echo from the bedroom. But when she stuck her head out of the door, she saw him standing next to the little writing table where she'd surprised him, very carefully crossing things out on one of his loose pages.

'You're not listening,' she said.

He turned around, pen in hand, looking suddenly like a guilty schoolboy caught in the act.

'Of course I am,' he protested. 'You were saying ...'

'Are you writing a new play?'

'Yes,' he replied nervously. 'I mean, it's only a draft. It's the story of a man who ...'

He began to stammer. Béatrice returned to the mirror, put the brush back on the shelf, and looked at herself. She didn't like what she saw. The little wrinkle, that line next to her mouth, seemed more pronounced. She hadn't been on top form that evening, despite the applause. She was also far away from Paris. Suddenly she felt terribly alone. And, much later, in the middle of the night, she found herself staring wide-eyed at the sad wallpaper and the reflection of headlights on the ceiling. While a contented Édouard — for she had been more tender and more passionate than usual — slept quietly at her side.

6

When he awoke the following morning, Édouard found himself alone, except for a letter pinned dramatically to the pillow beside him. Before he had a chance to open it, and while he was still emerging from the painful and fragile fog of sleep, he felt his heart stop beating and his blood turn to water. He hesitated a long moment before opening the envelope.

'Darling,' Béatrice had written. 'I'm leaving – for your sake as well as mine. We shouldn't see each other during the tour because your presence keeps me from concentrating. And I know the rôle of camp-follower is no good for you. You're a writer (this last underlined) and I don't want to be the woman who stands in the way of your work. Believe me, this separation will be as painful for me as for you. Love, Béatrice.'

There was a hasty and far more illegible PS:

'Don't forget that I'm an idiot, that I'm not worth what you are, and that even though I don't do it on purpose, I can only do you harm.'

The PS was the most important thing, but in his bewilderment and his violent and childlike chagrin, Édouard paid hardly any attention to it. All he thought about was getting away as fast as possible. An hour later, he was driving back down that triumphal road he'd come up two days before.

He drove badly, nervously, ruminating on his defeat. For it was well and truly a defeat. He'd gone to join his mistress and spend a week with her, and in two days she'd left him. All the signs along the autoroute seemed to be firing 'Defeat! Defeat!' at him at point-blank range; he would never ever drink Munich beer with Béatrice, and TWA with its handsome planes would never ever take them to tropical islands in the sun. Once he just missed ramming the back of a lorry and, trembling with retrospective terror and confusion, he pulled off the road and fled into a café, or, to be more exact, into one of those sinister jam-packed places that harbour fugitives from the autoroute. He would have liked to order a steaming cup of coffee from some golden-haired waitress, but instead he had to change a ten franc note into coins and push one of them into a cheap, dirty, metallic machine, only to get back a jet of tasteless coffee in a paper cup. The modern world was decidedly not for him. He opened his suitcase, took out a little bottle of the stimulants he took from time to time, and sadly swallowed one. He would gladly have injected himself with heroin in order to write ten first-rate pages, but the idea of chemically stimulating or smothering his moods humiliated him profoundly. The pill, though, did keep him awake until he reached Paris.

On arriving, he pulled up automatically in front of Béatrice's building, *the* building, hers, theirs. As he gazed at it, he suddenly remembered the Magritte painting and was overwhelmed by a profound depression. There he was, parked in front of a closed door; he no longer had the right to the blue bedroom; perhaps he'd even be excluded from it for ever. He sat there for an hour, inert, his head pressed against the car window, sightlessly watching the people walking by in the distance, all in a hurry and all looking so glum. Unable to make up his mind to go home, he ended up telephoning Nicolas who, thank God, was not only in but would be delighted to see him.

Corrupt, aimless, and amoral as he was, Nicolas had none the less remained a fundamentally tolerant man. And although he was still fond of Béatrice, he couldn't understand how any-one could suffer because of her. Having once conquered and then left her, he was perfectly willing to concede that Édouard, whom he liked and admired a thousand times more, might be desperately in love with her. It even seemed to him perfectly normal that on the corpse-strewn battlefield of Parisian amours, an implacable war machine called Béatrice would triumph over an unarmed civilian like Édouard. Such things were simply a question of natural law.

'You've become involved with a wild animal,' he told

Édouard. 'With a woman like her, you have to love less than you're loved. Or in any case, you have to pretend to love her less. If you don't, you're a loser from the start.'

'I'm not a loser from the start,' Édouard replied calmly and deliberately, in dramatic contrast to his broken and anguished account of their disastrous weekend. 'I'm not starting out a loser because I'm not trying to win. I hate power struggles.'

'But that's what it always comes down to,' Nicolas said. 'Especially with Béatrice. You're acting like a fool.'

Édouard sighed. He was in Nicolas's poor but charming little studio flat, the lair of an unemployed, skirt-chasing bachelor. He'd lamented his fate, he'd even talked of his real feelings, which was something he never did, or hadn't done for a very long time. For five years, in fact, because for five years – since Béatrice – he had loved no one.

'I may be a fool,' he replied. 'I may be a coward and a push-over, but I don't care. The one thing you just don't understand about me, Nicolas, is that when Béatrice threatens to destroy me, I care so little about it that it makes me virtually indestructible. The minute she embraces me, I don't care if a thousand people are laughing at me.'

'But among those thousand people, isn't it possible there might be just a few who are more intelligent or worthy or sensitive than Béatrice?'

'Let them keep their beautiful qualities,' Édouard said, irritated. 'The woman I love is more beautiful than they. And evil too perhaps, as you say. But the only time I feel alive is when I'm with her.'

'All right, my friend!' Nicolas laughed, throwing up his arms. 'Go ahead! Suffer! Love and suffer! What more can I say to you? Maybe it'll be good for your play.'

'Speaking of which,' Édouard began unthinkingly, 'I've come up with a sensational idea!'

He stopped short suddenly, feeling as if he'd committed some sacrilege.

'What I don't understand,' he went on quickly, 'is the end of her letter.'

He pulled it out of his wallet, reread the PS and looked uncertainly at Nicolas.

'She says she's too stupid for me. Isn't that strange? And she keeps me from writing.'

Nicolas smiled. 'That's the first time I've known Béatrice to have an honest thought, or rather a humble one.'

'Do you think she really thinks that?' Édouard asked. 'Do you think she's really afraid of ruining my life?'

And then, because that hypothesis was suddenly the only one that could deliver him from his grief, could even transform it into happiness, Édouard felt he'd discovered the truth, that he'd understood at last. Béatrice, that beautiful tender, crazy Béatrice, really did feel herself intellectually inferior to him, and really believed that was important.

'Don't get carried away,' Nicolas warned. 'Béatrice is no *Dame aux Camélias*, you know. She has absolutely no sense of sacrifice, I can assure you.'

But Édouard was already on his feet, shaken and triumphant.

'When I think!' he cried. 'When I think I missed the whole point! Last night, when she got back to the hotel, there I was, working away. Why, she must have thought ... Oh, but she's mad! She's marvellous, but absolutely mad ...'

He was already running for the door, already flying to Béatrice, burning to comfort her, to reassure her, to apologize. Then, seized with belated gratitude, he turned around.

'Good-bye, Nicolas,' he said. 'And thanks.'

'Think nothing of it,' Nicolas replied with a little smile.

From the window, he watched Édouard dash across the street, jump into his car, and take off towards his Destiny. He reminded Nicolas of one of those collapsed moths lying prostrate in the darkness, which, the minute someone lights a lamp, flies off with the same intoxication to crucify itself again. He shrugged.

On the autoroute to Roubaix, steins of Munich beer now offered themselves to Édouard and Béatrice, and planes pawed the ground in their impatience to carry them to golden beaches. Édouard sang. He couldn't know that Béatrice – believing in what she'd written to him, forgetting that it was because he'd bored her that she'd declared herself boring, forgetting that it was because he weighed on her that she'd felt herself so lightweight – Béatrice had that same afternoon sincerely and painfully renounced her rôle of muse. Resigned to being only a terrestrial actress, she had, on the spur of the moment, allowed herself to slip for two hours between the sheets of the young male lead.

Édouard arrived in the early hours of the morning, had himself announced, and went upstairs immediately. Béatrice was stretched out wearily in bed. Agostini, her partner, had been a poor excuse for a lover, had finished before she came and had left her with circles under her eyes. (Coming, on the other hand, always made her look childlike and well-rested.) Édouard immediately attributed the circles to lover's grief; after a hellish day of pills and autoroutes, he himself was looking none too splendid. He was haggard, unshaven, and seemed to float, a stick figure, in his corduroy jacket. By this time, however, Béatrice had completely recovered from her courtesan's rôle and was asking herself how she could ever have preferred that abominable hack actor to the seductive young man who stood so touchingly exhausted before her. How could she ever have made him suffer so? And how could she have so grossly cheated him? But she'd asked herself these same two questions in the past so often – and so vainly, since she could never bring herself to ask them aloud – that she'd given up looking for the answers. She held out her arms and he threw himself into them, into the familiar scent, the warmth, the soft skin, the low voice. He'd come home again. *It's insane*, he repeated over and over to himself. *It's insane to be so happy.*

'Calm down,' Béatrice said, alarmed at the beating of his heart. 'You're trembling ... Wherever have you come from at this time of night?'

'From Paris. I was furious this morning when I woke up, so I went home. Then I read your letter again, and I came back. The moment I understood ...'

'Understood what?'

Béatrice had forgotten exactly what she'd written. At the time, it had seemed very clever, even moving to her. And for a large part of the day, very accurate. As she remembered it now, after the deplorable interlude with Agostini, the only thing she could do was deny it. After all, the last thing she would like to be considered was an easy woman. Easy to satisfy, that is. Her head, like her heart, had its demands. In short, feeling frustrated, she grew soulful. Édouard, who had no way of knowing about all these moral, or at least mental, vicissitudes, talked on.

'You're mad, Béatrice. In the first place, you're intelligent. Often more intelligent than I am. You inspire me to write, you inspire me to live. I can't do anything without you, I don't want to. Don't you understand?'

He raised his head and gazed at her. He seemed utterly sincere. Béatrice smiled. Of course he wanted her now because he loved her, and of course she'd prevent him from writing one day if she made him suffer enough. And of course he'd get over it too, eventually. But for the time being, he was a child. She ran her index finger along his eyebrows, across his cheekbones, down the curve of his cheek, over his lips, then closed her eyes. He was a child, of course, but he was also a lover, and a very good one. That much she remembered clearly enough.

'Take your clothes off,' she told him.

'Yes,' Édouard murmured. 'Yes ...'

He was disconcerted. He'd come back to talk about quid pro quos, about misunderstandings and fine feelings. But instead of finding her haunted eyes shining with tears, he found a look that had grown opaque, animal, distant, an expression completely absorbed in desire. What had happened while he was away? What had happened during that day of madness, that day of endless kilometres covered in order to return to his source of life, to this full mouth with its arched upper lip and straight lower one, now covered with a fine film of perspiration? *My Destiny*, he thought. *She's my Destiny ...* His fatigue, coupled with the sudden drop in tension, intensified his desire for her and he trembled at the edge of the bed. She closed her eyes and he leaned forward.

'Be quiet, be quiet,' she said later, several times, even though he hadn't uttered a word. And later still, she bit into the base of his throat, then turned over on her stomach.

'You know,' she said, 'in the end, when I write awful things about myself, like that PS, it's because I really do mean them.'

Afterwards, though, she refused to answer his questions, and fell asleep all of a sudden, one arm folded across her neck as if afraid of the cold, or of fragments from a bursting shell.

7

The morning arrived, grey-blue, a morning filled with odours and street noises, and with variations in light that seemed to have been orchestrated by a single person; Proust, for example. Someone out there was directing the gigantic and naïve world machine; someone was choreographing the clouds, winds, the horns of buses and the scents of lilacs, directing them with the adroitness, fervour and talent of a great artist. Édouard, who did not believe in God, found in this harmony proof of the existence of Art. Stretched out in bed, alone, he closed his eyes in perfect contentment. It was rare these days for his life – which seemed to be running off in every direction – to stop suddenly, then turn towards him and blurt out: Yes, I do exist, and Art exists, and Beauty and Harmony, and it's up to you to describe them and to prove to the world that we exist. A violent feeling, compounded of happiness and impotence, surged through him. He wanted simultaneously to thank Heaven that he was a writer, and to break all his pencils. At this moment, he wanted never to have loved, never to have been loved. He would have liked simply to be more intelligent, more sensitive, and to remain where he was, eager and attentive, ready to take it all down, understand, translate it into words. For himself first, and then for the world. Of course, his translation would in a sense be false, since words once assembled turn traitor. Yet his own arbitrary and unique way of assembling them would none the less help him to get to his own truth.

He knew too that despite all his efforts to bridge the gap, it was in this difference between what he would have liked to say and what he would wind up saying that his style, his voice, even his talent lay. Words were both his masters and his slaves. He knew that often he was a distressing and sorry partner in life, in this bad but realistic play the others all insisted upon performing solemnly or monotonously, depending on the moment. He knew that with others he stammered, and that he was angry with himself when he left them. But later – very soon, in fact – he would be alone with his white paper, and all the horses and all the violins of his imagination would begin to gallop and sing alongside him. What did it matter then if all the horses were nags and the violins out of tune? They would drag him along anyway and life would become real again, pulsing with blood and meaning. He would throw himself into the whirlpool; he would scavenge in the darkest corners of his mind like some blind and frantic deep-sea diver. All that would remain of him on the surface would be his body, his head, his hands lying on the table. His look, too, would remain – if someone disturbed him – but it would reflect nothing but what he himself saw in the periscope of his imagination. And those things were invisible to anyone else, unless of course they decoded the black scrambled figures he traced on the paper like some cataleptic teletype operator.

Afterwards, of course, he would have to reinhabit his body, his hands, his look. He would have to *see* the others, to plunge back into life as they say. But that was precisely the moment he would feel himself taking leave of it, would feel himself merging fully into the dream. He would see himself resurfacing, like a drowned man, on to the empty and colourless plane of reality, that terrifying sea of reality where the only islands were called Béatrice. Or at least the only islands he could reach. For loving her was like writing. With her he dreamed, which meant he came alive. The rest of the time he was afraid; he inhabited his body and his age only with effort. And others felt it as well, no matter how lost they might be in their own suppositions. 'You're thinking about your characters again, aren't you?' they would ask. 'You're thinking about your stories.' And they would smile indulgently. More than satisfied with this noble excuse, Édouard gladly acquiesced. Actually, he never really thought about his characters, except when he was working. Most of the time, it was like a film running through his head, a confused and badly-edited film, a patchwork of bits of poetry, unfinished tunes, lost lines, and inextricable situations he enjoyed rendering even more inextricable.

In these particular scenes, it was always Béatrice who played the leading rôle. He didn't dream of rescuing her from the flames or having her prostrate at his feet, hysterical with passion. For him, the reality of her was already so dazzling that, despite his doubts and fears, he never thought of adding to it. He didn't want it to change, simply to continue. Neither better nor worse, since nothing could be better than Béatrice gliding into his arms, and nothing worse than her leaving them; which were things that happened ten times a day. He trembled at the idea that this wonderful imbalance might be upset, the feeling of freefall aborted, order re-established. He didn't want anything or anyone to move inside the wildly spinning top of his passion. And that included her as well as him.

In the meantime, however, spring had come to Paris. Béatrice would be back the following day, her tour finished, and he was there, in her flat. The windows were opened wide and he was perfectly happy. What's more, he knew it. He could lie around in bed, or get up and read the newspaper in his hammock, one of two Béatrice had installed together with the wrought iron table in the little garden outside her ground-floor flat. Both seemed as lugubrious in winter as they were romantic in the summer, but Édouard adored this spot. Or he could phone his friend Nicolas and meet him for lunch somewhere where people would ask him for news of Béatrice – for already, everywhere he went, people asked him for news of Béatrice, which gave him no end of pleasure. Or he could go and find Kurt at the theatre and watch one of those fierce and meticulous rehearsals to which only the director had the secret. He could also work. But suddenly, at the thought, there were a thousand ties binding him like an old man to the bed; laziness, doubt, fear, impotence, humility, dizziness. He would have to jump through all those burning hoops, like a dog in a circus, in order to get back to his hero, Frédéric. 'You are so lucky!' the others said. 'You write what you want. You're free!' It was true; and what was worse, on certain days he would have been only too happy to turn over all that freedom to them! Certainly, he was free – free also to submit to the anguish and despair he dealt himself when things went badly.

Just then, Béatrice's maid came in, the gentle Catherine, or

Cathy, as she was known to everyone. Cathy had a weakness for Édouard. She'd known all Béatrice's lovers over the past ten years, and had the habit of judging them mostly by their courtesy and their generosity. Édouard's obvious sensitivity touched her, though, for it led her to foresee an imminent break-up, and thus placed her squarely in the rôle of a nurse. When Édouard saw the fully-dressed sixty-year-old woman standing at the foot of the bed well after noon, he was jolted out of his lethargy, and chose the most austere of his various projects: he would go and see Kurt and talk over his play in more detail. Seeing Frédéric's reflection in someone else's eyes, and knowing that Frédéric already had an independent existence, would reassure and encourage him. And besides Kurt, there was no one else he could talk to. He was sure Béatrice would understand nothing whatever about Frédéric; she simply had nothing in common with him, either in kind or character. The notion saddened him, as if he were being forced to introduce a beloved mistress to a hostile brother. He sensed that Frédéric would fail to please Béatrice and, what was even more curious, that she might not please him. The eventuality of a meeting between them, in the little sitting-room for example, filled him with horror and unease. Then he realized he was hallucinating, laughed aloud at himself, and got up.

The theatre was small and dark and, on the empty stage, two heavily bearded actors were clearly waiting for something to happen. Seated in the shadows of the first row, Kurt van Erck also seemed to be waiting. Édouard put his hand on his shoulder and sat down silently next to him. He was more than familiar with Kurt's technique: silence. Let the actors reflect. Let them think. Sometimes Édouard had the impression they took advantage of these pauses to think about something else entirely. And – sacrilege! – that Kurt did too. Still, he knew it would be unthinkable for him to disturb their silence; his arrival itself seemed an intrusion. Kurt was rehearsing a rather esoteric play by a Czech playwright, one Édouard had read and reread with difficulty, although he thought it had a strange kind of beauty. He was curious to see what Kurt could do with it. 'What you don't understand, what you don't see,' Kurt always said, 'it's my job to show. What's important is what's between the lines.' Édouard had a tendency to believe it was the lines themselves that were important but he knew that was a fairly primitive notion. People had told him so often enough.

In any case, he didn't much care. As long as his own words were spoken in the appropriate tone by a cast with the appropriate physical features, he was satisfied. In his opinion, everything depended on the actors and their talent; the job of director should be limited to clarifying their rôles, making them go on and off at the right moments, lighting them when necessary. But after an initial and very stormy argument with Kurt, he had never brought up the subject again. Kurt had called him egocentric, blind, and retarded. (Their mutual affection sometimes seemed absolutely incomprehensible to both.)

He was bored to death after two minutes. It was a beautiful day, the street was so alive and cheerful in the sunshine. Whatever was he doing there in the dark with all these prostrate people? Kurt must have read his mind, for he finally got to his feet.

'Let's do it again,' he said.

The two actors went back to their places and the girl, a small blonde who seemed very weary, turned slowly towards her partner.

'Just where do you think you're going?' she demanded. 'You don't have a ticket, you don't have ticket for anything, not even for life, not even for the bus!'

Her partner sulked.

'You're right; I don't have a ticket, I've never had a ticket, I'm a man without a ticket ...'

'Stop!'

Kurt's voice rang out, imperative.

'Listen, Jean-Jacques, when you say you don't have a ticket for life, why do you say that? You think you're schizophrenic? Or you just don't care? What do you think about it? And you Armanda, when you tell him he hasn't got a ticket, are you pitying him or reproaching him? Well .. ?'

'I don't have the vaguest idea,' the one called Armanda replied. 'I wish you'd tell me.'

'But what do *you* think?' Kurt insisted.

She looked at her partner, then at Kurt, then shrugged her shoulders with an air of hopelessness.

'All right, why don't you try thinking about it,' said Kurt. 'Or try reading the text again. I'll be back in ten minutes.'

He led Édouard into the café across the street.

'You heard that?' he grumbled. 'We've read it ten times, I've explained to them twenty times who they are, we've been rehearsing for a week and look at them ...'

'The girl doesn't seem so bad,' Édouard replied, trying to be kind.

'And what about you?' Kurt interrupted. 'Let's get down to what's important. How far have you got with the play?'

All of a sudden, Édouard had absolutely no wish to talk about Frédéric. A ray of sun crossed the café, foamed the pale beer in front of a heavy-set man at the bar, woke up the flippers on the pinball machine, played with all the gleaming surfaces on the counter and tables. Frédéric was warm and comfortable in the shadows of Édouard's mind, dependent exclusively upon him to come to life. A new sensation swelled his heart for an instant, a feeling of pride, of ownership, and of secrecy.

'It's fine,' he said. 'Just fine.'

He raised his hand in a decisive way that he knew would keep Kurt from insisting. Thank God this pompous and comical convention existed – the one known as the mystery of artistic creation. The most timid author, even Édouard himself, could hide behind it with an air of both modesty and arrogance.

'O.K., I won't insist,' replied Kurt. 'So (and he suppressed, or pretended to suppress, a yawn), so how's your love life?'

'Good,' Édouard said in the same light tone. 'Everything's fine.'

'If you've got nothing to tell me about your work or your love life, what do you want to talk about?' Kurt asked, with a hint of reproach.

'I just came to say hello,' answered Édouard, innocently. 'I didn't mean to bother you.'

They fell silent and studied each other. Once again, Édouard noticed distractedly that Kurt had very low eyebrows, a protruding jaw, blue eyes, and square hands, 'workers' hands' as he liked to call them. He also noticed that he seemed to be getting on Kurt's nerves.

'I was just passing by,' he repeated. 'And as I had nothing to do . . .'

'But we do,' said Kurt. 'As you may have noticed, we're rehearsing.'

'Fine,' said Édouard, getting to his feet. 'Excuse me.'

Kurt grabbed his sleeve and pulled him back down.

'Listen, let's forget it, O.K.?' he said. 'I'm glad you came by. I must talk to you anyway. (Here there was a long pause, a very long one, as in his productions.) Your Béatrice is worthless. She's all right as an actress, but she's no good for *you*.'

'But . . .' Édouard, stunned, began stammering. 'But I know what I'm doing.'

'No, you don't,' Kurt replied. 'You're a child and you know nothing. Suppose you tell me what you *have* been doing for three months? Have you written anything?'

'Yes,' said Édouard. 'One scene. And I've thought about the rest, I assure you.'

'Yes, you thought about it in the station between two trains, I suppose. Between two beds. You thought about it when Madame Béatrice Valmont let you think about it. A play that started so well! It should be finished by now, and because of some bird . . .'

Édouard stiffened. It seemed to him that simply because they'd known each other since they were teenagers, Kurt was refusing to admit that, thanks to Béatrice, Édouard had grown up. But, above all, it was the first time Kurt had said something so vulgar to him, and so coarsely. Édouard hated it when people talked about 'birds' or 'blokes' or 'real people'.

'Do you know what work means?' Kurt demanded.

'Yes,' Édouard replied quietly.

And he stood up and left.

Once outside, he walked off with a determined stride in an effort to calm down, heading instinctively towards 'their' house where Béatrice's clothes, her scent, their bed, their hammocks, and his white paper were all waiting for him. No one was going to come between him and them.

Yet he felt a kind of sadness. After all, Kurt really was one of his best friends, as were ... who else, in fact? As he walked, he tried to remember the names of a few human beings with whom he'd shared time, feelings, even his bed. He tried to remember a face, a voice, just one single character in the great human comedy of his past. But all he saw were anonymous actors. It didn't matter, though. He himself had wings, and in the overpopulated wasteland of the city, he paid no attention to the red lights and pedestrian crossings he had always respected so religiously. The only traffic regulations he would respect from now on, he decided, were those of his own personal biology. Because yes, he did know what it was to work; he might even have told Kurt a thing or two about it. Because work was something more than forcing a bunch of stupid drones to mimic someone else's text. Oh yes, he knew what it was to work all right. And as soon as Béatrice got back, he'd introduce Frédéric to her.

8

Almost the moment she'd arrived, and after a quick embrace, Béatrice took off again, rushing around Paris with the frenzy of a provincial or a long-term exile, although she'd only been away for two months. She didn't have a thing to wear, she said, and Édouard would have to decide whether to spend another afternoon in his hammock or to tag along on her shopping spree. And so he found himself hunched on a little stool in a couturier's salon at five in the afternoon, totally exhausted, overseeing Béatrice's tenth fitting. He felt superfluous, old-fashioned, and somewhat ridiculous; he thought he looked like some elderly Edwardian suitor. With an occasional brief glance, Béatrice would ask his opinion about her choices, but when she finally realized that he was interested only in her bare skin, she stopped bothering him. Little by little, her desire for new clothes turned into a veritable need – like all her desires, in fact – and she became impatient, grumbling at and scolding the beleaguered saleswomen. At the moment, she was watching a small and very young woman who knelt before her, a redhead who had been rather arrogant and sure of herself at first but who was quickly abashed by her client's imperious tone and curt manner.

'That's the fourth time you've pricked me!' Béatrice snapped. 'Do you think I'm Saint Sebastian or something?'

To Édouard's great consternation – and in fact, to Béatrice's astonishment – the girl burst into tears and stumbled from the room. The head saleswoman hurried over, overflowing with apologies.

'You must excuse Zoé, Madame,' she told Béatrice. 'It's the heat. We're all terribly on edge at the moment. Don't give it another thought; I'll finish the fitting myself.'

'I'll wait for you in the café over there,' Édouard said, and walked out, furious and upset. He couldn't stand people attacking waiters or salesgirls or *maîtres d'hôtel*, or anyone else who couldn't defend himself. He felt it was the height of vulgarity. Therefore, when Béatrice entered the café triumphantly, smiled at him, and happily demanded a large Gin Fizz, he repeated the order flatly to the waiter without raising his eyes.

'My God!' Béatrice exclaimed. 'What an afternoon! The orange one's gorgeous, don't you think ... ? Well, what's the matter with you?'

'I'm just thinking about the girl,' Édouard replied. 'She's probably crying all by herself in the backroom over there. You must have spoiled her whole day ... and her evening.'

'She was trying to make me wear a length that's no good on me,' Béatrice protested. 'Believe me, if you think I'm difficult, you should see some of the women ... Oh listen, Édouard, please, what's wrong? I don't understand.'

Whereupon Édouard launched into a garbled, humanitarian speech (becoming less humanitarian and more garbled as he went on) about social classes, power struggles, people's dignity, and so on. Béatrice listened in silence, tapping her glass from time to time with her ring. Her face was perfectly composed and when he finally came to a stop, halted by his own pomp, she looked at him so amiably and so approvingly that he was totally disconcerted.

'You're right,' she said. 'I was definitely too hard on her. Let me go and try to repair the damage.'

For some time she'd been watching the street and suddenly she stood up, leaving her bag behind, and strode purposefully across to the other side. The dress shop was emptying and a stupefied Édouard saw her head straight for a group of employees, grab one (her victim) by the arm, and begin a pleasant smiling conversation. Oddly enough, the girl seemed to be denying something, to be defending, or even excusing, herself. Then she gave in suddenly and followed Béatrice over to Édouard. He stood up, terribly embarrassed.

'Mademoiselle,' said Béatrice, 'allow me to present Édouard Maligrasse. Édouard, this is Zoé, who I brought to such grief. But to prove she doesn't hold it against me, she's agreed to have dinner with us tonight.'

'That is ... I mean ...' stammered the aforementioned Zoé, casting a sequence of delighted and embarrassed glances at Béatrice. 'I mean I was just telling Madame that it wasn't her fault. It's just that I've got personal problems at the moment, and the heat ...'

'Have a little champagne,' said Béatrice cheerfully. 'We've all had it today. I've just got back from tour and hardly know what I'm doing myself.'

In a daze, Édouard stared at her. So their first dinner in Paris after the interminable tour, the dinner he'd imagined in the garden in the cool of the evening, would now take place instead with some insignificant little person they didn't know, but whose spirits were already reviving and who was calling Béatrice by her first name, as requested. He should have got up and left, but he was afraid Zoé would think him a snob, or that later on Béatrice, in the best of faith, would criticize his change in attitude. Dinner was, in fact, awful. The two women talked about clothes and about the glories of the cinema. Zoé got a little drunk, burst into peals of laughter, and said at least ten times that no one would believe her, no one would believe she'd had dinner with Béatrice Valmont. When she left, she kissed Béatrice on both cheeks. Béatrice, of course, had been exquisite during the entire meal. She was gay, even amusing, and her eyes had often, candidly and with no apparent trace of irony, met those of her depressed and exasperated lover. It was ten thirty. They stood on the pavement in front of the restaurant, watching their guest vanish into the metro.

'Charming, isn't she?' said Béatrice cheerfully. 'Do you think she feels better now?'

She turned on a smooth, sincere, almost worried face to Édouard. He stared at her for a good ten seconds before she burst out laughing and collapsed on to a near-by bench. She laughed so hard he could hardly understand what she was saying. 'Oh, my God!' she gasped. 'Your face! If you could just see yourself!' and she went off again in hysterics. People turned to stare at the beautiful dark-haired woman sobbing with laughter on a bench in front of an obviously furious young man. At last she declared that they'd have to drink to that and Édouard followed her into a nightclub, resolved to get roaring drunk.

It was always the same nightclub, and the same crowd; Nicolas, Tony d'Albret, and a few other regulars. Delighted, Béatrice threw herself into their midst and immediately launched into a description of their dinner which everyone found hilariously funny. Nicolas and Tony roared with Béatrice until they were all gasping for breath. The portrait she drew of Édouard was as sweet as it was comic, and made it impossible for him to get angry. In fact, the only thing that made him uncomfortable about the whole idiotic episode was not, he realized, how ridiculous his rôle had been but how insignificant. Any one of Béatrice's companions inclined to attacks of sentimentality or vaguely leftist sympathies could have played the part. What really made him feel terrible was that he was Béatrice's lover, that she had just returned, and that rather than dining *tête-à-tête* with him, she'd preferred to teach him a lesson. It didn't help that everyone else seemed to find this perfectly normal. 'In any case,' Tony was saying as she wiped her eyes, 'with Béatrice, nothing's surprising!'

'If the truth be told,' Béatrice added triumphantly, 'our little Zoé really did try to ruin my fitting. She was tearing through it as fast as she could, all because it was six o'clock. I have no patience with people who do sloppy work.'

Her voice had become serious and her audience nodded its collective head quickly and with dignity. Édouard ordered a third vodka. Vodka made him feel carefree. He knew that in half an hour he'd be like the rest of them; he too would be laughing and making fun of the naïve young man driven to sham sympathy by the tears of a poor seamstress's assistant. And he wouldn't be entirely wrong to laugh. He might well have been the one who'd lectured on the odiousness of social distinctions, but it had been Béatrice, and Béatrice alone, who'd known how to put aside these distinctions and who'd made Zoé put them aside as well. At least for the space of a dinner. She'd left her victim – for the girl had clearly been a victim – enchanted with her evening, while he, Édouard the pathetic,

Édouard the champion of equal rights, had done nothing but chatter hypocritically and sulk.

'So you're a leftist, are you, Édouard?' Tony d'Albret was smiling maliciously and pointing her finger at him, insisting. 'It doesn't surprise me in the least.'

'I'm not a political animal,' Édouard replied. 'But yes, I suppose you have to say I'm a leftist. What do you mean you're not surprised?'

'First, the business of Zoé,' replied Tony. 'And then (bursting into laughter), you won't be angry, will you? It's just that I don't understand a word you write and usually when I don't understand what someone writes, it's because he's a leftist.'

She'd also had too much to drink and suddenly seemed to realize it herself – thanks to that prodigious instinct of hers which in the midst of a shipwreck would have made her offer the last life-jacket to the richest passenger, even if he were some faceless figure in cotton pyjamas. After all, Édouard was an author, and critics these days were so unpredictable that he had every chance of success, leftist or not.

'I'm talking to you like this,' she said, patting Édouard on the arm, 'but I always exaggerate. I really do like what you do, and we're good friends now, aren't we? Anyway, we haven't seen the last of each other, my sweet, at least not with that wild bird there.'

She gestured with her chin towards Béatrice who was dancing – smiling, eyes closed, in Nicolas's arms. They danced very well together.

'Handsome couple, wouldn't you say?' Tony remarked. 'But don't let them get you down, my sweet. They've already done time together. And if things do get you down, just give me a call. If there's anyone in Paris who knows Béatrice, it's me.'

There was a brief silence.

'No, thanks,' Édouard said at last.

In spite of being slightly drunk, he was horrified, first by Tony's proposition, then by the pause that preceded his refusal. There was no doubt that Tony disgusted him, but perhaps it would have been wiser to make a friend of this fake Oenone? Already he saw himself phoning her at dawn, begging her for clues, for ways of tracking Béatrice down when she disappeared.

Already he saw himself sucked into a hellish circle, a sort of vicious melodrama with him the cuckold, Tony the confidante, and Béatrice, of course the fierce coquette.

'Just like the theatre,' he said aloud.

The word 'theatre' rekindled Tony's professional consciousness.

'How's your play coming on?' she asked. 'You must tell me, tell me everything, since we're friends now. Has it got a part for Béatrice?'

Édouard stared at her stupefied, as if she were mad. Then he suddenly understood: he was a writer. Béatrice was an actress, and he loved her. And he realized that he had never imagined writing a part for her. The idea was so totally incongruous, so vulgar; it was an insult to the pure gratuitousness of their affair. His love was one thing, his work another, and the idea of combining them seemed by its very logic obscene. None the less, he felt a twinge of guilt.

'No ... no,' he stammered. 'You see the main rôle's for a man. Actually, I'd already begun the play before I ...'

'Yes, of course. But perhaps we'll have to give that some thought,' Tony said cheerfully. 'Yes, some other time. Anyway, we're positively flooded with offers at the moment. Hasn't Béatrice said anything?'

'No,' replied Édouard, surprised. 'No, nothing.'

It was true. Béatrice hadn't said a word to him. She never talked to him about her work, except to grumble about the obligations to the press. Thankfully, she seemed as reticent on the subject as he was.

'How strange,' Tony murmured. 'Yet that's all she thinks about ... Except when she's in love, of course,' she added obligingly.

Far from making up for the first, Tony's second remark only succeeded in crushing Édouard. Obviously Béatrice thought only about that, about her work. Of course. There was no doubt about it. And obviously she didn't trust him enough to discuss it with him. And obviously, she fell in love from time to time. There'd been someone before him, and someone was doubtless already looming over the horizon to take his place. She may have been his Destiny, but he obviously wasn't hers. He realized that he'd been considering this notion for a very long time, but suddenly it seemed so clear and bright and definitive that all he wanted was to get up and run. The only trouble was their friends were still dancing, Tony was still mumbling and waiters were bringing more drinks. He was paralysed. He felt as if he'd climbed on to a whirling, jangling, jolting, catastrophic merry-go-round. That he'd be thrown off one day without warning was perfectly clear, but for the moment he was pinned to it by sheer speed and the laws of gravity. He ordered another drink and the evening wore on in a sequence of fuzzy theories and fanciful projects. It was four in the morning when Édouard Maligrasse, the notorious teetotaller, was escorted by his mistress back to her flat, dead drunk. She undressed him, kissed him on the forehead and feeling marvellous herself, fell asleep at his side.

9

At eleven the next morning, Béatrice, fresh as a water-colour, was swinging slowly back and forth in her hammock. Édouard, very hungover, sat stiffly on a chair and tried not to look at her.

'I feel so marvellous!' Béatrice exclaimed. 'It's terrible, really. As soon as I go on a binge, I feel marvellous. Unfortunately, I've got to work today.'

The words reverberated like a gong inside Édouard's throbbing skull.

'You look very under the weather, Édouard,' she went on, laughing. 'But we did have a good time last night, didn't we?'

She was wearing a summer dressing-gown and, with no makeup and her hair uncombed, seemed very young and very gay. She tapped the manuscript next to her.

'Raoul Dantys' new script,' she said. 'He wants to do it in October. A dreary subject, but interesting. You wouldn't want to read for me, would you?'

'Of course,' replied Édouard. 'Is it a good part?'

'I don't know if it's good, but it's the biggest. And Raoul has the money to make it. I think I'll do it. Raoul's always got good subjects, a little vulgar maybe but effective. Anyway, I need the money. I always need the money, I know. But honestly, I don't know where it goes ... And you?'

'Oh, me,' said Édouard. 'I have my royalties. They're not bad, and Kurt handles them for me.'

'You ought to give Tony your business,' said Béatrice. 'She's a pro.'

Édouard laughed.

'But she told me herself that she didn't understand anything I wrote.'

'All the more reason,' answered Béatrice. 'That annoys her so she'll sell you for twice as much. Are you writing now?'

Édouard flinched.

'A little – just the beginning. You know, what I was doing in Lille ...'

He stopped short, searching for words. He wasn't feeling particularly brilliant this morning, or particularly sure of himself. He would have liked to talk about his play after making love, for example, in the darkness. Perhaps if he were sure of himself as a lover, he'd feel sure as a writer. But here, in the pale sunlight with the cold taste of stale tobacco in his mouth ... Béatrice put out her hand and tenderly stroked his hair.

'You know,' she said. 'If it upsets you, we won't talk about it. But I love what you write. We're friends too, aren't we, you and I?'

There was an oddly gentle and worried inflection in her voice that astonished him. *Aha*, he said to himself. *So it's true! It's true she thinks I'm too intelligent, too intellectual for her.* She'd certainly made him look more or less ridiculous the previous evening, but perhaps she'd done it only to reassure herself? The dark eyes watching him had no trace of irony in them. They were simply attentive and tender. A small gust of happiness stirred in him. Of course he feared she was capable of anything, but then there was a big part of himself – oddly enough, an unsentimental part – that gave him a peculiar confidence. She might torment him one day but she'd never fail him. Of that he was sure. And he also knew that the only way he was going to find the answers to those innumerable questions he'd never really formulated, but that had been whirling around inside him since childhood, would be in the suffering she inflicted upon him.

When she smiled at him then, he thought she'd understood him. He thought she already knew everything about him, about herself, about their relationship. For the first time, he had the clear if mad impression they were accomplices. (Which, after all, was as it ought to be for people who were trying, separately but together, to escape from their chronic solitude.) The trouble was that neither of them could ever admit to this complicity. Neither of them could ever prove it, much less find refuge in it. It was an unnatural complicity; it went against the very nature of everything that bound together man and woman, or lover and lover, or even subject and object. This complicity rejected all notions of force and power, and so it made their love – past and present – false. Artificial. The truth was, however, that Édouard set great store by this blind and rickety love, the way certain mothers are especially attached to their mongoloid children. It was a strange child indeed, this love of theirs. From the very moment of its birth, it had been beaten and rejected by an undeserving mother and a vulnerable father, but it had none the less returned after five years, cunning and triumphant, and had settled in again between them. Édouard wondered if, of the three of them, this child might not just be the most alive and the most important, no matter what they might do later on to deny it.

'I'd love to read you what I've written,' he said. 'But I don't think you'll like it.'

'Look,' replied Béatrice. 'Why don't you climb into the hammock, drink your coffee, and try breathing very slowly. Not too deeply, mind you. You should never breathe too deeply. You shouldn't do callisthenics every day either, or avoid fatty foods, or make sure you've taken all your makeup off before you go to bed. If you do, you'll be dead in ten days. Or in ten years, which is worse.'

'You don't believe the experts?' Édouard asked, surprised.

'Not on your life!' exclaimed Béatrice, stretching slowly and arrogantly. 'There are some people who need all the advice they can get, people who thrive on permissions and prohibitions. Now, for example, they say it's all right to make love with five people at the same time, but you mustn't smoke. Thank God there are the others, like you and me, and the *concierge* over there, and my taxi driver yesterday. Happy people, intelligent, liberated. You know, Édouard ... when all is said and done, I really do love the French!'

'What's come over you?' asked Édouard. 'I thought you didn't give a damn about such things. I mean, about generalizations.'

'There's a lot you don't know about me,' said Béatrice tenderly. 'In fact, you don't really know anything at all about me. You just love me. What's your hero's name?'

'Frédéric,' he replied. 'He's young and a little mad and has a very comfortable and orderly family life. Then óne day he finds he's inherited a lot of money and he forces each member of his family to play outrageous rôles: his mother has to fall in love with him, his father has to hate him, his sister to make him ashamed, and so on. After a while, they all get so involved in the game that they end up believing it, and even going beyond it. So Frédéric's little comedy turns sour.'

'But that's an awful story!' said Béatrice, indignant. 'What gives him the right to want to change people?'

'To start with, he just wanted them to pay more attention to him, you see. Like everybody else in the world, he just wanted more attention. So he put masks on them. But then the masks became real ...'

'The phone!' Béatrice interrupted, and rushed into the house. *With relief*, Édouard thought. Obviously, he had no idea how to tell a story. Furious with himself, he picked up Béatrice's script.

'I cannot live,' the heroine, Clara was saying. 'Without your love, I cannot breathe. I walk through the streets like a robot. I don't even notice what colour the sky is any more. You *have* to love me; it's your blood that runs in my veins ...'

Disheartened at first, Édouard suddenly began to laugh. After all, if you didn't worry about style, it was exactly the same story. Both he and Raoul, or Raoul's script writer, wanted to tell the same story, the same endless supplication, the same terror, the same demand; Don't leave me alone! It wasn't really worth looking any further. Every piece of literature and every piece of music came from this cry, or from its sometimes absurd corollaries. Like jealousy, for instance, which struck him suddenly. Who had Béatrice been talking to for so long? Why had she jumped out of the hammock so fast? Had she been waiting for the call? Expecting it? And who was responsible for her flattering opinion about the French?

When she came back with the announcement that Tony d'Albret had invited herself for lunch, Édouard, despite the fact he found the woman increasingly odious, was ashamed to feel such enormous relief.

'How utterly charming!' Tony cried. 'You look just like a Peynet drawing! And the garden's perfectly divine!'

The garden was indeed charming, and wholly unexpected at the Alma, not far from the Champs-Élysées where Tony d'Albret spent her days dispersing her vital forces. She put a heavy briefcase down beside her and collapsed into an armchair.

'A real oasis,' she went on. 'Paris is killing. Béatrice dear, Raoul is on tenterhooks; he keeps ringing to find out if you'll do it. Have you read the script?'

'Just when did you expect me to read it?' said Béatrice. 'None of us got to bed before four.'

'Four thirty,' Tony corrected. 'And I was up at nine. Feeling better, Édouard? You were rather smashed last night, it seemed to me ... But I haven't forgotten a word of our conversation.'

Édouard blushed. Was she alluding to their brief exchange about Béatrice, alluding to it right in front of her? This woman obviously stopped short of nothing. There she was, square and solid in her beige gabardine suit, with short cut hair, flashing eyes, a thin mouth outlined in translucent lipstick, gleaming fingernails, and an incredibly pretentious Berber ring on her index finger that heightened the maniacal feverishness of her gestures. In fact, inside this little fortress of craft, cunning, ambition, and common sense, her nerves offered the only conceivable crack.

'I ran into Maddison,' she declared in a ringing voice. '*The* Maddison. In *Fouquet's*.'

Édouard looked puzzled, so she plunged on quickly.

'Don't tell me you don't know E. P. Maddison? The king of Broadway? I had an absolutely ingenious idea, Édouard. I sent him your play and he's coming to see it tonight! Luckily, he didn't have any other plans.'

'Not bad,' Béatrice murmured admiringly.

'It's just the kind of theatre they love over there at the moment,' Tony said, as if evoking some oddity in the customs of New Guinea aborigines. 'The less they understand, the better they like it. I took the liberty of saying I was your agent, since Maddison trusts me. Who *is* your agent, by the way?'

'I don't have one,' Édouard answered weakly. 'Kurt read my play first. He found the theatre and took care of getting it put on in London and Stockholm.'

'You don't have an agent?' Tony exclaimed, totally incredulous.

Had Édouard declared himself blind from birth or destined for an early death, she couldn't have been more upset. Béatrice laughed.

'Édouard's an orphan, you see,' she explained. 'He fell from the sky into this hammock and it's all you can do to get him to give Cathy a few shirts to wash.'

It was true that out of a combination of superstition and delicacy, Édouard had not yet hung a single suit of clothes in Béatrice's flat, a state of affairs that obliged him to keep running between his functional and empty studio and the blue room he felt to be his only real home.

'This is no joking matter,' Tony replied gravely. 'I can't force myself on you, Édouard, but you do know my credentials.'

Édouard, who knew nothing of them at all, nodded his head. He too began to feel like laughing.

'I doubt if there's anyone in the entire Paris marketplace who'd say a word against me,' Tony continued. 'I'm a little blunt, I know, because I always say exactly what I think, and because I love art, as silly as it may sound. But before everything else, my clients are my friends. Get that into your head, Édouard. If you join my stable, it will be as a friend; before all else.'

'But *after* the ten per cent,' added Béatrice quietly.

'Let's not worry about money,' Tony declared, unperturbed, dismissing this trifling detail with a wave of her hand. 'Édouard's not a money man. I've always felt that. Édouard's an artist, my dear,' she added reproachfully, turning to Béatrice.

'And it's for this artist that I, Tony d'Albret, am going to assure a luxurious life, free of all material anxieties,' Béatrice went on, imitating Tony to perfection. 'Thanks to me, he'll be able to consecrate himself solely to his art. Tony d'Albret, synonym for flair and efficacy ...'

The imitation was so perfect that Édouard burst out laughing. Tony stood up and walked over to the hammock.

'Let's shake on it, Édouard. As far as I'm concerned, that's worth more than any contract.'

Édouard hesitated and glanced at Béatrice who was now laughing openly.

'You're impossible, Tony!' she cried. 'The frank and open handshake! Now I've seen everything! Édouard, for the love of God, shake her hand so we can all get down to the champagne!'

Édouard shook, and Tony went back and sat down with dignity.

'We'll have to start by getting your second play put on,' she said. 'Woodward could stake it, for example. Yes, a brilliant idea, Woodward.'

'But ...' Édouard stammered weakly. 'But they used Kurt's production in London. Kurt was there ...'

'Kurt, Kurt,' Tony snapped. 'Your Kurt's an intellectual director who happens to be fashionable at the moment, though God only knows why. The Americans do things very differently, let me tell you. You're the one who *wrote* the thing, aren't you? You didn't sign anything with Kurt, I hope?'

'No,' replied Édouard, desperately. 'But really, he's the one who ... who helped me in the beginning and ...'

'It doesn't matter,' Tony interrupted. 'Kurt or no Kurt, your play would have been done. With a talent like yours ... Oh yes, yes, my dear Édouard, you can't hide a light like yours under a bushel for long. Kurt was just lucky, believe me. Not you, *him*. But from now on I'll take care of everything. And it's none too soon, I might add.'

As if to stress the urgency, she swallowed the champagne Béatrice offered her at one gulp. Édouard was still slightly queasy but, out of sheer politeness, felt obliged to empty his glass as well.

'You must give me your manuscripts,' Tony continued, warming to her subject. 'Who's your publisher?'

'Not only will you have to give her your scripts, you'll have to explain them to her,' Béatrice said, sending him a little smile. 'Maybe you'd do better to give her a synopsis of the plot. You can give us both evening lectures, in the moonlight, right in this garden. We'll learn together, Tony and I; we'll learn to decipher the codes and silences of the modern theatre. You'll have a lovely little class, very attentive, very well-behaved.'

There was a sadness in the irony that surprised him, and he looked at her questioningly.

'When I first knew you five years ago, you were like a little baby goat. A kid,' Béatrice went on dreamily. 'An accountant? In an insurance office? And now, my poor darling, between your one talent and Tony's many talents, you've turned wolf. You've become a successful author ...'

'You have something against success?' inquired Tony, a hint of sarcasm in her voice.

The look the two women exchanged was charged with everything but friendship. Béatrice turned away first.

'No,' she said firmly. 'I have absolutely nothing against success. And speaking of which, have you heard from our friend Jolyet?'

Édouard jumped. It was the last name in the world he wanted to hear. Jolyet was a casual, jolly, and seductive fifty-year-old man whose intelligence and free spirit might well have appealed to Édouard enormously when he'd first met him five years ago. Unfortunately, however, André Jolyet was the owner of a theatre and, unfortunately, at the time Béatrice was more than a little appealing to him – physically, that is – and, unfortunately, Jolyet also felt she was a very talented actress. He'd offered her two leading rôles: one on the stage of his theatre, the other in his bed. Édouard, who'd been living with Béatrice for a few months, had been politely shown the door. He'd never known – and the ignorance had poisoned his grief – if Béatrice had been attracted to Jolyet for reasons other than professional ones. He hadn't been able to imagine the truth, which was simple enough: Béatrice had loved Jolyet because he'd given her an opportunity for success. And she'd loved him sincerely, without pettiness or sordid calculation. (After all, one does sometimes let oneself love other people, even though love deprives one of everything one has : intelligence, sense of humour, courage. So why not love people who let one keep – and even use – these things? It's no more moral to love someone who makes one suffer than to love someone who gives one pleasure, so why not love someone for his money if that money gives one the time to dream about him, buy him flowers, find ways of making him happy?)

When he'd first known Béatrice, Édouard had been entirely devoted, nothing more nor less than the particular reflection of herself she'd been looking for. Jolyet, however, had turned this reflection into a reality. For Béatrice knew there were a thousand good-looking men in Paris ready to fall at her feet, but only one theatre owner ready to launch her career. And so she'd calmly announced to Édouard that she no longer loved him. It was this that he couldn't bear. Had she slept with Jolyet and then taken the trouble to lie to him about it, to hide her new affair from him, he could at least have drowned his sorrows in jealousy or derision. But she'd been honest, which was far worse. She'd simply told him truthfully that she didn't love him any more. The trouble was that, although lovers are always screaming for sincerity, there are times when sincerity bears a strong resemblance to callousness. Indeed, because their break-up had been so easy, so obvious, so frank, Édouard still had the feeling that apart from a purely sensual interlude – and scarcely even that as he'd been very young at the time, and very awkward – he'd meant nothing at all to her.

With Béatrice, Édouard would always be what he'd been for an hour in that café on the Avenue Montaigne where she'd given him his notice: a lost and trembling young man who found his dismissal as normal as it was atrocious. There'd been no mirror on that café terrace, but he could still see his miserable self in his old grey tweed jacket. (Memory can lie, as much as imagination, of course, and its lies can be every bit as cruel.) In any case, until now both he and Béatrice, as if by some tacit agreement, had carefully avoided the name Jolyet.

'I ran into him yesterday on the Champs-Élysées,' Tony replied. 'A walking scarecrow ... But there he was, strolling along in the sunshine and whistling as if nothing at all were the matter.'

'As if nothing were the matter?' echoed Béatrice. '*Is there something the matter?*'

'Don't you know? They say he has ... oh, well, you know, some sort of tumour ... You know what I mean ...'

Tony's voice had dropped, but it was so unusual to hear her whisper that her listeners started.

'What? You mean cancer?' asked Béatrice. 'Why don't you just say what you mean, Tony? Discretion isn't exactly your forte.'

'All right. He has cancer of the throat, to be precise,' said Tony. 'But I don't think he knows about it himself because he walks around whistling. Ignorance, you know, is often ...'

'Not for Jolyet,' Béatrice broke in. 'The blessings of ignorance aren't for him. It's just that he's always lived in a state of grace; he's always felt he even had enough grace left over to share with others. With life, actually. Only now he's sharing it with death.'

Instead of annoying Édouard, the warmth and tenderness in her voice moved him. He imagined Jolyet walking along, accompanied by frivolous memories and on his way to meet a very real death. He imagined his resolute smile as he strolled beneath the chestnut trees he'd never again see in flower.

'That's nice,' he said, looking at Béatrice. 'What you just said is nice – the idea that someone can have grace to spare. Did you love him very much?'

She turned towards him and he saw, to his astonishment, that her eyes had misted over and were filling with tears. It wasn't that he feared the rivalry of a dying man, nor even that his former jealousies had been re-awakened by the mention of the name. No, he was simply afraid of this suddenly tender woman who was so sensitive to other people's dignity, afraid of this compassionate stranger who seemed so far removed from the pagan idol he loved.

'Don't worry,' she reassured him quickly. 'I'm only crying about myself. As usual.'

IO

Ten days went by, all deliciously identical. Béatrice read her script and looked after her plants with a professionalism that disconcerted even Édouard, although he'd been brought up in the country. She saw almost no one. 'I don't have any friends,' she said, to his surprise. 'I've never wanted friends. Or had the time for them. I have my work and my lovers. That's plenty.' She said this with such a tranquil sort of pride that he didn't know whether to congratulate himself or not. For him, friendship meant constancy and confidence, two words Béatrice knew nothing about. On the other hand, this particular lack of knowledge permitted him to be alone with her. She listened to records, walking about humming, and from time to time, in the middle of the day or night, she ordered him to come to her. Upon which they'd retire to the blue room, close the shutters against the sun, and make love. There was an opera Édouard particularly loved that spring. He knew where it surged forward and where it held back, and he always tried to make both Béatrice's moans and the violins arrive at their respective paroxysms together. The record remained permanently on the record player and he would switch it on without even thinking whenever they made love. Béatrice noticed but said nothing. Her sense of modesty was as strange as her immodesties were extravagant.

Sometimes, as he lay across the bed dying of thirst and exhaustion, Édouard watched the evening shadows stretching across the garden, and the silhouettes of the hammocks and the old tree against the dying light. A tranquil and innocent picture, an incongruous backdrop for the ravaged sheets and the carpet strewn with clothes, and it reminded him of odds and ends of poems he'd learned at school. *Avec ses baisers et ses étreintes amies*, he remembered, *c'était bien un ciel, un*

*sombre ciel où j'entrais, et où j'aurais aimé être laissée, pauvre,
sourde, muette, aveugle ...* Snatches of Rimbaud, and of
Béatrice's soft voice on the telephone behind him, a voice so
posed, even composed, yet one he had heard so decomposed, so
little posed, a mere half hour before. Without turning around,
without taking his eyes from the green of the garden and
from the curtains swollen by the evening breeze, he reached
out behind him and touched a warm consenting thigh. While
outside, the wild and tender birds played childishly and protested the coming of the night settling rapidly upon them.
The birds seemed to be warning him about something. They
were telling him to pay attention, to take a careful look at the
patterns of light, to fill himself with the near-by warmth, to
inscribe the picture precisely and for ever in his mind's eye.
For it was the picture of his happiness and one day when it
was gone, when he no longer possessed it, it would still remain, perfectly preserved in his memory.

What Édouard didn't know, of course, was that memory
has no respect for aesthetics, that it has no taste, and that the
image of his lost happiness would be perfectly synonymous
and banal. It would be Béatrice turning around to look at him,
for instance, before getting into a taxi. (For, when someone has
stopped loving one, one never remembers his voice saying
'I love you'. All one remembers is a voice saying 'It's chilly
tonight' or 'Your sweater's too long'. One never remembers a
face convulsed with pleasure; all one remembers is a dis-
traught and hesitant countenance in the rain. It's as if memory, like intelligence, deliberately ignores the movements of
the heart.)

Sometimes during these moments, Béatrice would turn towards him and say 'I love you', either because she'd been moved
by the felicity of the moment itself or because Édouard's happiness was so contagious. And he would smile, although he didn't
believe her. These words of love enchanted him, but they also
sounded too much like lines from some old-fashioned comedy,
lines he himself might have written five years before in a moment of aberration. At best, he felt Béatrice was giving a bad
performance. After all, didn't the fact that she hadn't loved him
once before prohibit her from loving him now? For, once again,

Édouard didn't know that people can change their minds about their indifference as well as their passion. He didn't know that time delights in these strange little games, in these abrupt reversals that always astonish their witnesses. He didn't know that people can find themselves burning with desire one evening for someone they'd wished to see burning in hell ten years before. Yet since she so seldom said these words, he felt a kind of desperate happiness in hearing them, in having her repeat them, even in having her swear to them. If he told himself they weren't true, it was only because he lacked the lucidity to tell himself it was all too late. But had he been able to do that, he would have had to explain to himself just why it was too late – after all, at that very moment he was there and he loved her. Beyond that, he simply couldn't go.

In the meantime, he worked. He worked hard, until his play began to reverberate inside him like something with its own existence. One evening, after he'd drunk several glasses of port with Béatrice in the garden and felt himself particularly inspired, he tried reading a passage to her. But instead of beginning at the beginning, he naturally started with what he'd written that afternoon, and which seemed to him, of course, more brilliant. Thrown abruptly into the company of a hero she knew nothing about, Béatrice only became thoroughly confused, then annoyed, and finally visibly bored. Édouard's voice dropped lower and lower as he felt her attention wandering, until suddenly he became furious and with one dramatic sweep, leaped to his feet, tore up the pages, and threw them at her feet.

'You're right!' he shouted, to her amazement. 'You're absolutely right! It's worthless!'

He stormed inside and threw himself on the bed. Once he'd calmed down, his first concern was to reconstruct in his head the scene he'd just destroyed. Thank God he knew almost all of it by heart and, thank God, there was surely an early draft somewhere in his desk. An immense wave of relief washed over him. The main thing was there; the text itself was there. Whether Béatrice liked it or not suddenly seemed irrelevant; or at least of secondary importance. It was all his fault anyway; he ought never to have thrown Frédéric's tirade against his mother at her without first explaining the reason for the tirade. Not even the most partial critic would have appreciated the violence he'd hoped he'd given that scene. The trouble was that now he'd have to overcome Béatrice's resistance if he wanted to read her any more. For Béatrice was – a priori – always wary of boredom, concerning not only his play, but him as well. Could she in fact be bored with him? Boredom itself was so foreign a concept to him, each moment seeming to him so fragile and so intense, that he'd never dreamed of asking what she, the mistress of their Destiny, thought about their shared solitude. Perhaps outside their moments of passion, she found it a little flat, a little tepid? Perhaps his impression of shared tenderness and laughter was his alone? In fact, it was entirely possible she was bored. The fact that an inmate on death-row never gets bored is no reason to think that his executioner might not yawn once or twice before tackling the job in hand.

The executioner entered the bedroom with a serious expression on her face and sat down at the foot of the bed. She had one hand hidden behind her back.

'Forgive me,' said Édouard. 'I was ridiculous.'

'But very amusing,' replied Béatrice. 'The outraged author tearing up his manuscript and throwing it in the face of his obtuse audience. I didn't know you were so sensitive.'

'It's not that,' said Édouard lamely. 'It's just that I suddenly realized how bad it was ...'

'It's not because the play is bad,' Béatrice broke in. 'It's because you read so badly, my poor Édouard. The next time, just give me the play to read for myself. Here.'

And she held out the complex puzzle of torn pages that she'd put back together again with scotch tape.

'Here's your work,' she said. 'I can't stand seeing someone destroy what he's done in anger. It's too precious – someone who invents people, ideas. You have no right to do that, to tear it up. And besides, it's absurd.'

She talked to him as if to a child, and she seemed suddenly sad and a little weary. Édouard wanted to ask her forgiveness, but he didn't know what for exactly. He laid his head on her shoulder; she put her hand on the back of his neck and stroked his hair. And they stayed like that, numb and immobile, each knowing that the other was following an independent train of thought and, in some obscure way, both resigned to it. They leaned against each other like two tired horses and for once there was no flare-up of desire, no violent flaming. For once, there was no sensuality, burgeoning or replete, in the touch of their bodies. At last they shared a feeling, even if it was only one of melancholy.

Béatrice was the first to snap out of it. She stood up, started towards the garden, then turned around. The bones in her face, the swell of her lips, the lines of her body were accentuated by the light as she stood by the french windows, and Édouard was seized again by desire and hesitation. Then the clocks began to tick once more and they were no longer equals, but lovers.

'I invited Jolyet to lunch tomorrow,' said Béatrice. 'If that bores or bothers you, you can eat out. Maybe you can phone your friend Kurt.'

For the first time in ten days, her tone was definitely disagreeable.

'What do you mean?' asked Édouard.

Suddenly, he panicked. He'd been wrong to hang on to her like an albatross for ten days, to follow her, interrogate her. He'd been wrong to want to read her his play. He'd been wrong to want to share anything at all with her. He'd gone outside his margin of security. She couldn't stand him any more.

'I mean that you're being a little casual with your friend Kurt,' Béatrice replied. 'You ought to tell him about Tony, first of all. Because you're playing a really dirty trick on him, aren't you?'

Édouard started.

'But you yourself saw how it happened! And in any case, nothing's really been decided. I mean I haven't really thought about it . . .'

'I know,' said Béatrice. 'You haven't really thought about anything. But don't come to me afterwards and start sermonizing about my lack of delicacy with others. As for Jolyet, I intend to cheer him up tomorrow and I don't think the presence of someone sulking in a corner is going to be much help.'

'But why would I sulk?'

He was totally lost now. The day had been turned upside down and in this suddenly hard and scornful silhouette, in her black and stony look, he couldn't recognize the tender and weary woman who'd been caressing his hair and talking to him about his work only two minutes before.

'You'll sulk because you'll be thinking about how I left you for him five years ago. And you'll stew over your old sad memories and wallow in self-pity. I sometimes wonder just what you've been doing for five years, Édouard. You may live in the past, but I'm bored by it. I hardly remember what you were like then. A little thinner maybe, and a little less skilful in bed. When you talk about our old affair, I feel as if you're talking about someone else. You were an accident for me, Édouard, just a vague accident. And don't you forget it.'

'I knew that then,' replied Édouard. 'And I know it now. I've never been anything but an accident. That's the only rôle I can play, isn't it?'

'I've never had anything but accidents, my little Édouard. Some short, some long. And how long they were was something that didn't always depend on me, no matter what you may think.'

'You're bored with me, aren't you?'

Édouard heard the question with horror. How could he have asked something so direct and dangerous? He'd promised himself to slip into step beside Béatrice, to slip into life at her side, to get her used to him, and not to question their relationship. On the contrary, he'd promised himself to make it seem inevitable, to make it seem to her the most natural thing in the world. And if she said that yes, yes, she was bored with him, what would be left but to leave, to go somewhere far away from her, to exist quietly, like a living corpse? He knew she was perfectly capable of answering yes. He knew that with one blow, she could repudiate these last two months and all their nights of love and all the cries and sighs. He knew she could forget him all at once and for ever.

'If I were bored with you,' she said, 'I'd leave you. At the moment I find you a little tense, but not exactly what I'd call boring.'

She laughed then, completely relaxed.

'There's a good western on TV,' she said. 'Why don't you put all these little papers away and not tear any more up? I'd rather not spend the rest of my life taping them back together again.'

Édouard stayed on the bed, exhausted, like someone who'd been within a hair's breadth of certain death. He felt as if he'd been beaten to a pulp, and not only physically. All the evidence had been thrown at him at once: Béatrice didn't love him, had never loved him, would leave him one day. But when she'd turned back into the cruel stranger of yesteryear, he'd been surprised to feel a sort of pleasure in his despair.

II

'You get lovelier all the time,' Jolyet remarked thoughtfully.

Installed in an armchair at Béatrice's feet, he reached out and gently swung her hammock. With Édouard sitting on the other side, both men – one young, one dying – appeared to frame her like some sort of allegory. As always, Jolyet was slender, alert, and elegant. Only his eyes had become large and troubled and seemed strangely out of place, like two ice-blue pools encrusted in an ever-ironic face. He'd been gay and nonchalant while they'd talked about literature, politics and the theatre, coughing from time to time, a little absent-mindedly. At those moments, Béatrice looked him straight in the eye, but he never blinked. Édouard had wanted to leave as soon as lunch was over, and had started fumbling for an excuse, but Jolyet, polite and authoritative, had told him he mustn't leave so soon and that he was terribly pleased to see him again.

'You've become better-looking, too,' he went on, turning to Édouard. 'You had a certain charm five years ago, but now you have something else. I like your plays very much, you know. Especially the last one, although it's a bit depressing for a man of my age.'

He seemed very sincere and Édouard was touched. People hardly ever talked to him about his plays without his feeling uncomfortable, but there'd been a sort of tranquil approval in Jolyet's voice, the suggestion of authentic complicity, of two professionals discussing their trade. It was then that Béatrice, who had been looking and listening to one, then the other, stretched and got out of the hammock.

'Excuse me a minute,' she said. 'I have to ring Raoul. I think I will do that film of his after all.'

The two men watched her walk into the flat. Jolyet's eyes met Édouard's.

'You seem as much in love as before,' he remarked, smiling affectionately.

Édouard returned the smile without effort. Now that they were alone, he noticed the little wrinkles at the corners of the mouth and eyes, like a series of small attacks, of scars due not to age but to something else, perhaps to the habit – acquired too soon – of suffering in silence.

'You made quite an impression on me at the time,' Jolyet went on. 'Does it upset you if I talk about it?'

'No,' Édouard replied. 'Quite the contrary.'

'It was because I felt you were completely defenceless. If I'd known you wrote, I wouldn't have been so worried.'

He lit a cigarette, coughed, eyed it with a detached sort of rage, and inhaled a second time with obvious satisfaction.

'Even so, I was very unhappy,' said Édouard.

'Ah, yes,' Jolyet admitted. 'That was obvious. I told Béatrice to go easy with you, but going easy is not exactly one of her strong points. As you well know.'

He laughed, coughed again, then suddenly threw down the cigarette and ground it out with his heel.

'It's so tedious,' he said. 'Dying apart, it's all these perpetual little battles with the weed. Odious.'

He glanced at Édouard who sat immobile in his chair.

'You know about it, of course,' Jolyet continued. 'I expect that horror Tony d'Albret has told you everything. Béatrice would love me to talk to her about my impending demise, but my provincial education forbids me to speak of my ailments in the presence of women. And yet they do seem to love it.'

'Do you suffer very much?' asked Édouard.

Jolyet hesitated, then surprisingly, glanced at his watch.

'Not yet,' he replied. 'But as soon as it becomes truly disagreeable, I have everything I need to end it. Perhaps a month from now. Or two. There's no sense making a big production out of it, you know. In fact, it's rather amusing in a way to walk around the city and look at people and never feel particularly concerned by anything. If I'd made a habit of living in the future – I'm sure I'd be absolutely desperate, but I've always made it a point to live squarely in the present. But we shouldn't be talking about this, really. What about you? Are you happy?'

'I don't know,' said Édouard. 'I've never asked myself the question. I haven't had time.'

He was very tempted to confide in Jolyet. He seemed to be the only person to whom he could explain his life, the only person to whom he wanted to explain it, the only person – perhaps because of his detachment – who he thought might be able to help him.

'But I know I'm miserable without her,' he went on.

'Béatrice is worthy of great esteem,' Jolyet said. 'Fierce, of course, but eminently worthy. I lived with her for a year, you know. The play she did for me made her, and for a year she believed in me heart and soul. Or in my luck. Then some English actor came along. Or American, I can't remember which. She tried to justify herself; she tried to lie to me, but I told her one ought never to justify or excuse oneself for anything or to anyone. Except perhaps to those people one makes suffer. But since she was incapable of making me suffer ...'

'Is that true?' Édouard broke in.

'Partly. Anyway, we parted friends, which is a miracle where Béatrice is concerned. She does love to leave a mass of smouldering ruins behind her. But I'm delighted to see you've managed to re-emerge from them.'

Jolyet got to his feet and began wandering around the garden. He leaned against the tree and rubbed his cheek against the bark for a moment, a soft and animal gesture, already nostalgic, as if he'd stumbled by accident on some half-forgotten tune. Then he stepped back, glanced at Édouard, and sat down again opposite him. Fascinated, Édouard followed his every move. Jolyet removed a splinter of bark from the lapel of his jacket, and Édouard noticed how slender and beautiful his hand was. Indeed, Jolyet was one of the few directors in Paris whose reputation was based more on an aesthetic than a business sense.

'You should pay more attention to the secondary characters in your plays,' he continued. 'Penelope, for example, in the last one. She would have been superb if you'd developed her a little more. But that's just a detail, of course.

You're a fine writer, Édouard. I'm delighted to have been able to tell you that. And if it reassures you . . .'

'One is never reassured about what one does,' said Édouard.

'I'm not talking about that. What I mean is that you have little to fear as long as you keep writing. It's a well-known fact that writers – or all artists, all people who create things – know how to control their hearts and their bodies extremely well. They feed both with the same facility, as soon as they begin to create. Their appetites may be violent but they're of secondary importance; their emotional well-being, as it were, is reduced to a kind of tedious necessity. If they make a mistake, even if they suffer because of it, they do so rather casually. It's the light-heartedness that comes from knowing that no matter what happens, mistakes are not things they're capable of making. Not really.'

'I don't agree,' said Édouard, feeling rather more irritated than reassured. 'If Béatrice left me, I'd be incapable of writing.'

'For how long?' Jolyet demanded.

He stood up, walked over to Édouard, and studied him for a moment.

'You must find me either very restless or terribly solemn,' he smiled. 'Actually, I'm restless because I enjoy feeling the muscles in my legs moving. I was once a great walker, you know. Or an old hiker, if you prefer. But then, it doesn't really matter, does it? If you find me solemn, I mean. The fact is, I suppose, that I couldn't care less about your judgement. In spite of the affection I feel for you,' he added, smiling.

For an instant, Jolyet's charm, his famous charm, resurfaced, lighting up his blue eyes, bringing colour to his cheeks, smoothing his brow.

'I think I'll go and see Béatrice now,' he said. 'She must be waiting for me. And since I feel in a good mood, I may even let my hair down and cry on her shoulder, just to make her happy. It'll be a nice memory for her. Later on she can say that beneath that indifferent exterior, I was really a very human human being. I even cried on her shoulder exactly one month – or two – before . . . and so on.'

He laughed, clapped Édouard on the shoulder, and went off into the house. Édouard watched him disappear with a curious sort of despair. He would have given his right arm at that moment if this man he'd hated so violently could live for one more year. It seemed to him that in that circle – that at once brilliant and nauseating circle into which his success was dragging him – Jolyet was the only truly elegant knight, the only one who still had a genuine passion for that 'Art' Tony d'Albret was always evoking so complacently. He knew he'd found a real friend just as he was about to lose him. He knew too that Jolyet was right about Penelope, that he was telling the truth, for after all, he had no time left for lies.

When Béatrice came back into the garden an hour later, her eyes were red. She sat down on the arm of Édouard's chair and, in a wholly uncharacteristic gesture, hid her head on his shoulder and said nothing. He asked no questions. Later, during the night, she asked him softly, almost pleadingly, in a voice Édouard had never heard before, if he wouldn't like to come with her and spend a few days in the sun, in a villa in the Midi where Jolyet was going the following week to rest.

'Of course,' he replied.

Tenderly, he kissed her eyes, her cheek, her forehead, as one kissed an unhappy child.

'Of course we'll go, of course . . .'

For the first time, he felt himself to be stronger than she. More mature. For the first time, he had the vague impression she needed him, a happiness for once uncoloured by fear or constraint. His eyes filled with tears.

'Anyway,' Béatrice's voice continued at his side, 'it wouldn't be a bad idea to get a little suntan.'

Two weeks later, Édouard was leaning against a balcony railing above the sea. In the distance, a sailing boat tacked into the wind and on the boat, thanks to the powerful binoculars he'd found in Jolyet's house, Édouard could just make out the shapes of Béatrice and a very young man who happened to be kissing her on the lips. Her hands were crossed behind his suntanned neck and she was smiling, her body golden and harmonious, her hair swept back by the wind. She was beautiful. Then the young man abandoned her mouth and moved to her breasts.

The binoculars slid from Édouard's moist hands and he fumbled feverishly to raise them again.

A few yards behind him on the balcony, Jolyet watched too, elegant in white twill, a burnt-out cigarette dangling from his fingertips. He was smiling sadly, as if he too were looking through the binoculars. As Édouard watched, the sea began tossing about at the end of the glasses, became fuzzy, foamy, then empty. When he finally located her again, Béatrice had stopped smiling. Her body was arched, her eyes closed; the young man had disappeared from his field of vision. Édouard watched her jerk backwards suddenly, saw her mouth open, and in a last mocking reflex action, he put his hands over his ears. The binoculars smashed on to the rocks below. When he turned around, there was no one behind him. There were only some faded mimosa trees and a pretentious deserted terrace on which he seemed to see, already propped up for him against a pillar like some tragic vaudeville queen, the grotesque and terrifying figure of his jealousy.

12

'Won't you have a little more soufflé, Édouard?' Jolyet asked.

Édouard didn't answer. Intrigued, Béatrice glanced at him, then smiled. She was enjoying herself, thinking what a mad idea it had been to go off alone with Gino on the boat. It had certainly been a long time since she'd seen such a handsome creature. And so brazen, so naturally brazen. She'd protested at first, but then the burning sun, the swell of the sea, and the freshness of his mouth had suddenly come together in one brutal and irresistible wave of desire. Confronted with this argument, her body – like an honest mathematician faced with a surprising and unforeseen piece of evidence – had surrendered with its usual tranquil obedience. Far from feeling ashamed, however, Béatrice had felt instead a certain pride in discovering that the independence and the appetite of her intractable body were still intact. Indeed, she'd always had a triumphant and untroubled picture of her own sensuality; she'd always acknowledged her desires and had almost always satisfied them. All sexual predilections were blameless as far as she was concerned, unless of course they were hopelessly sectarian, and the exhibitionism, the fantasies, the embarrassing guilts and secrets that ravaged her contemporaries were completely beyond her understanding. In the final analysis, she found the pleasure-is-obligatory dictum of her age to be as ridiculous as the dictum of ten years ago that had prohibited it. And so tonight she felt oddly reassured and wholly at ease, as if her treachery had proved that where Édouard was concerned, her body could protect her even against herself.

When she'd returned, late, she'd found both her men sitting on the terrace silently contemplating the sea instead of discussing books and plays as they'd been doing for a week.

What had happened was that she'd just begun to feel bored when they'd run into Gino and his mother, one of Jolyet's ex-mistresses. It wasn't Béatrice's fault if Édouard didn't like the sea, just as it wasn't her fault if the consequences had been so dazzling. *Édouard has no reason to sulk*, she thought, and she smiled at Jolyet who was at great pains to keep the conversation going. She even winked at him, a wink of complicity which to her great surprise, he didn't return.

'What've you two been doing all afternoon?' she inquired.

Édouard stared at the ground, Jolyet coughed.

'I was tired, my dear. I stayed in my room and read. Édouard did the same, I believe.'

'You ought to have come along,' said Béatrice. 'It was a marvellous outing. Little Gino took us all the way to Cap Martin. We even passed right in front of the house.'

'Who's "we"?' demanded Édouard.

'He and I,' answered Béatrice calmly. 'At the last minute, his mother decided not to come along. He's a nice boy,' she added. 'Very well brought up.'

Jolyet pushed aside his plate and stood up.

'You'll have to excuse me,' he said. 'I'm really terribly tired this evening, I'm going to bed.'

This was the first time since they'd been there that he'd admitted to being tired. Béatrice was worried. Up to now, he'd been so charming, so gay, and so seemingly unconcerned about his condition, that this sudden confession of weakness was a shocking reminder.

'Are you all right?' she asked.

He reassured her, kissed her hand, tapped Édouard on the shoulder, and headed for the stairs. Béatrice watched him closely, then turned to Édouard, who seemed paralysed.

'I'm terribly worried about him,' she said. 'And you? What's the matter with you?'

Édouard raised his eyes, then lowered them immediately. He was having great difficulty, an almost mechanical difficulty, in opening his mouth.

'Jolyet has a beautiful pair of binoculars,' he said flatly. 'I was trying them out this afternoon and I happened, by accident, to focus on to your boat.'

There was a moment's silence. He ran his fork over the tablecloth, his eyes still lowered, his ears ringing.

'I see,' Béatrice replied pensively. 'What an unfortunate accident.'

Édouard had been prepared for everything except her placidity, and, for a moment, he went numb. He'd been waiting for this scene for the past three hours, the way one waits for the crash of cymbals in a symphony. But instead of cymbals, all he'd had was a tranquil bassoon.

'Does he make love well, this Gino?' he demanded.

Slowly and deliberately, Béatrice lit a cigarette.

'Pretty well. Not as well as you, but not badly.'

She stared at Édouard who closed his eyes. In his mind, he could still see that mouth, now so relaxed, opening wide with pleasure. He felt that the ecstatic face he'd seen in the twin circles of the binoculars would always and for ever be superimposed on the expressionless face now opposite him. Not the slightest shadow of remorse or fear had crossed this face, and the infernal tension he'd been subjected to dissolved suddenly before the obvious : it would do no good whatsoever to beat her, or to shout, or to beg. There was only one possibility : he would have to leave her. This he could never bring himself to do, and she knew it as well as he.

Béatrice stood up, started for the door, then turned around.

'You know it's really not as serious as all that,' she said, her voice becoming tender and indulgent as if it were she who was forgiving him. 'Don't torture yourself so much, Édouard. Have another drink and go to sleep in the room next door. Everything else'll take care of itself.'

'But you don't understand!' he shouted, springing to his feet, almost imploring, absurdly, desperately, demanding not only understanding, but consolation. 'You don't understand! I saw you, I saw you both, just as I see you now! And just at the moment when ...'

Béatrice nodded. She seemed genuinely moved.

'It must have been terrible. Really ... I really am sorry, Édouard.'

She appeared to be estimating the misfortune or unhappiness of some close friend – she even appeared disconsolate – but a misfortune for which she herself was in no way responsible. As the realization of this struck him, Édouard brought his hand up to his eyes.

'So why?' he cried furiously. 'Why?'

But Béatrice had already left the room. She was on her way upstairs to take off her make-up, get undressed, and fall asleep, one arm across her neck, bored and perfectly intact, while Édouard was left behind, alone in the big living-room. He stared at the casual furniture with hatred, at the record player where the same record was still playing, at the bottle of whisky he was in the process of emptying on Béatrice's advice. He understood nothing of his pain. At first, it had been physical, but now it had become something moral, even intellectual. The detailed and tightly woven story he wrote every day in his head – the story of his passion for Béatrice – had coalesced into one big final close-up, indecent and incredible. It seemed to him a colossal error, as if an enraged editor had suddenly decided to slip, between two intelligent chapters of some nineteenth-century novel, three pages of comic strips.

Curiously, however, this final scene was not really repugnant to him. It made Béatrice more exotic, more perverse, more desirable than ever. It didn't matter what she did with her body; that still belonged to him. She'd given it to him and once given, it couldn't be taken back. There was no question of someone taking away this warm, familiar, and generous body; it had been created for him, now and for ever. He was the only one who valued it to its full extent, something that body knew perfectly well even if the addled brain of its owner was tempted to forget. Even when she was sleeping – and perhaps she was unfaithful to him in her dreams? – he could clearly see it draw closer to him, like a faithful horse, as he lay awake in the darkness. He saw the thighs, which undoubtedly opened for others during the day, seek his. He saw the languishing hand, that undoubtedly signalled to strangers during the day, feel for his forehead or his chest, mechanically, as if in secret, so that the dark, blind, and solitary head on the pillow would know nothing of it. And if he leaned over the cruel face, if he gently placed his lips on the inert mouth, he felt it awaken and accept him well before a conscious Béatrice had even recognized him. No, this naked woman's body was not his on loan; it had been restored to him and was his to keep.

When the clock struck three, Édouard could no longer walk steadily, but the alcohol was in no way responsible for the wave which swept him up the stairs, across Béatrice's room, and on to her bed. In the pitch blackness, he recognized through the blanket the shape of the woman who belonged to him, who was his property, his virtue, his strength, his only love. In no uncertain terms, he told her precisely that; he praised her, then insulted her, then became hopelessly entangled and fell asleep. While Béatrice, who hadn't lifted an eyelash during this flood of verbiage, had a certain amount of difficulty doing the same.

Béatrice and Jolyet were eating breakfast, unconsciously keeping their voices down to a whisper. Édouard lay nearby, perfectly immobile and eyes shut tight, like a convalescent.

'It's odd,' Jolyet was saying. 'I was standing behind him yesterday, watching him looking at you, and I had the impression I was looking through those damn binoculars with him. I would have been embarrassed if he'd turned around. The poor boy ...'

'There's no reason to feel sorry for him,' Béatrice interrupted. 'If you'd heard him last night ... He was rambling on as if he owned me but in such a weird sort of way, as if he weren't talking about me at all, but about my double. I tell you I was almost frightened ...'

'But of course you're a double to him,' Jolyet replied. 'By definition. After all, at the moment you're the woman he loves but you're also, potentially, the character he'll write about one day.'

'Do you mean he's going to *use* me?'

She seemed genuinely horrified.

'Of course,' said Jolyet. 'Even if he doesn't know it yet. All the heroes in the plays he wrote after you left him were men who had been deserted. I wonder what the new heroes will be like ... Unrequited lovers? Masochists?'

'Why not just plain, old, happy men?' Béatrice demanded, severely.

'Because happy men make lousy heroes,' replied Jolyet. 'No matter what you think, happiness is the last thing Édouard's looking for with you. For the moment, he loves you blindly.'

'That's the way I've always been loved,' said Béatrice bitterly. 'Blindly. Except that the men weren't blind at all. It's just that they loved only my faults.'

'A nice nuance,' Jolyet remarked. 'But perhaps your faults are more exciting than your virtues? Perhaps they lend themselves more easily to fantasy, even for someone like Édouard?'

Béatrice raised her cup to her lips, then set it down sharply.

'Listen, André,' she said. 'I've always told you the truth – more or less. You know perfectly well I feel free only on a thirty by sixty foot stage and that I feel honest only when I'm speaking someone else's lines. And Édouard's no different – he's only honest in his fiction.'

'Ah, but there's a slight difference,' Jolyet replied. 'When you act, you're trying to forget yourself. Whereas when Édouard writes, he's trying to find himself. And what's more, actors are like musicians or painters. They can hear when they're in tune; they can see their colours. You have echoes, you know; all you need is the audience's silence or its applause for instant proof of your talent. You have immediate, even sensual rewards. But a writer never does. Except once in a while, at dawn, when he has the impression he's discovered something he already knew. But that's an abstract pleasure, one that no one else knows anything about. It's not Édouard I fear for, you see. It's you. I'm afraid you're going to end up performing his plays.'

Béatrice made a vague gesture of protest and Jolyet laughed.

'Thank God,' he went on. 'It's your faults that protect you better than anything else, better than your frantic ambition, your appetite for men, your love of deception. You must hang on to your vices, my dear, no matter what I've told you before. They are, or they might be, your virtues. After all, it's the best victims who make the worst executioners,' he added, motioning towards Édouard who had risen to his feet and was making his way towards them.

He felt sodden, physically and morally, dazed by the sun and ravaged by his memories of the preceding day. Try as he might, he couldn't connect that evening of torment with the dark woman and the peaceable gentleman before him, nibbling toast under a sun shade. He couldn't even remember Gino's face. He would have liked to sit at their feet and listen to music with his forehead resting on Béatrice's knees. He would have liked to sit there for a thousand years and then die, without anything else having happened. Instead, they were going back to Paris. They were going back to the city, the studios, the stages, the others. And undoubtedly back to other Ginos as well. Next summer, Jolyet's periwinkle blue eyes would no longer be around to study the sea, but they would be there, he and Béatrice, and even more inseparable than before. There was nothing she could do about it. Yesterday's betrayal suddenly reassured him. She'd been able to betray him, he'd been able to accept it, and the fact that things had resolved themselves in such a way meant that nothing irreparable could ever come from such an act.

Yet he still refused to admit that his acceptance of Béatrice's treachery was not what had worried him. No, what had worried him was whether or not she could tolerate that acceptance. Some women were unfaithful to their men cheerfully and even affectionately, but the minute the men found out, the women couldn't stand them any longer. It was a question of their self-respect which they saw dissolving in the other's gaze. Béatrice, thank God, didn't respect herself enough – or was simply indifferent enough to her image – to demand that her reflection remain pure and intact in Édouard's eyes. He had, none the less, run a terrible risk in confessing that he'd seen her. And it was only a sort of virile and rather summary arrogance which kept him from realizing how terrible that risk really was.

They were returning to Paris, and he would be able to write again. The sunshine didn't inspire him; on the contrary, it turned him off altogether. Instead of feeling wonderful in this lovely and already deserted villa, he felt stultified. He needed troubled and changing skies, temporary rooms, dreary afternoons, sleepless nights. His words sprang from tepid ashes, not from flames. He waited impatiently for the moment he could decently pretend to have forgotten Gino, unsure, in fact, whether or not it would really be a pretence.

A telegram from Tony d'Albret made them bring their departure date forward, and Jolyet didn't try to delay them. Despite his impeccable courtesy, he seemed increasingly absent, to them as well as to himself. Édouard had often seen him skimming pebbles over the water with a kind of bitter but nostalgic pleasure, for despite his calm and courage, Jolyet must have felt angry at this sea for being so blue, so consistently blue in all its caprices, and so indifferent to the fate of its admirers. They went out for dinner in Beaulieu on their last night and afterwards Jolyet, who seemed in top form, persuaded them to have a last drink in the hotel nightclub. And then Gino arrived, smiling, more handsome than ever, and obviously delighted to see them again. He asked Béatrice to dance and when she refused, he insisted. Although he'd had almost nothing to drink and hadn't fought, as far as he could remember, since his military service, Édouard suddenly found himself rolling around the dance floor in a confused and wholly ineffective brawl. Horrified and delighted, the waiters quickly separated them and the next thing Édouard knew, he was in the gents with Jolyet who was brushing him off and straightening his clothes. To his immense satisfaction, little Gino was sporting a ridiculous and very bloody nose.

'An excellent performance,' Jolyet said, reflectively. 'It's very difficult to fight without working up to it, you know. And you didn't want to at all, did you?'

Édouard laughed. He felt relaxed and marvellous, as if he'd just made love.

'No,' he replied. 'But I thought it would be the correct thing in the circumstances. *Vis-à-vis* Béatrice, that is. I'm not fond of fighting, but then I'm not afraid of the Ginos either. Physically or morally.'

'And do you know why?' said Jolyet. 'Strangely enough, because he's handsome. And Béatrice beautiful. And all those beautiful people, those people who make a living or a vocation out of their beauty, form a separate sex in which homosexuality and equality simply don't exist, for once.'

They had gone out on to the terrace and were waiting for Béatrice.

'But why do you say the beautiful people form a separate sex?' Édouard repeated, his curiosity aroused.

'Because they're so used to being admired they can't satisfy each other in bed,' Jolyet replied. 'It's so obvious every time a marriage between two actors goes on the rocks. Imagine: while one's stretching out voluptuously on the pillow, the other's leaning gracefully out of the window. Both in close-up, of course. Front and centre stage. The only trouble is there's no audience, and that's the worst thing imaginable for both of them.'

Then Béatrice emerged at last, and congratulated Édouard on his uppercut.

'I didn't know I'd been keeping company with such a sportsman,' she declared. 'These intellectuals are full of surprises.'

She was smiling, however. To be sure, virility was something to be proved in bed rather than in the ring, yet she appreciated the fact that the gentle Édouard had felt he should fight over her, that he should play the stud. For Béatrice, relationships between the sexes had at least a slim chance of becoming real, or staying that way, only if these sorts of childish and conventional pretences were respected. Both as mistress and as actress, Béatrice could not have put up with loving a coward for long without feeling ashamed.

13

It was the interval and Kurt's dress rehearsal was already a disaster. Édouard had read the play and wondered where its fragile charm – slightly anguished and Chekhovian – had gone. During the first act, he'd watched a group of robots execute a series of what appeared to be completely arbitrary manoeuvres. He'd watched them rearrange the metallic scenery, then fall into heavy silences. The clever lighting – which consisted of leaving the speaker in darkness and illuminating some banal object – hadn't been clever enough to spark the spectators' interest, even though this particular audience was more than ready, given Kurt's reputation, to pronounce the pathetic exercise superb and filled with originality. In the theatre lobby, people whispered to each other with expressions of consternation on their faces, an attitude that was essential in such situations, and that concealed a far more pernicious satisfaction.

Édouard was depressed. He was worried about Kurt's morale. As for Béatrice, she'd been admirable during the entire ordeal; she'd crossed her hands under her chin, focused her eyes on the stage, and hadn't moved. She hadn't permitted herself a single stretch or yawn or cough, even though her entourage hadn't been quite so disciplined. There were a few young people, of course, partisans of the avante-garde, who'd looked at the old bourgeois regulars with contempt and derision, but their menacing attitudes were more reminiscent of café revolutionaries than anything else.

A critic passed them in the lobby, then did a double-take when he saw Béatrice's beautiful and perfectly made-up face. Béatrice introduced them.

'André Beretti, Édouard Maligrasse.'

'Delighted to meet you,' the critic bubbled. 'For heaven's

sake, Béatrice, whatever are you doing here? Can you possibly tell me what in God's name you see in all this pathos? What a bore!'

'On the contrary,' Béatrice replied. 'I find it very interesting.'

The two men stared at her. She wore an unmistakably sad but absolutely loyal expression that she herself clearly felt was perfect for the occasion. At the same time, she seemed to be telling Beretti that she knew that he knew what she really thought but that she'd rather play the fool than the traitor. It was so transparent and such an unusual rôle for Béatrice Valmont to be playing – insofar as she'd always opted for brutality and had never understood the meaning of the word loyalty – that Beretti couldn't help laughing.

'Really,' he exclaimed, 'Béatrice, you're marvellous!'

He kissed her hand and turned to Édouard.

'My compliments,' he added. 'I believe van Erck is a friend of yours?'

Édouard had followed their little comedy and was exasperated by it. He would have preferred Béatrice to come right out and say it was deadly, boring, odious, and demand that they leave, rather than put on a show of commiseration and loyalty she couldn't possibly feel. What Édouard didn't realize was that Béatrice played this comedy only when she wanted to hide her real feelings. She hated Kurt and was immensely gratified by his failure, and so she pretended the opposite merely so as not to make Édouard unhappy. She smiled at him, sweetly and tenderly, the smile of a loyal wife, and he couldn't help feeling annoyed. Did she really take him for an utter fool?

'So you found it *that* interesting, did you?' he asked.

She looked at him for a minute and saw immediately that she'd chosen the wrong tactic and was on the wrong tack altogether. With the lightning speed of which only she had the secret, she shifted gears and in a split second had changed from posturing actress to a sincere woman.

'Actually, I found it ghastly,' she declared.

Now it was Édouard's turn to be disconcerted, the more so as Béatrice kept repeating 'ghastly', louder and louder, in a strong and jubilant voice. Several heads turned in their direction. He took her arm and pulled her over to a less populated spot overlooking the foyer. They leaned on the railing.

'It's grotesque,' she said, suddenly calm. 'It's pathetic. Grotesque. Your friend Kurt, my good man, is a fascist.'

'A fascist?'

Édouard began to protest, but she had already put out her hand, grabbed his tie, and was shaking him gently while delivering an eloquent and utterly sardonic tirade.

'You come from a nice provincial family of nice provincial lawyers, my dear Édouard. And Kurt from a family of German lawyers, if I'm not mistaken. Whereas my family was strictly lower-class Parisian, and I've spent my life trying to climb out of it. I know "the people", as you call them, better than Kurt. What's more, when he puts on these plays he claims are for "the people", the people come out looking pretty pathetic and depressed, if you ask me. If not furious. Because "the people" in general, just like other people, have only thirty decent years to live. And they know it.'

Édouard stared at her, open-mouthed. Anger became her; it deepened her colour, made her duskier, more dangerous. And a lot more real than Kurt's theories. It was just that he couldn't get rid of that old memory, the memory of Kurt's early belief in him, of his help, his advice, his rehearsals, of their mutual hopes. It was true that Kurt's abstract attempts exasperated him, but the more concrete pronouncements of the modish and worldly made him sick. Basically, Édouard had no idea where he stood or whose side he was on, but he knew that one day, in the midst of the whirlpool of false truths and half-lies, he would have to define a very precise image of himself. Be it here in Paris or somewhere else. The truest image, of course, would be defined by his work. But whatever it was, it was sure to be misinterpreted, misunderstood, betrayed. He'd be judged by people who had no sense of justice, admired by people he despised. That was his destiny as a playwright. And one day, without a word, they would all come to an agreement at his expense, so to speak. They would all agree upon a certain image of him. It was an age of classification, yet Édouard knew he would remain – like all other artists, good or bad – what he knew himself to be at heart: unclassifiable. Then, too, it was obvious there was only one judgement that could set his heart pounding, only one judgement to which he bowed, even if it were wrong, and that was Béatrice's. What he didn't know was that he felt this way because he was young and a writer, and because his lover's heartbeat was still louder than all the fifes and drums of success.

The second act was just like the first, except for a few guests who thought it chic to be rude and so left the theatre with great commotion before the curtain. Afterwards, Édouard found Kurt backstage – bitter, sarcastic, and furious. He gave Édouard an off-handed pat on the shoulder, as if to push him away with the rest of the crowd, with all those corrupt souls who couldn't appreciate his skill as a director. The pat seemed to signify that Édouard was part of this crowd and should stay part of it. And all Édouard's friendly and awkward stammerings were to no avail. He was terribly depressed and very relieved when Béatrice suggested they go home.

That night, Béatrice took him in her arms. She called him her fascist, her little fascist, just the way certain irresponsible mothers call their children their little monsters. It was a warm night and the smell of the mock-orange tree outside seemed to recall an old friendship, a lost confidence, a fortuitous disaster. Béatrice leaned over him, smoothing his eyelids with her fingertips and telling him not to worry, that he had talent, that he had a voice all the actors in Paris, London, and New York were just waiting to borrow from him. Or would be waiting to borrow one day. With an almost sickening tranquillity, she also told him that such ordeals were part and parcel of their work. After all, wasn't it true that the moment he'd first put pen to paper, the moment he'd written the first lines of his first play, he'd wanted to be performed? Of course, and so automatically and in advance, he'd consented to the thousand betrayals, the thousand intrigues, the thousand loathsome episodes of theatre life. Tenderly, in a melancholy voice he'd never heard before, she told him he must never count on anything, that just as theatre always followed fiction, so did pretentiousness follow talent, and that in this world, purity and intransigence were only cover-ups for impotence and failure. And she reminded him that he knew all this already. He knew perfectly well that every sentence he wrote was calculated for its effect, and that he was only too happy to linger over each one to make sure. And although he might envy Shakespeare and Racine, she said, although he might regret not being one of 'the greats', he was none the less rather content with himself in the final analysis. At least on certain evenings. The way she was when she thought she'd found the proper accent or tone for a character she didn't like or felt she didn't resemble.

That evening, for the first time, she made love to him in a deliberately unselfish way, like a whore or a nurse. She was the one who put on their record and it was she who guided him to a climax at the precise instant he was used to guiding her. Fulfilled and happy, Édouard wanted to tell her not to bother, that his suffering was strictly moral and his wounds fake, but this new form of sensuality hadn't really altered his stature as a lover. Instead of making him the priest, she had simply made him the sacrifice. At first glance, that might have seemed a reversal of rôles but, since it was she who'd made the decision, nothing had really changed. There was clearly a kind of melody in their story and no matter how it was orchestrated, no matter what key it was played in, no matter what inevitable improvisations its players added, Édouard knew it would always be the same melody and that he would find it everywhere, intact and unforgettable, and for ever at his ear.

14

Contrary to what he'd expected, Édouard had trouble writing, Paris was empty, Béatrice sweet and tender, but he couldn't find the words. He spent hours in the garden scribbling notes that he tore up in the evening. From time to time, Béatrice asked him to read her script with her, as she'd agreed to do Raoul Dantys' film in September. Ironically, albeit an irony of the most banal sort, she was to play a noble and faithful wife tormented by a jealous husband. Édouard at first found the dialogue flat and verbose, then absolutely odious. When, for the second or third time, he'd flatly asked Laure (the heroine) whether she'd been unfaithful to him and heard her reply with admirable obstinacy that such a thing was impossible, he flew into a rage and heaved the manuscript to the other end of the garden. Stupefied at first, Béatrice finally realized what the matter was and burst out laughing.

'Listen,' she said. 'Try to be just a little bit serious. I have to learn all those words. I *do* work, after all ... And I have more important things to worry about than a gallery of hypothetical Ginos.'

His indignation was genuine, however, and the faithful Cathy finally had to take Édouard's place. Béatrice was growing increasingly short-tempered as the days went by. She herself began declaring the dialogue impossible. She paced up and down in the little garden, following a precisely defined perimeter. She tossed her head, stamped her foot, leaned against the summer-dried trees as if they were part of an imaginary stage set. Uneasy, Tony d'Albret took to dropping by more and more frequently, asking Édouard prying questions he didn't know how to answer.

A phone call came in the nick of time. The *Théâtre des Buttes* had decided to revive *L'Après-Midi*, the play that had originally launched Béatrice's career. Barberini was in charge, an aged director always on the verge of bankruptcy despite continuing support from critics. The revival had for once promised a long and successful run, but then the female lead had suddenly fallen ill. Playing the part created by Béatrice, this particular young actress had given the heroine Claire a more intellectual interpretation; her Claire was more internal – or more modern – and more than a few critics had rushed to point this out in terms favourable to Béatrice. And so, his back to the wall, Barberini had rung to ask if she'd step in just for a month. To everyone's surprise, she'd accepted. After all, she had nothing to gain by it and she was not exactly known for her professional altruism. People waxed eloquent over her acceptance, praised the great solidarity of the theatre and the sudden generosity of the implacable Béatrice Valmont. After a few rehearsals which proved superfluous, given Béatrice's excellent memory – at least for her rôles – she was back in the limelight.

She had refused Édouard and Tony's company and entered her dressing-room an hour before curtain time. Actually, they made her nervous; Édouard because he believed she'd accepted out of pure unselfishness, and Tony because she believed on the other hand that she'd done it strictly for revenge. Béatrice herself knew both were wrong. She dressed and made up her face quickly, and was ready half an hour early. When the stage manager came down the hallway crying 'Curtain in half an hour!' she started, surprised to find the blood rushing into her face. The face in the mirror had nothing in common with the now almost forgotten reflection of five years ago. Then she'd been gambling with both her career and her life, while now, this evening, she had nothing to lose.

Yet her hands were trembling. She brought them down sharply on her dressing-table, as if to crush something. Fear perhaps. Or anger. Béatrice didn't like being surprised by herself. She wasn't used to it. She called the dresser, asked her for a brandy, then began interrogating her about her life, about how the theatre was run, about all the backstage gossip she generally disdained. She invested a great deal of frantic energy in filling up the void, but when she arrived on stage at last, behind the dark curtain, she was still trembling, and still surprised by it.

There was the usual rending sound of the curtain being opened, and then she found herself in the spotlight opposite a vague and anonymous mass of pale faces in the darkness. She took a deep breath, spoke her first line loudly and clearly, then let go of the piano she'd been leaning against and walked towards her male lead. And then, suddenly, it hit her – freedom, happiness, invention, sincerity, power. All at once everything was restored to her. Her heart stopped pounding and took up a new rhythm, deep and regular. It beat strongly, her voice rang out clearly, for at last she was speaking the truth. The impression of lies, fantasies, conflicting feelings, and nostalgia that made up the backdrop of her everyday life had disappeared. All the faces before her fused into a single one, a face she loved because she didn't owe it anything and because after tonight, she'd never see it again. And this face demanded that she lie to it, that she make it dream, laugh, cry. This face demanded everything from her, everything except the 'truth', that banal, arbitrary, and graceless truth that her family and friends and lovers had always solicited from her. In vain. Whereas here, the frantic and profound fraudulence that was her rôle would never be enough for these people who constituted her public. She would always fall short of their demands. But through these words written by someone else, these gestures defined by someone else, and before all these others she didn't know, she could at last be herself. She said 'I love you' to her lead (a notorious homosexual) a thousand times more sincerely than she'd ever said it to her lovers. This fake English furniture, rented by the month and unused twenty-two hours out of twenty-four, was more familiar to her than her own house, and the sky painted on the backdrop through the fake window reflected in her eyes an authentically beautiful day. And when, as Claire, she began backing offstage out of this miserable décor, her voice filled with real torment when she heard herself begging her partner to be sure to water the green plastic plant every day. She didn't love any of them, of course, neither the young man with the brilliantined hair nor the fake furniture nor the borrowed objects, but she was none the less gripped by a wild and irreplaceable love for their impermanence, even their factitiousness.

The audience gave her a standing ovation and, for once, she didn't try to prolong it with curtain calls. When her partner came up to her at the door of her dressing-room and said with all apparent sincerity: 'You were marvellous, Béatrice! I really believed in it!' he was astonished to hear her reply – unsmiling and with a sort of listnessness and exasperation: 'I should hope so. That's all there is to believe in.' (He found the line so nicely turned – a memorable actress's phrase – that he rushed off at once to spread it around.)

Alone in her dressing-room, Béatrice took off her make-up in a kind of rage, her hands cold and tears in her eyes. But fifteen minutes later, when she joined Édouard and Tony who, moved and admiring, were waiting for her in the lobby, there was a smile of triumph on her lips. She kept up a perfectly natural conversation during the dinner given by the director, who was delirious with gratitude, and if the compliments and commentaries bored her, she didn't show it. It didn't matter because tomorrow, after she'd been through one more night and day, after she'd made love and discussed her film projects, she'd be back again behind the dark curtain, her blood flowing normally. It was only a question of patience. But she drank so much that evening, not only to keep pace with the others but with her own existence as well, and she felt so ill when she went to sleep that, for once, Béatrice lied to herself, attributing her melancholy to too much alcohol.

Propped up on an elbow, Édouard watched her sleep. He'd left the french windows open, and from time to time the wind lifted the hair of the stranger next to him. He'd heard her say 'I love you' on stage. He'd seen her wounded, hesitant, pursued, vulnerable. In fact, odd as it seemed, he'd seen her resemble the image he had of *himself* in relation to her. He'd wanted to ask: 'Who hurt you? When? And why haven't you got over it yet?' But that woman up there wasn't the woman he loved. It was another one, the one who'd made fun of him, who'd deceived him with Gino and been unmoved by his pain. So why had he been so upset when she'd looked so anxiously at that green plastic plant? Why had he suffered with her when she'd had to leave that idiot? And why had he wished she'd stayed behind the piano after her opening lines, as if behind a barricade? Béatrice was an actress and a good one. That he already knew. There was nothing so strange about her expressing a feeling she herself didn't recognize, and refused to recognize. And so, leaning motionless over the blind and mysterious face now turned away from him, he asked himself where this terrible anxiety had come from, this pretence of remorse that was keeping him awake at her side like a spy or a criminal. What was he guilty of? Ever since he'd known her, he'd loved her, and he'd always told her so. He'd always suffered because of her and he'd always accepted his suffering. He knew she trusted him more than his predecessors; he knew he was not only a friend but a superior lover. And he knew that in Béatrice's uncertain, impulsive, and egocentric life, he represented the only certainty, the only security, and perhaps the only tenderness. But what of it? All he wanted was the revival to be over and Béatrice to take off her mask and become once again the brutal and disconcerting object of his passion.

Dawn found him at the dining-room table. It was as if he'd needed all that doubt and sadness for Frédéric to come back. Once again, Édouard could see a kind of consistency in his indecisive young hero, and some sort of meaning in his indecision, but the reason for this rebirth, or reappearance, made little difference to him, particularly since it was sure to be fairly troubling and indecipherable. All that mattered was that, like Béatrice twelve hours before, he'd found his own voice again. And so it was that one, sleeping and safe in her sleep, and the other, insomniac and clutching his insomnia, spent the first few hours of the new day in perfect harmony. Even though neither was aware of it. And thanks to these moments of perfect solitude, they shared, during the next two weeks, their finest period of happiness.

15

Édouard sat in a meadow on a wooden crate borrowed from an obliging stagehand and watched Béatrice fifty yards away, arms outstretched, an ecstatic expression on her face, walk towards a young blond male and collapse sobbing on to his shoulder.

'Cut!' shouted the director.

To Édouard's enormous relief – for in spite of himself, after three weeks of filming, he still suffered terrible pangs of jealousy during these love scenes – Béatrice extricated herself from her partner's arms. She glanced over at him and he sent her a small silent bravo. She appeared not to notice. In fact, she appeared not to notice him at all. Of course, they were shooting the final scene and she had to concentrate in order to play one of those famous 'smiling-through-her-tears' scenes Raoul Dantys was so fond of. But this was the sixth take, the technicians were nervous wrecks and Béatrice's assuming a mystical out-of-this-world posture did seem somewhat excessive. Édouard clapped harder, making his bravo a little more obvious. Béatrice looked at him again, then turned away immediately as if he were some out-of-place milestone that had strayed on to the scene. Édouard let his fingers slip down gently into the palm of his other hand, put both hands between his knees, then stretched out his legs and studied his shoes. Ever since he'd been watching the shooting, he'd invariably found himself in the same posture: undesirable spectator by day, burdensome lover at night. The sound of someone laughing behind him made him jump.

'You look exactly like a hunting dog,' Nicolas said as he sat down beside him on the ground, broke off a blade of grass and began chewing on it, apparently delighted with life in general. Béatrice had got him the principal supporting rôle with such authority and such an exemplary *esprit de corps* that Édouard had been enchanted. It was only after some ten days that he'd finally realized that like a gypsy, Béatrice needed to take a few members of her tribe along with her when she did a film or play. This time, her maid, Tony d'Albret, Nicolas, and himself made up the caravan. Unfortunately, however, after a period of moroseness, Béatrice had begun to enjoy the game and to play her rôle for all she was worth. And once the caravan had been shaken up, only productive gypsies were allowed to stay. Which meant Tony, who argued over the bills, Nicolas, useful despite the constraints of his rôle, and the ever-faithful Cathy who spent her days peacefully sewing and ironing at the hotel.

As for Édouard, he had no specific function. It seemed to him that the lowest stagehand was more useful than he in Béatrice's eyes. In the evening, when every last soul from the make-up man to the director sat around discussing the day's takes, Édouard – despite the fact he'd been there for all of them and knew their every wrinkle – invariably felt himself to be a parasite, a stranger, a foreigner, excluded from the troupe.

In vain, he'd made several trips between Paris and the Loire Valley, where the film was being shot. In vain he'd tried to talk about his own work, his own meetings. But none of it seemed to interest anyone, besides Tony d'Albret who'd finally managed to sell the rights of his play to a first-rate Broadway theatre. But when Tony talked to him about contracts and projects, it was always in a whisper, almost in secret, as if after three weeks it would have been indecent to mention anything but Raoul's film. The general indifference didn't particularly bother Édouard, for he'd always felt a kind of obsessive horror in talking about his writing. What did bother him, however, was the fact that, as far as Béatrice was concerned, the public and daytime indifference had also become private and nocturnal. Even when she was buried in the bedclothes, even when she was in the midst of making love, a part of her was always absent. There was something foreign and solitary about her, something she refused to share with him and that he didn't really understand. In the film, she played the rôle of a touching but rather stupid woman – a pain in the neck, as she herself laughingly put it. She made cruel fun of the part but did everything in her power to make everyone else believe in it. Little by little, the distance she'd felt from her rôle in the beginning had disappeared; she was playing Emma Bovary in modern dress and, being neither Homais nor Rudolphe, Édouard could only be a nuisance.

'Basically,' he said to her one night – the third in a row she'd refused to make love – 'basically, you'd much rather make love with your young lead, your little Cyril, than with me.'

Béatrice pondered the idea for a moment.

'It's true,' she admitted. 'And yet God knows I don't like him.'

Édouard hesitated an instant, then continued.

'So why don't you? It wouldn't be because of me, would it?'

But she'd burst out laughing before he'd even finished his sentence.

'Don't be so idiotic, Édouard! When someone wants someone, he can always find a time and a place for it, even with seventy technicians around. As far as things like that go, the cageyness of actors is quite well known. No, what bothers me is that if I already know I don't like him and if I've got enough trouble as it is trying to pretend to love him and if, on top of everything, I find out he's no good in bed, it'll be even more impossible.'

'And Raoul?' Édouard went on in a flat and quiet voice, knowing it was the only kind that could get the truth out of her. 'Your director's in love with you, isn't he?'

'Of course,' replied Béatrice. 'But that doesn't matter. In fact, I can guarantee he'll bide his time until the film's over. There are certain close-ups, my darling, certain framings and certain effects that a director can only get out of an unknown woman – in the biblical sense of the word, so to speak. Otherwise, I'd have to surrender right at the beginning,' she added, laughing, 'and then play the adoring female during the whole film. In which case you wouldn't still be around, my dear. And anyway,' she went on, pulling him to her, 'it's you I'm in love with.'

Indignant, Édouard had repeated these cynical remarks to Nicolas, who'd confirmed the fact that this was the classical ABC of film-world relationships. Yet there was such an aura of chastity around this crew so absorbed in making a film highly-coloured by the erotic; it was as if the activity of simulating love and watching one's gestures being repeated mechanically ten times a day had turned everyone off.

'I think it would be better if I left,' Édouard said to Nicolas.

'I've told you at least ten times already,' Nicolas replied, sympathetically offering him a cigarette.

Nicolas, however, was completely at ease stretched out in the grass and chewing a piece of straw. The low hills of the Loire region were bathed in an oblique, soft, yellow, September light; the tiles on the roofs were turning mauve, and into the beauty of all these reds and yellows interspersing the already vanquished green of summer, a sort of melancholy was gently slipping. The winter frightened Édouard. For him, winter was noise, furor, the city, the others. He'd never spent a winter with Béatrice. When he'd first known her, it had been springtime, a springtime that had ended with his defeat. And it had been spring when he'd found her again. That made almost three seasons he'd spent with her, and he asked himself why he was so frightened of a fourth.

'But why should I leave?' he asked. 'You can't imagine how bored I'll be in Paris now that I've finished my play.'

'But at least there's that,' said Nicolas. 'Especially because you know it's good.'

He leaned forward and shook Édouard's shoulder affectionately.

'You know,' he said. 'It really was very nice of you to give it to me to read. I was very touched.'

Édouard smiled back. It was true. He didn't know why but this good-for-nothing Nicolas, this funny little man, this gentle drunkard, was the only person to whom he could show his play. With his too-handsome face (heavily made up at the moment), his too perfect teeth, his fake boyishness, in fact his caricature of everything sympathetic and seductive, he had none the less become for Édouard the very image of trustworthiness and friendship. And oddly enough, even though everything Nicolas did was always a little off – his laughter, his jokes, his gestures, his declarations when he'd been drinking – what he managed not to do, on the other hand, was always sensitive and intelligent. Nicolas had a way of keeping quiet, of turning away, of not laughing, that bespoke a pure heart.

'My play apart,' said Édouard, 'do you think I really bother Béatrice by being here?'

'Absolutely, my dear fellow. You're not part of the film. You're superfluous. Maybe you haven't noticed, but you're always in the way. If there's a shadow, it's yours; if there's someone in front of the camera, it's you. And if there's a strange sound on the tape, it's because you coughed.'

'True,' said Édouard. 'But I can't help it. I'm so miserable without her.'

And he gestured towards Béatrice, who was staring up into the sky as if to shoot down the aeroplane that purred overhead. Chin in the air, she was tapping the ground impatiently with her foot; of all the people waiting for the inopportune plane to disappear, she seemed the most impatient, the most ferocious.

'What a tough nut!' Nicolas laughed, and Édouard joined in, repeating the word 'nut' with the terrified delight of a pupil mocking his teacher.

'But what can I do?' he said finally. 'What in God's name can I do to make myself useful? I mean, I can't exactly go around sweeping the floors.'

'No,' replied Nicolas. 'You don't belong to the union. And you're too clumsy. I don't know, old man, we'll have to think of something. Well, here we go again,' he said, getting to his feet.

He took up his position in front of the camera. An artificial silence fell as Béatrice, her eyes glittering with tears, ran towards her young blond lead and threw herself into his arms. Suddenly, at that moment, Édouard had an ingenious idea.

That evening, all four of them were installed in front of the fire in the hotel bar, listening to the rain which for once had waited for the day's work to end. Tony d'Albret, who'd just returned from Paris (she'd vanished once she'd seen Béatrice well ensconced in her rôle), seemed beside herself with delight. Not only had Édouard's American contract been signed, but photographs of the filming had already appeared in the newspapers and were remarkable. As far as she was concerned, all was for the best in the best of all possible worlds.

In fact, Tony was so fascinated by the private lives of her clients (as well as by their careers and the profits she reaped from them) that she completely forgot about having one of her own. Sometimes she would remember suddenly – as if for reasons of decorum – that she was a woman and would thrust herself at some dazed but willing debutant, take him to her bed, and then show him off afterwards, triumphantly, for a week or two, at cocktails and parties, like a lap dog. And then, just as suddenly, she'd forget him one day in some dark and sombre corner. Later on, when someone mentioned Gérard L. or Yves B., she would remember. 'Ah yes, that one,' she would sigh. 'If I wanted to, I could ...' Which suggested that the young man in question had not only wanted to but could have, and that it was only through lack of time and out of devotion to her clients that Tony had been unable to guarantee the unfortunate young man's career, or rather his happiness. The way she talked about it, it was even possible to think that he had kept a double image of her: Tony the Fairy Godmother overwhelmed with responsibilities, and Tony the passionate and delirious mistress. That was where her emotional life apparently stopped, if you didn't count a sick and aged mother in the provinces whose suffering was invoked only when the subject of Tony's percentages came up. Even Béatrice, who combined machiavellian astuteness with a natural ferocity, had never been able to find out whether there really was a Madame d'Albret, much less one as persistently on her deathbed as Tony made her out to be.

'I'm afraid I have to leave tomorrow,' Édouard declared sadly.

Three different expressions settled on to the three faces around him: sympathetic vexation for Nicolas, curiosity for Tony, and for Béatrice, relief.

'Why tomorrow?' she asked, although the tone of her voice seemed to suggest 'And why not the day before yesterday?'

'No choice,' Édouard replied, as if apologizing. 'I need to put some finishing touches to the play. Which is annoying, particularly with this *Show* magazine thing.'

'What thing?' inquired Tony.

Show was the most widely read show-business magazine in the United States, the mere mention of its name enough to set all the agents and actors in Europe and America aquiver.

'Oh, didn't I tell you?' Édouard replied, nonchalantly. 'When they found out my play was being done in New York, they asked me to write an article on whatever I wanted. I suggested something on Raoul's film.'

'And then?' Tony urged impatiently.

'Maybe you don't realize it,' Édouard continued, 'but Raoul's fairly well known over there since his last film. I've forgotten the title ...'

'*Les fruits de l'Aube,*' Tony interrupted.

'Yes,' said Édouard. '*Les fruits de l'Aube.* It was a big success, wasn't it?'

'Of course it was,' snapped Tony, exasperated. 'Everybody knows that, but what of it?'

'They like the idea of an article by a Frenchman about a Frenchman making a film,' Édouard went on calmly. 'That's all.'

The expressions on the three faces had changed completely: a sort of incredulous amazement on Nicolas's, stupefaction on Béatrice's, aggravation mixed with anxiety on Tony's.

'And then?' both women squealed in chorus.

'And then,' Édouard went on, feigning surprise. 'And then they sent me a telegram a week ago and I've been trying to take notes right and left ever since, but I feel I'm disturbing everyone all the time. I haven't dared insist. With my questions, that is. Things like the camera angles, or the relationship between the actors and their scripts. That sort of thing.'

'Really,' Béatrice grumbled. 'Why didn't you tell me?'

Nicolas had left the circle and was leaning against the bar at the far end of the room. His shoulders shook as if he were sobbing. Édouard had to take a deep breath to keep himself from laughing as well.

'But Béatrice,' he replied. 'I didn't want to bother you. You work hard enough all day long without my asking you questions all night. The same goes for Raoul. How do you expect me to talk to Raoul? And about what? I don't know the first thing about films! Which I made very clear to the people at *Show*.'

'What!' Tony exclaimed. (She too had risen, had even gone pale. Édouard almost admired her.) 'What! So you refused?'

'Of course,' said Édouard. 'I wrote them a letter. I don't remember if I sent it or not ...'

He stood up and pretended to search through all his pockets. Nicolas had finally calmed down and rejoined the group, glass in hand, only to drop it suddenly. He bent down precipitously over the debris.

'Well, well,' said Édouard. 'Look at this! I forgot to send it! I'll do so tomorrow from Paris.'

There was a moment of stupefied silence. Nicolas was still bending over his broken glass and groaning. Finally, he stood up, then sat down, his eyes full of tears.

'Let's all sit down,' Tony said curtly. 'Édouard, you must do the article. You must. Do you understand? You just must. That's all there is to it.'

Édouard sat down again, really astonished this time and trying desperately to avoid looking at Nicolas.

'But what do you want me to write?' he asked. 'I don't want to bother Raoul and I'm always in the way and ...'

'So?' Tony rang out. 'There's always someone in the way. And believe me, it's not always a reporter from *Show*, for God's sake! And Raoul? What's Raoul? He's a director, isn't he? With a film coming out soon in the States, isn't that right? And you're worried about whether or not he's got the *time* to answer your questions? You go right ahead and ask him, my little Édouard. You go right ahead and ask everybody. Everybody'll answer you. I'll make sure of that myself. Even Beatrice'll answer you!'

Édouard turned towards Béatrice. She was eyeing him pensively, a vague look of admiration on her face.

'But who at *Show* asked you to do this?'

'Millane. Edward Millane. Or something like that.' (He'd spent an hour on the telephone getting the information.) 'He's

Matthews' assistant, the editor-in-chief, I think. It's funny, you know they pay by the word? A dollar a word! Quite a sum, don't you think?'

Tony had already rushed over and thrown her arms around him, pressing him feverishly to her heart, kissing him, calling him 'my little genius, my pet dove, my darling Édouard'. Then she turned to Béatrice.

'My dear,' she pronounced theatrically, still pressing Édouard's submissive head against her thigh. 'For once, I say bravo! You've found us a real gold-mine here, a veritable gold-mine!'

'If I stay,' said Édouard, half-hidden in her perfumed sweater. 'If I stay, will you answer my questions too, Béatrice?'

'If they're not too personal,' she laughed and standing up, came over in turn to kiss him tenderly on the brow, like a mother happily surprised to find her little monster suddenly coming first in his class. Nicolas ordered champagne; he too seemed happily surprised, although for different reasons. Someone went to wake up Raoul and his assistant. Édouard – now the hero of the set instead of its most pathetic actor – repeated and embellished his rôle with a kind of dismayed maliciousness. His treachery would doubtless be discovered and, when that time came, he wouldn't give two bits for his life. But in the meantime, he and Nicolas were sure to have a good laugh.

And thus it was that although he was thirty-six years old and had always been a writer, Édouard Maligrasse suddenly discovered the joy and anguish of telling lies. And thus it was too that later, during the night, when Béatrice smiled at him and said: 'You want me to show you how French women do it, Monsieur le journaliste?' he thought he was the cleverest, and possibly the guiltiest, of lovers.

16

Although Nicolas was officially considered a parasite, he had a family and took care of them. In fact, he was one of those rare people who not only proclaimed that money was not important in itself and that it was only a means to other ends, but who also applied this doctrine both ways : that is to say, he found it as natural to give as to receive. Partly out of production money, therefore, and partly out of his own pocket, he summoned one of the most penniless Irishmen in Paris to play the rôle of photographer from *Show* magazine. Equipped with an old rented Leica, Basil Keenan arrived one sunny morning and, after a short and confidential talk with Édouard, was introduced to Raoul and to the other members of the crew.

Basil Keenan was tall and very dark, with blue eyes and all the notorious gaiety and charm of the Irish. He and Béatrice took to each other straight away, they understood each other perfectly at first glance. Consequently, they set about avoiding each other for a whole week, but were so ostentatious about it that they finally wound up upsetting – albeit belatedly – the imprudent Nicolas. Édouard, on the other hand, was so intoxicated by this new rôle that he noticed nothing whatsoever. He was too busy seeing himself as a hero out of both Machiavelli and Feydeau and, as far as he was concerned, the apparently clumsy and phlegmatic Basil was just a minor ally. And naturally enough, after a cautious and well-choreographed mating dance, Basil and Béatrice finally found themselves face to face. And alone.

They were shooting out of doors that afternoon and when it suddenly began to pour, everyone ran for cover into the near-by houses and cafés. As if by accident, Basil found Béatrice in a barn. The air was filled with the scent of grey and gold freshly cut hay, a tender reminder of summer, and with the smell of earth soaked by a rain that joyously heralded the arrival of autumn. Béatrice's hair was plastered on to her forehead; her eyelashes and mouth were wet, and there was a wild expression on her face. Without a word, Basil advanced on her, smiling. She returned the smile. As he kissed her and then lay down quietly beside her, she marvelled at the miraculous and infallible instinct that always and everywhere allowed a man and a woman devoted to pleasure to recognize each other, as if they had been branded with the same iron. Devoted to pleasure, yes, but more accurately it was a question of being received into an omnipotent and highly selective secret society. Basil made love to her with skill and violence and, transported, she had to bite his shoulder to stop crying out.

Later, feeling mellow, she gazed with genuine tenderness at the forever unchanging profile of that most eternal of passersby – a new lover. The rain had stopped and they were calling for her. She sat up. Propped up on an elbow, Basil smoothed back her hair and removed a few pieces of hay with his big fingers while she buttoned his shirt and knotted his tie. Their movements were calm and harmonious, like those of a couple who had been together a long time. Then, in a gesture of gratitude, he kissed her hand and carefully, slowly, she kissed his before going out.

Nicolas was waiting for her in front of the camera, and she smiled at him like a spoiled child. He understood the situation immediately and, to his own great surprise, flew into a rage.

'You can't do that to Édouard!' he hissed at her between his teeth.

Béatrice stared at him.

'Do what to Édouard?' she repeated.

Taken aback, Nicolas hesitated, unable to come up with an answer. After all, there was no reason for Édouard ever to know anything about it; neither he nor Basil was particularly indiscreet. So he abandoned the unfamiliar rôle of judge in favour of that of advisor.

'You know,' he said to Béatrice, 'Basil's strictly a good-for-nothing.'

'I can't say I agree with you,' she replied, breaking into such happy and suggestive laughter that it became contagious and Nicolas couldn't help joining in.

'You're so wanton,' he said between gasps. 'You're absolutely indecent. And wanton ... and ...'

Béatrice stopped laughing and looked at him.

'Of course I am,' she admitted with a little smile. 'But that's why Édouard loves me, isn't it?'

There was a sad question mark in her voice and it disconcerted him.

'You're a strange woman,' he said.

'In what way am I strange?' she repeated, shrugging. 'You know I've never been able to resist someone with blue eyes.'

She leaned against him and, for a moment, the proximity of this woman fresh from lovemaking flooded him with old memories.

'Seriously, Béatrice, he's no good, this Basil.'

'But why?' she said. 'After all, he *is* a photographer. You wouldn't be getting snobbish in your old age, now would you?'

She really was very surprised, for she herself had always been completely without snobbery where her choice of lovers was concerned. There had been producers, hairdressers, cameramen, and men-of-the-world, and Béatrice had always taken them along to parties, premières and dinners with perfect equanimity. She'd shown off the most doubtful gigolos this way, something she freely and rather proudly admitted to. In fact, it was in just this way that Édouard, the little accountant, had got his first big chance.

'It's only my body that's a snob,' she'd said one day to Tony who had reproached her for some insignificant freelancing lover who was more embarrassing than the others. 'But my so-called carnal snobbishness is a lot more consistent than yours, believe me. And a lot less incomprehensible,' she added, punctuating her accusation with a thrust of her chin at Tony's cherished circle which some bored journalists had once christened the *Tout-Paris*.

'They all think they've made it,' Béatrice had continued. 'But when you ask them where to, they don't have the vaguest idea. But I, I know where. And I know it each time.'

And she'd smilingly rejoined her too-handsome escort.

Nicolas didn't insist. After all, it wasn't his problem.

Although he'd been nervous at first, Édouard had finally been caught up in his own game and had become a rabid film fan. Poor Raoul was bombarded with naïve questions to which he always replied with a mixture of satisfaction and irritation. From their conversations, Édouard learned that this blustering, heavy-handed, and ambitious director was passionate about his work. At times he became almost lyrical on the subject (lyrical being the last adjective in the world anyone would think of applying to Raoul Dantys). He was a full-blooded man, he told Édouard, a kind of self-styled colossus, and so obliged continually to play at Orson Welles; although minus his genius, unfortunately. He had acquired the habit of sharing his bed with his leading ladies – a custom observed more or less out of duty, like some exhausted feudal lord who still insisted upon his rights – and so he had been displeased at first by Béatrice's amiable but firm refusal. Displeased not for emotional or even sensual reasons, of course – like other forces of nature, Raoul lacked a certain forcefulness in bed – but for hierarchical reasons. If it were permissible for the feudal lord to choose not to exercise his rights, it was not permissible for the serf to balk at this exercise. What made Béatrice's refusal worse was that her infidelities, as well as her indifferences, had long been legion. Thus, until now, Édouard had only represented an odd but easy alibi for Raoul. Once transformed into an emissary from *Show*, however, he took on a certain consistency. He became a pawn on the great chessboard of Raoul's career, although a pawn Raoul liked considerably. 'The boy has charm,' he would say, grasping Édouard's shoulders. And Édouard would cast a troubled glance behind him, as if this charm were a huge mad dog he hadn't been able to train.

As for Béatrice, she was waiting with a certain maliciousness for Édouard to do his duty as a journalist. She even went so far as to feed him a series of slick and hollow phrases. 'Art is life,' she would tell him, or 'Every actor carries in himself a double who is both his better half, and his worst'. Despite their incongruity, these inanities were delivered with such seriousness, with such insistence that they be taken down, that Édouard – speechless and embarrassed – finally began to wonder if his beautiful mistress might not in fact be a complete fool. He also began to wonder, on the other hand, if she might not have got wind of his little joke and be making fun of him. At such moments, a small icy chill blew through his mind, filling him with terror. In fact, however, he was quite wrong : Béatrice sincerely believed in the article and was bent on occupying as much space as possible in it. And so she amused herself by deliberately exaggerating the pompous absurdity of her remarks, primarily because she hoped to provoke Édouard into a critical response that would help her become a real person. But since he never showed any response at all, she began to think that if these stupidities didn't surprise him, it was because they came from her, the obvious conclusions being that he thought her feeble-minded. This exasperated her beyond measure, for Béatrice was as sure of her love as she was of her desire and where men were concerned, that was generally enough for her. Now, however, she found she also wanted to be sure of Édouard's esteem, which was the last thing in the world Édouard was concerned about. In fact, he was about as interested in Béatrice's moral value as a drug addict in the molecular composition of morphine. It was only natural, then, that a certain tension bordering on open warfare should develop between them. And the original goal of Édouard's plan – to protect himself from Béatrice's displeasure – wound up exposing him even more to her peevishness.

Things came to a head one Saturday night. Since Béatrice didn't have to work the following day, she dropped all aesthetic concerns and proceeded to drink heavily. And as usual, with each drink she felt an attraction for the truth that was as irresistible as it was ill-fated. For once they were alone in the little hotel parlour. Nicolas had gone off to seduce another member of the cast.

'You haven't asked me how I decided to become an actress,' Béatrice said suddenly.

Édouard started. He'd completely forgotten his rôle as a journalist.

'True enough,' he replied. 'Yes, you're right. I've never asked you. How did you decide, in fact?'

'If you really want to do the article,' Béatrice said curtly, 'it would be best if we finished with it once and for all. Ask your questions, I'll answer them, and then we won't talk about it any more. I feel as if I've been living one perpetual interview for the past ten days and it's exhausting.'

'But you know it's not really an interview,' said Édouard, embarrassed. 'It's more a collection of thoughts, ideas ... I mean a collection of my personal impressions.'

'What you do mean,' Béatrice interrupted, 'is that it's so personal, this article of yours, that no matter what Raoul and Cyril and I say or do, it doesn't matter.'

'That's not really what I meant ...' Édouard began.

But seeing the expression on her face and the determined way she was pouring herself another vodka, he felt he'd better make an effort.

'All right,' he said in a voice he meant to sound playful. 'Just how did you begin?'

Béatrice swallowed her drink in one gulp.

'I always knew I was destined for the theatre,' she replied emphatically. 'When I was just a child, when I was two years old to be precise, I was already an actress. Nothing and no one could have kept me from following my path. I knew that even then ...'

She gazed directly at Édouard as she spoke, with a look of challenge in her eyes. Not knowing what to do, he blushed and was embarrassed for her.

'So?' she said. 'You're not writing it down. It's not serious enough? Not sufficiently stupid? Or grandiose? You want me to tell you about all my wretched years at the Conservatory? My adolescent fantasies about playing Phaedra? The sandwiches I existed on so I could pay for my classes?'

'But what's the matter?' Édouard exclaimed, completely confused.

'What's the matter is that I'm fed up!' Béatrice cried. 'If you want to know the truth, it's very simple. And banal. I became an actress accidentally. I became an actress because my husband – my first husband – was very rich and very boring and one of my lovers was an actor. What's more, I've told you all this a hundred times! So why are you asking me these asinine questions?'

'But you're the one asking the questions!' Édouard replied. 'You're asking yourself these questions. I haven't asked you a single one!'

'And why not?' cried Béatrice. 'Why haven't you asked me any?'

She lowered her head suddenly and burst into tears. *My God*, she thought, *I'm drunk. This is ridiculous, vodka always does this to me. But I'm in such a good mood!* It was true. She didn't feel like crying at all. She didn't feel sad. She couldn't understand the reason for this rush of burning tears. As for Édouard, he was completely lost. He couldn't remember ever having seen Béatrice cry. The most he'd seen, if anything, had been some furiously held-back tears, whereas now she seemed to be giving herself over to them with a kind of relish. She even seemed to approve of them. He knelt down beside her and took her hands.

'I don't understand,' he said. 'I don't understand what's wrong.'

Béatrice cried even harder. Then she wiped her face on Édouard's jacket and gulped down another mouthful of vodka like a prisoner on his way to the electric chair.

'I don't either,' she said brokenly. 'I tell you these stupid clichés and you seem to find it normal. Do you think I'm as stupid as that?' she asked, her voice suddenly becoming gay.

Then, just as suddenly, her head dropped back on to Édouard's shoulder and she burst into tears again. With his arms around her and feeling protective, Édouard let the guilt wash over him. Ever since that night in Lille, he'd known she had her complexes, her doubts about her intelligence. And he also knew, more objectively, that she was an intelligent person. He'd behaved like a conceited boor. Now he had to reassure her. And the thought that it was up to him, Édouard, to reassure Béatrice filled him with pleasure. He cradled her in his arms and murmured tender words, marvelling that the tears of the fierce and beautiful creature he held were his responsibility.

Béatrice, on the other hand, had already forgotten whatever explanation she might have come up with and was smiling to herself about how complicated Édouard was. Basil, for example, would never ask her to talk about her art. In fact, she would grant him an hour tomorrow, dear little Basil. Hadn't he practically been begging her for one since their first? He wasn't without talent, this Basil ... But in granting him his hour, Béatrice refused to see that her favours were less a response to the memory of Basil's charms than to a blind rage against Édouard.

Édouard, meanwhile, was thrilled. He drank her tears, his lips following them down her cheek, catching them just at the angle of chin and neck with an eager and tender movement. *He's a vampire*, she told herself. *Behind all that innocence and vulnerability lies a real Othello. My little goat's turned out to be a sadist.*

'Basically,' she said finally, 'you're delighted to see me cry, aren't you?'

For the first time, she looked at him with genuine curiosity, and for the first time, Édouard felt that she was both seeing and judging him as something other than a passing fancy.

'It's strange,' she said pensively, 'it's strange that my crying makes you so happy. I would never want to see you unhappy. Even later on, when I'm not around.'

'That's because you don't love me,' Édouard replied immediately.

'But I do,' said Béatrice, stroking his hair. 'I can see you very well twenty years from now in a wicker armchair on a terrace in the evening, correcting the proofs of your next play. There's a blonde woman, and a porcelain lamp, and a dog, and a lime tree. And maybe even a child with brown eyes like yours ...'

Without knowing why, Édouard was filled with rage at her fantasy, but it was an impotent anger, as if the image were in some way inexorable.

'What a charming picture,' he replied ironically. 'Who painted it, Vuillard?'

Béatrice knew nothing about painting, or at least no more than she did about literature or music. And this was because, given the rigours of her profession, the finer arts that passed through it were completely transformed. All characters became rôles. She loved Stendhal because of Sanseverina, a part she desperately wanted to play one day. She liked Goya because one of her rare lovers with some culture (Jolyet probably) had once compared her to his Naked Maja. She liked Dostoevsky for Philippovna in *The Idiot* and Grouchenka in *The Brothers*

Karamazov. She even liked Proust because of the bizarre, sensual, and icy interpretation she planned to give Oriane de Guermantes; already she heard herself replying 'You exaggerate!' to Swann's anouncement of his imminent demise. Indeed, Béatrice fascinated her directors because she brought to her rôles a real inventiveness, one inspired by her perpetual desire to deceive. And she worked hard at it. In fact, because of this taste for deception, she'd read a great deal and, in the evenings, loved playing all the characters an astonished and delighted Édouard asked for. Once she even did Phaedra for him and was so marvellous that Édouard renounced his imitation of Hippolyte's angelic chastity and took her between two stanzas. But Vuillard was an unfamiliar name to her and she was troubled.

'And you?' she replied, avoiding the question. 'How do you see me?'

'Naked,' answered Édouard. 'Naked and dark, lying in front of a mirror studying yourself. Or spreadeagled on a beach in the sun. Alone. Yes, above all else, alone.'

'You see how evil you really are,' Béatrice said, laughing. 'But seriously Édouard, in ten years you'll have forgotten all about us. And so will I. All our passion will seem awfully excessive to you and you'll be consoled by some other woman's tenderness.'

She spoke so serenely and her description of this meaningless and derisory existence of his, this wasteland of his future, was offered so matter-of-factly that he stepped away from her, furious.

'And you?' he almost shouted. 'Where'll you go for consolation?'

'Nowhere,' she replied. 'In ten or twenty years, I'll still be acting. I'll be old but with make-up I'll still be beautiful. And I'll be living with someone who'll love me. Or who'll pretend to.'

'Who'll love you the way I do?'

She hesitated before saying no, but only because for once she was sure that was the correct answer. In her distorted and alcohol-blurred prism, she still saw him as he really was: a kamikaze lover, ardent and suicidal, flaming and aflame. She saw his eyes liquid with a desire that was still pure and intact after eight months, and she was surprised at her own astonishment.

After all, there'd been other fanatics, other men madly in love with her. The difference was that what she saw in Édouard was the fanaticism not of the possessor, but of the possessed. She could do what she wanted to him: she could say whatever came into her head. He would never have enough of her. He would go on forever demanding kisses, looks, even blows. Not that he was masochistic; when she was inadvertently tender with him there were long and inimitable sighs of satisfaction, like those of a contented child. And inadvertently was definitely the word. She had always deliberately refused all forms of *détente*, just as she had always refused to make things easy, not only for him but for herself. She was the one who set the pace and drove the team; she was the one who forced him to wear the double yoke of anxiety and desire. But why? Who was forcing her to play animal tamer? Who or what was pushing her – if not tomorrow, then the day after – into the arms of a Basil who made love no better than Édouard? Who kept her from saying 'we' when she talked about herself and Édouard in the past or future? And who was keeping her from even imagining this future? She'd always maintained that her passions were strictly provisional, but this idea had been no more than a flat and abstract judgement, based on past experience. So why did she insist on reminding herself of it now? Why did she exhaust herself trying to be like her image and why did she feel secure only when this fierce and primal image coincided with the reflection she saw in Édouard's eyes? Édouard wasn't exactly the public, after all! It was his job to look for her truth, even find it. But which truth? After all the lies and lives she'd lived, who was she?

All of a sudden, she saw herself at twelve, in a black schoolgirl's smock on a rainy day in Rouen. She was standing at the window and her mother was shouting terrible things at her. 'But what's the matter with you?' she was screaming. 'I can't understand you! I don't know what to do any more! Who are you?' The little girl was terrified because she didn't know the answer. She'd never thought about that particular question before. It seemed to her that, by definition, her mother was the one with the answer, and that she'd give it to her when the time was right. Yet here was her mother shouting that she didn't know, her mother demanding the answer from *her*! It was all so horrible and confusing. So who did know the answer? Who could know? Once again, she saw the reflection of her black smock on the windowpane, the sun-bleached rain glancing off the other side, the angry red face of her mother that suddenly went grey, then disappeared without a word, without even apologizing for having let out such a terrible secret. Now Béatrice's eyelids really were burning, but this time she knew where the tears were coming from and she choked them back, rubbing them away with her fist like the schoolgirl in her mind. She tried to laugh at herself; after all what difference did it make whether she was this or that, whether her existence had such a meaning? She'd never paid attention to anything other than her ambitions, her desires, her pleasures. She'd never loved or hated herself. At most, she'd admired her strength when the going was rough, her cleverness in dodging dirty tricks, and her indifference to hard knocks. They just didn't matter to her. And if sometimes she was pleased with herself, it was only because she'd done something that made her laugh, even though the laugh was as ironical as it was joyous. She knew that gratuitousness, kindness, trust, and fidelity were not empty words for everyone, but she also knew that they were just that – empty words – and, as far as she was concerned, would remain so. For two reasons; her nature and that of her work. She never lied to herself about this; she was entirely lucid and proud of it. She even felt it was one of her strengths, whereas it was probably her sole weakness. For, while Béatrice imagined that it was she who had refused all illusions, it was in fact the illusions that had been refused to her.

There are times, it is said, when lucidity is worse than the worst blindness. The moment you accept your reflection as definitive, it doesn't matter whether it's been deformed by the mirror or the eye. It doesn't matter because the reflection must be beautiful, or at least try to be, for if it isn't, and if you're resigned to that, you invariably wind up looking for the worst. You try, for instance, to exaggerate your ferociousness, like those fairgoers who are already ugly enough but who suddenly recognize their caricatured reflections in a house of mirrors and apply themselves to accentuating their grotesqueness rather than simply taking to their heels in horror. In fact, these fair-goers even get together and laugh openly at their ugliness because now they see it with a capital letter, whereas in private, when it's in small letters, all they can do is smile nervously. But in the house of mirrors, their insignificance has finally been noticed! And what do the insignificant and the idiotic seek, if not to be noticed? Everyone who walks down the street wants someone else to turn around; or when he can't sleep, he wants someone to worry about him; or when he laughs or cries, someone to understand him. And when he's happy, someone to envy him. Which is perhaps why all separations, all divorces, are so painful. It's not the loved one – opposite or complementary, master or slave – you miss, it's the 'other', the spectator, the perpetually plugged-in microphone or camera. It doesn't matter whether you are watched with desire or hatred; what's important is that there should be someone to see you get up, get dressed, smoke, go out, someone to hear you whistle, yawn, or fall silent, even if that someone doesn't really look or listen. And then, suddenly, there's no one. Because even if you can't stand him, for whom do you stub out your cigarette in an ashtray rather than in the middle of the rug? Even if you feel no more desire for him any more, for whom do you put out the light and get undressed? Even if you hope he won't be there in the morning, for whom do you shut your eyes and try to go to sleep? Even when you're an adult, for whom do you go to sleep, if God doesn't exist? And for whom do you wake up? Who'll be around the next day to notice how carefully you've brushed your teeth? Who'll be there to watch you do it?

These weren't exactly the sorts of questions Béatrice tended to ask herself, but they were, on the other hand, very much a part of the interminable self-interrogations – be they tender as lilacs or fierce as orchids – that had always populated Édouard's secret garden. They were the questions that had inspired his two plays (already performed), his novel (unfinished), and his poems (thrown out or lost). In a way, his work was nothing more nor less than the incoherent monologue of a gardener overrun by his flowers and his words, a crazed gardener who has only the stakes to water because the plants themselves have all been ravaged from too much digging and pruning. Yet this same gardener is also sometimes amazed and delighted to find a fragile, but succulent rose rising and swaying in the midst of all this carnage, a wholly unknown variety of rose, a rose made of words and petals miraculously intertwined – namely, a felicitous turn of phrase. And it was through these four flat and academic words – felicitous turn of phrase – that Édouard understood the incredible joy of self-expression and the possibility, the delirious possibility, of being understood.

17

Autumn was upon them. The days grew shorter, as did the time allotted for the shooting of the film. But it rained nonstop in the Touraine Valley and the team continued to sink ever deeper into the muddy yellow fields. Béatrice had to replay the opening scenes of the film because of a cutting accident, and she was annoyed. It poured, and when it stopped, steam rose from the meadows; even the poplars seemed to be waiting for winter, dreaming about something else altogether. From the window of his hotel room, Édouard watched the slippery landscape without really seeing it. He unconsciously filed it away in the huge album of his affair with Béatrice, an album begun at the beginning of time and therefore hopelessly eclectic. One day, however, certain still vivid memories would coalesce, although for the moment they tended to stand side by side in a false but cordial equality – memories of the autoroute, the Magritte, an open bed, words, words stammered and unpolished, the sleek line of a sailing boat, a naked mouth in the night, an old opera tune, the sea. He had already given up looking through the jumble for that particular profile of Béatrice ringed in pleasure in the circle of his binoculars that summer afternoon. Instinctively, he remembered only the happy moments and wondered why his memory was so selective, so deliberately turned towards a happy past, whereas his imagination remained hideously defeatist and kept insisting on a heartbreaking future. He supposed that in the final analysis his cowardice – or his courage – was fake; he was the sort who withstood the hardest blows without flinching but fell to pieces before the unexpected, even if it turned out not to be the worst. Furthermore, he knew he could never hold a grudge. The memory of Gino and the sailing boat was still as sharp as some terrible wound, but he had no idea as yet who'd inflicted it upon him. If he'd had to name the culprit, he would have said 'life'. Life, yes, but Béatrice, never. Never, because since then she'd taken him back into her arms, kissed him, loved him, had given him pleasure and had taken the same from him. No, if anything, the fault lay with his carelessness. One should never take other people's natures for granted and given the sort of person Béatrice was – free, sensual, and unfaithful – he should never have let her go off alone on the boat with such a handsome escort. After all, one would have to be terribly small-minded and terribly contemptuous not to accept Béatrice as she was, or to refuse to protect her. Of course, she'd played the whore in his eyes, but he must have seemed every inch the imbecile in hers. In any case, when it came down to it, he preferred Béatrice's rôle in the whole affair; like all dreamers, he had great admiration for people of action. The problem was that he feared Béatrice too preferred that rôle. And if he respected her for the suffering her escapade had caused him, that didn't mean, alas, that she respected him for having felt it. And she was right. Absolutely right. No amount of pain was worth a moment of pleasure, no melancholy worth a surge of feeling, no regret worth a desire. Of that he was sure. In fact, as far as he was concerned, not the least of Béatrice's charms was that each day she pushed him to feel rage and starvation and fulfilment. In short, she made him feel like a man.

The following morning, Béatrice ran into Basil in the hotel corridor. One look was enough to see that everything was still not only desirable between them, but also possible. His room was two steps away, he smiled at her, she wanted to follow him, and she did. She followed his broad shoulders and long legs and the confession of desire in his eyes. A confused but automatic urge to obey – one she knew well – made her suddenly want to surrender to that desire, made her feel that desire as a command, even an obligation. She had decided to obey a sort of ancestral obligation, and her hands, her legs, her very blood acknowledged its justice. Once, for an hour, she'd belonged to this man and he to her. They'd pleased each other and there was no reason to break this tacit and perfectly natural bond in the name of some unknown person or thing. Because there in that dark and empty corridor, Édouard had suddenly become an unknown, an idea, almost a memory. At that moment, Béatrice had only one friend, one close person, one equal, and that was Basil. And she knew it. She'd always been taken aback by the irreversible aspect of these accidental and purely sensual encounters. Taken aback, and completely fulfilled. For her, these were the only circumstances where a man and a woman enjoined equality, because both were victims of the same delicious necessity of joining together. So she let the tall demanding body press up against her, and like a music lover recognizing the opening bars of a favourite andante, she instinctively fluttered her eyelashes out of sheer gratitude for the warmth of this contact. Odd as it may seem, she felt that it was the purest and most honest part of her that lay down on the hotel bed. And that this resolute and lustful body of hers now abandoned to a mere passerby was perhaps the only proof of her respectability.

Indeed, Basil was most respectful in his disrespect, exasperated as it had been by a week of disappointments. He was surprised to find he really had been waiting for her, and he avenged himself for the delay with gusto. As Édouard was in Paris for the day, they had more than enough time after making love to talk. Weary, their desire satisfied, encouraged by a kind of melancholy sweetness – for they knew they would probably never see each other alone again – they exchanged confidences. In certain circumstances, and between two people who scarcely know each other, confidences have a tendency to become indiscretions. And because neither dared go as far as to tell each other their dreams, they stuck to the basic facts. Which meant that Basil, usually the soul of discretion, told Béatrice why he was there; he told her about Nicolas's conspiracy and Édouard's little game. No sooner were the words out of his mouth, however, than he felt guilty. Béatrice seemed to be taking it very phlegmatically even with amusement, but Basil knew that the reactions of a woman just after making love could be quite different from those of a well-rested woman back on her feet. He begged her to forget he'd ever mentioned it, but she laughed in his face.

'Are you out of your mind?' she retorted. 'Do you think I'm just going to keep my mouth shut and go on playing my part in this little comedy? Édouard's my lover. Which means there's no question of secrets between us.' (This last added without the slightest sign of a guilty conscience.)

She left the room humming to herself and Basil went in search of Nicolas whom he couldn't find. Meanwhile, Édouard, who'd had plenty of time to embellish his rôle on his way back from Paris, arrived at the hotel looking every inch the perfect, overworked, blasé, and efficient journalist.

'They're all very pleased with the beginning of the article,' he announced later by the fire. 'I spent an hour with their correspondent, a fellow named Williams. They think the pictures are fine, and they're even thinking about another article once the film's out.'

They were all together in the little parlour and Tony d'Albret was exultant, having spent the afternoon taking one of her discreet health walks after she'd noticed the simultaneous absence of Basil and Béatrice.

'I wish you'd show us the article, Édouard dear,' she said. 'After all, I don't really think it's asking too much.'

'I'd rather keep it a surprise,' Édouard interrupted quickly.

'I don't like surprises,' Béatrice said in a flat voice which presaged the worst. 'In fact, I think it would be only decent ... yes, decent, if you showed us the piece before it comes out.'

This unexpected and somewhat laughable reference to decency definitely signalled a storm and Tony, caught off guard, frowned. When Béatrice was in a good mood, she was perfectly and deliciously natural, but when she began talking morals – a vocabulary completely unfamiliar to her – you could be certain the good mood had vanished. For, contrary to most women, Béatrice always felt more tender and considerate of her lovers after she'd betrayed them, an attitude prompted by neither condescension nor pity nor even shame – a feeling even further removed from Béatrice than decency. What she felt, quite simply, was gratitude. Tony didn't know this, of course, but it was gratitude that welled up inside Béatrice when she saw her lover returning, calm and happy, whistling a tune. The very lover she'd spent the afternoon forgetting in someone else's arms. It was gratitude for the fact that he was sufficiently blind or confident or busy to let her enjoy her little escapades without making a scene. It was only natural, then, that Tony found Béatrice's irritation so difficult to understand.

'And you, Tony,' Béatrice continued. 'Don't you find Édouard's a bit irresponsible?'

There was such panic on Édouard's face that Nicolas didn't know whether to laugh or protest. It was really too much that a man with Édouard's talent, charm, and sincerity should find himself not only laughed at but accused of some sort of crime.

'I'm waiting until the film's finished,' Édouard repeated lamely. 'After all, I'm an outsider here. I have a different point of view and my article might influence Raoul. Unconsciously, that is.'

'Now wait just a minute!' Béatrice protested. 'Don't tell me you're going to lecture us about a fresh eye and a new way of looking at things and all the rest of that slush! As far as Raoul's concerned, he couldn't possibly be influenced one way or the other. Everyone knows that's his one great strength.'

Not quite sure how to take the compliment – if indeed it was one – Raoul gave a short triumphant laugh and bowed.

'And speaking of which,' Béatrice went on, turning to Raoul, 'have you looked over dear Basil's photos to see if they're any good? After all, we do want to look like worthy representatives of the French cinema and not a bunch of old fashioned puppets!'

'What's got into you?' Tony broke in. She'd grown increasingly alarmed as Béatrice went on and was now waving her short arms in the habitual gesture that made her look very much like a penguin. 'Why are you getting so worked up? As long as *Show*'s happy ...'

'I'm not getting worked up,' Béatrice snapped. 'It's just that I'd like to read the beginning of the article. That's all.'

She turned a steady gaze on Édouard and he knew then that all was lost. Not because he thought that Basil might have betrayed him, but because he'd become so comfortable in his rôle that he felt guilty because he hadn't been able to write the article. He'd actually tried: he'd wanted to look serious and he'd also wanted to pretend it was true. Unfortunately, however, he'd been forced to acknowledge the fact that he'd never make a good reporter. His memories of the shooting depended entirely on the state of his passion: the first week's work had seemed good, the second painful, the third ghastly, but these judgements were only a reflection of Béatrice's moods. As for Raoul's technique, it could be summed up in one sentence: he either directed Béatrice or left her to her own resources; and Édouard was utterly incapable of evaluating Béatrice's performance. She was always and everywhere front and centre stage, and as far as he could tell, in close-up. Like all the preceding weeks, these last two had been a continuous and almost morbid sequence of close-ups conceived and executed by an obsessed director. Édouard couldn't remember anyone telling a single joke on the set; in fact, he couldn't remember anything about what had really happened. Once again, he had to admit that reality – or truth – meant nothing to him; only his feelings and his fiction gave his life meaning. The trouble was that had this game been anything more than a joke, *Show*'s readers would surely not pay two cents to learn that Béatrice loved the smell of hay, that she detested omelettes, that she wore pointed high-heeled shoes in the worst muddy puddles, that she was on sickeningly familiar terms with technicians, and that she offered the camera enough looks, gestures, and semi-swoons to drive Édouard wild with jealousy. The absurd efforts he'd made in the past ten days to start his fake article had been utterly useless. Even the words themselves – his ever-faithful allies, his subjects, his troops – had turned out to be nothing but a mob of disobedient recruits in revolt. In fact, in order to crush the mutiny, he'd had to start a long and delirious poem that was still unfinished.

'In any case,' he declared, 'it won't come out for at least six months.'

'If "it" ever comes out at all,' murmured Béatrice so softly that everyone froze. Nicolas began moving in the vague direction of the door and even Tony, usually so prodigiously insensitive to atmosphere, put her drink back on the table.

'What do you mean?' she asked.

But Béatrice had already crossed the room, taken a firm grip on a petrified Édouard's arm, and was pulling him outside.

'We have things to talk about,' she declared from the doorway. 'Monsieur Maligrasse and I have some very serious things to talk about.'

Then, spinning around, she executed one of those dramatic exits that had made her such a success – in life as well as on stage.

Night was falling rapidly and it was very cold outside. In the courtyard of the hotel, the sky had turned dark blue. Béatrice turned to Édouard, took hold of his lapels, and studied him. Édouard saw that she knew, but the extent and the suddenness of the catastrophe left him defenceless. He stared back at her, arms dangling at his sides, the blood pumping in his ears. He couldn't remember having felt such terror since the day he'd been caught by the school principal smoking a cigar in chapel. At the same time, however, he couldn't help noticing that Béatrice's lower lip was fuller than usual, and he wondered confusedly who might have bitten her.

'So you lied to me,' her voice came to him, as if from a great distance.

He didn't answer and she shook him lightly. Docile, he nodded, wondering once again if this were pretext enough for her to leave him.

'Yes,' he replied finally. 'I lied to you. So what?'

She moved closer to him, put her arms around his neck and laid her head on his shoulder, the first submissive gesture he'd known her to make.

'My God,' she murmured. 'My God, how marvellous! You *do* have an imagination after all.'

Raising her head, she kissed him passionately. Stunned, Édouard wavered, deliriously happy, knowing he would never never get used to her. Or get unused to loving her.

'You don't know what it's like,' Béatrice's voice went on, half-smothered in his jacket. 'You don't know what it's like living with a man who has no imagination. I'd rather live with a crook, a pimp even. At least with them the percentage is strictly financial. But with a creative man, you know, the percentage is only in boredom. He lives off your inspiration and wishes you were dead when you can't distract him from the banality of his existence. But you, my dearest,' she added, raising her head and kissing Édouard's neck almost respectfully, 'I see now there's nothing of the pimp about you.'

She began to laugh and Édouard, who'd closed his arms around her, studied the night-blue sky that a minute ago had been bordering on catastrophe but now glowed with all its country softness and tranquillity. Then he too began to laugh, realizing that this was the first time she had really seemed to admire him and, for that, he'd had to lie to her.

The following day, however, he had time enough to forget his tender regrets. Béatrice was on top form and at seven o'clock, after the last take, she let loose. The technicians were gathering up their equipment in the courtyard of the farm. Raoul, Cyril, Nicolas, Basil and Édouard were splitting a bottle of white wine on the stone steps. With a wink and a smile, Béatrice had already reassured Basil who was filled with remorse over yesterday's betrayal (Édouard not having had the time to tell him about the failure of the whole conspiracy).

'And so, Tony,' said Béatrice gaily, 'Édouard finally decided to read me the first few pages of the article. It's really very good, very good indeed.'

Nicolas and Basil stared at each other open-mouthed.

'But I think it lacks romanticism,' she went on. 'Americans love their fairy tales, don't they? Especially fairy tales from the film world. I think Basil should take a few pictures of Cyril and me embracing tenderly.'

'But ... Well, that seems like a ... like a strange idea,' Cyril stammered, torn between the opportunity of destroying the vague aura of homosexuality that always hovered about him and the terror of provoking his wife's anger (like all homosexuals' wives, dark-haired Margot suffered from her husband's hypothetical female liaisons with a jealousy as morbid as it was absurd).

'For heaven's sake, Cyril,' said Béatrice, 'Margot's not here. You don't have anything to worry about.'

She sat down next to him and began arranging herself in suggestive poses. Laughing and joking, Basil snapped away while Édouard, hands tied by all his lies, sat champing at the bit, grumbling about how ridiculous it was, protesting that he wasn't writing a gossip column but a serious piece.

'Listen,' said Béatrice, 'did I read your article or didn't I? I promise you, it could do with a little spice, among other things.'

'It's true,' Basil added. 'Americans do love this kind of thing. I wouldn't mind reading a few pages myself, Édouard.'

'Look,' Cyril began, trying to disentangle himself from the arms locked firmly about his neck, 'when this article comes out, what'm I going to tell Margot?'

'You can tell her it was just a big joke,' answered Raoul. 'A publicity stunt.'

'She's already awfully suspicious of me,' said Cyril pitifully.

Raoul, Nicolas, and Tony exchanged leers.

'Well,' drawled Béatrice, getting up and stretching, 'since I'm the star, why don't you pose with me, Édouard? You can play the bashful lover. Get your Leica ready, Basil.'

She took Édouard's arm, assumed a languid expression, and laid her head on his shoulder.

'An excellent idea,' said Tony, suddenly remembering she was an agent. She gazed at them tenderly, although not without a certain curiosity. 'An excellent idea for both of you – the successful young playwright and the film star. Very romantic. And it *is* the truth, after all,' she added, in her most innocent voice.

Smiling and unperturbed, Basil shot off a roll of Édouard and Béatrice. Nicolas had difficulty trying not to laugh. *Only Béatrice could pull this off*, he thought. *Only she could persuade one lover to photograph her swooning in the arms of the other!*

'I find all this very embarrassing,' Édouard protested in a low voice. 'Embarrassing and ridiculous.'

'Édouard finds this ridiculous!' shouted Béatrice to the onlookers. 'Do I embarrass you, my dear? Are you ashamed of our relationship? (Here, she gave him a loud kiss on the cheek.) I can't imagine why. After all, none of these pictures will ever be published; and anyway, I find it amusing.'

'That's exactly what I find so unpleasant,' Édouard hissed back. 'This is the first time you've displayed your feelings for me in public, and I had to go and invent an article for it. And Basil ... Basil must think I'm God only knows what!'

Béatrice began to laugh, the laugh Édouard found particularly detestable.

'As for that,' she replied, 'I'm sure he does think you're God knows what. O.K. Basil, that's enough,' she cried. 'Oh, wait a minute, I want a picture of the two of you, Édouard and Basil. It's very fashionable these days, you know, to have pictures of the reporter and his photographer.'

The two men sat down a yard apart like two andirons, hands dangling at their sides, both of them embarrassed and furious and agreeing that the whole idea was in very bad taste. Béatrice aimed the camera at them.

'Smile!' she called. 'Really, you look like two straight men out of some old comedy. No, not like that, you're not at all funny, you know.'

'Neither are you,' Nicolas's voice said behind her.

He had been admiring Béatrice's little game in silence, and had to admit there really was something terribly funny about the devastated expressions of these two ageing boys each so profoundly convinced he was fooling the other.

'So why don't you go and stand next to them?' Béatrice hissed back.

He looked at her. A lock of hair over her forehead, her cheeks pink, her eyes dark and sombre, she had such a malicious and self-satisfied expression on her face that he was utterly disarmed. And she was seductive enough to indulge in this kind of joke. It was unfortunate he hadn't understood when they'd been together how genuinely funny she really was.

'No,' Nicolas replied softly. 'I don't think I will. It would be a chronological error.'

Béatrice burst out laughing, put the camera down, and threw her arms around him. Both laughed with that total innocence peculiar to the mildly and gently corrupt.

'It's up to you,' Béatrice whispered, nibbling at his ear, 'it's up to you to redress the error.'

But the two others, vastly relieved, had already joined them and so, escorted by all three handsome, distinctive, and equally enamoured suitors, she retraced her steps to the hotel, thoroughly pleased with herself and with life in general.

18

The curtain fell for the fifth and last time, but the applause was so meagre that the stage manager signalled for it to stop. Béatrice was beside herself with rage. Eyes glittering, she stormed across the stage to where a depressed Tony and Édouard were waiting in the wings. Despite the fact that the play had been pronounced an unqualified failure four days before, Béatrice couldn't get used to the fact. Her anger was as loud and demonstrative as her pleasure had been detached and discreet six months earlier when she'd triumphed in the revival of *L'Après-Midi* in the same theatre.

'What louts!' she exclaimed as she came up. 'What a bunch of imbeciles!'

'It's the play,' Tony said plaintively. 'I told you.'

'You told me nothing at all,' Béatrice snapped. 'It's a perfectly good play, well directed, well acted. By me and everyone else. It's the critics who are the cretins, just like everybody who reads them!'

She stalked off to her dressing-room and, fulminating, began rubbing off her make-up. Édouard smiled. In this drab and masochistic age, Béatrice's revolt seemed like a ray of sunshine. He'd seen too many artificially tasteful and elegant resignations, too many responsibilities sloughed off on to others, too much grating cheerfulness and heroic silence. In short, he'd had his fill of all the trappings that usually served to disguise failure, and so he was enchanted with Béatrice's vehemence and resolute faith. Her exasperation was in fact doubly justified for, in addition to everything else, Raoul's film had got off to a bad start. It had been edited too quickly and launched with too much publicity and Béatrice, who had in the meantime agreed (a little too casually) to do this supposedly brilliant play, was bearing the brunt of both disasters. For the past three weeks, her interviewers had all become judges and she'd been dragged in front of the TV cameras like some sort of defendant, even though she was clearly not cut out for the defensive posture. Of course, she should have kept quiet and let time take care of things, but she'd always refused to accept defeat. Or rather she'd always believed that the line between victory and defeat was a fine one in the entertainment world and thus there were always reasons to fight. So she'd lost her composure and begun flailing, striking out blindly and a little haphazardly.

Strangely, however, the continual combat, the defection of certain friends, and the increasing rarity of telephone calls did not depress her in the least. On the contrary, the unfamiliarity of such phenomena gave her a new cheerfulness. The beds of roses that came with success had always seemed natural to her, and therefore very banal. Failure, on the other hand, allowed her to rediscover her favourite scent – the smell of gunpowder. When they realised this, the journalists began backing off and although they continued to scream like a pack of jackals, they always made sure it was a group effort. In truth, however, this inhabitual caution had been inspired by the unfortunate experience of one Patrice Polivet, a journalist famous for his surly disposition, who had thought it would be amusing to welcome Béatrice on to his programme with expressions of sympathy and indulgence. He quickly found, however, that she was not exactly the sort of person who enjoyed pity. On the contrary, she was to be admired, not for her talent or her courage, but rather for her remarkable patience in replying to the treacherous inanities of her host. The interview had turned into a fully-fledged battle, and some of Monsieur Polivet's colleagues had been overjoyed when his guest, on the top of her form and marvellously illuminated by three judiciously placed spotlights, had exposed him as a perfect idiot in front of twenty million spectators. By the same token, the memories of many of these immutable and interchangeable people who made up the *Tout-Paris* of Arts and Letters had been permanently invaded by a respectful admiration and Béatrice, who up till now had had a 'character' only in the opinion of her lovers, suddenly became a character in the eyes of the general public. A new bond had been formed between her and that elusive public, an amused complicity that could never have come from any triumph based on her talent.

With two successive failures to her credit, Béatrice had never been desired by so many men – known and unknown. Her post was proof enough, as were certain looks and remarks picked up in those late-night restaurants where she and Édouard ate dinner after the show. For once, however, this kind of homage left her indifferent. She wanted to be admired, not desired; she wanted to be admired by men and envied by their women. She wanted to understand once and for all just what this blind, dumb, and indispensable public really wanted. (For the first time in her life, Béatrice was paying attention to the female opinion, not that she felt she really belonged to the species of course. On the contrary, she saw it as whining, overdemanding, and impossibly egocentric, and felt absolutely no solidarity with the other representatives of her sex. In her agitation, however, she signed a couple of feminist petitions which in normal times she would never have taken the time to read.) In the end, helped by a few courageous critics – whose courage consisted mainly of holding the opposite opinion from their colleagues for a week – Béatrice managed to wrest a kind of success from both her enterprises. Every once in a while, however, she felt like giving up; she'd been working too hard for too long and often found she'd been drinking too much.

In the meantime, Édouard had been overwhelmed by success. His first play had opened with a great fanfare on Broadway, and journalists on the other side of the Atlantic had discovered, or had decided to discover, singular talent in this young French playwright. As the first echoes of his vaguely-defined notoriety began to appear on the wires of Associated Press in Paris, Tony d'Albret, strutting about in seventh heaven, congratulated herself with her usual unconscious vulgarity and told everyone that she was the only person in Paris capable of selling all that hot air for so much – in advance. Édouard, who until now had shunned the limelight, suddenly found himself trapped in its glare. He was frightened, and automatically refused all interviews, including an invitation to go to New York to participate in the casting. His indifference was the talk of the town, and everyone put it down to shrewdness. But, in fact, Édouard was anything but shrewd. The only lie he'd told concerned the reasons for his refusal. He'd excused himself by invoking his new and barely finished play, but it was scarcely the play that took up all his time and kept him bound and gagged in Paris in the dead of winter. It was his love for Béatrice. As far as he was concerned, the sparkling aeroplane, the unknown and magical city of New York, the pleasures and battles that awaited him there and that all his friends, including Béatrice herself, described with so much feeling, all boiled down to the same few words: being separated from his love. All the skyscrapers in New York might not keep Béatrice from being unfaithful in the blue bedroom at the very moment he was seeing them for the first time. Nor would all those obsequious producers and enthusiastic reporters keep him from missing her long black hair as he fell asleep at night, that warm and silky mass he wanted to fall for ever between him and the outside world, his refuge, his protective shield, even his trap.

The more he was sucked into this frantic modern world, the more Édouard saw himself as some Edwardian character, a character from Vuillard. With a kind of quiet pride, he told himself that among all those famished, patented, and mechanical sensualists in pursuit of glory and pleasure, he was the only one – with his pigskin gloves and imaginary candlestick – capable of abandoning everything for one night with one particular woman. And this not only because he feared she might spend that night with someone else, but also, and especially, because of the pleasure her body was sure to give him. He had been using and abusing that body for over a year; it may have been unfaithful, but it was always submissive, always desirable, and it left him no choice but to make love to it.

Indeed, his despotic love that both dazzled and terrified him and that he never talked about, had become a kind of symbol in the eyes of the general public. People talked about the passion of Édouard Maligrasse for Béatrice Valmont with the sort of stubborn, amused, and envious astonishment only an undisguised happiness can inspire. In fact, it was this very passion that provoked an elegant and dying Jolyet to his final, notoriously scornful laugh in public, in response to a woman who had asked him, or rather had wondered aloud, what Béatrice Valmont could have done to that poor Édouard Maligrasse.

'Everything,' Jolyet had replied. 'She's done everything to him,' and burst out laughing, only to fall immediately into his customary indifference.

His dream interrupted, Jolyet stretched out his hand, touched the fresh crisp sheet, and sighed, content for an instant. Then the pain burst back into his throat and into his chest, growing in depth and intensity. With a groan, he sat up and reached for the switch that always lay in the same corner next to him; in these circumstances, speed was essential and he didn't have time to waste groping about in the darkness. He turned on the light and blinking his eyes, opened the drawer of the superb bedside table signed by Jacob and of which Jolyet was very proud. The phials were all arranged in rows, as if standing at attention, slender, sparkling, and ice cold. Next to them lay a large and brand-new syringe. Carefully, he peeled one of the phials from its box, grasped the top between thumb and index finger, and snapped off the cap. Then he picked up the syringe, jabbed it into the phial he held like a treasure in his hand, and slowly, carefully, siphoned out the contents. A fiercer pain, almost an insult, bent him in two, but he had already acquired the necessary reflexes and, even though his head twisted convulsively on the pillow, his two precious hands remained upright and immobile. It would have been better had he stopped for a moment or two, for pain can often provoke involuntary and disastrous movements. But he couldn't stand it any more and so – without alcohol or cottonwool – he bent his knees back against his chest and plunged the needle into his thigh. He had always despised hurting himself, and the necessity of giving himself these injections, of having to dig this bit of metal into his skin and through the nerves below, was profoundly contrary to his nature.

Jolyet waited, his knees still pulled up to his chest. The pain was too great; it was unthinkable that someone could be in such pain, unthinkable that pain did not cause madness, wars, revolutions, unthinkable that anyone could be concerned with anything else. He sank his teeth into the sheet and then, suddenly, he felt something begin making its way, as if guided by remote control, towards the beast devouring his neck. He felt the pain recede and sighed in anticipation of the immense relief to come. When he saw he still held the empty needle in his hand, he threw it into the waste-paper basket at the foot of the bed, for the débâcle was now well underway, the pain fleeing on all sides. At last he could turn over; his body had become supple once again, alive and warm between the sheets. He turned off the light, making sure the switch was in its proper place for the whole process could start all over again as quickly and as brutally as before. Now he had to sleep, he had to go back to sleep, not to maintain his equilibrium – a laughable notion for a dying man – but to forget the pharmacist's panoply, to forget the cruel and stubborn fact that he was heading for oblivion. He could sleep now. There were a thousand chemical molecules, a thousand policemen, watching over him – over his body, his warmth, his imperviousness – a thousand guardian angels to keep away that delirious nymphomaniac known as physical pain.

He sighed again, opened his eyes, and looked at the luminous dial of the alarm clock. It was three in the morning, but what morning? What season? Thank God tomorrow wasn't far off, bringing with it daylight and Béatrice. He didn't have much time left and Béatrice was one of the few people whose company he enjoyed. At the moment, she was obsessed by her failures and talked to him seriously about them. Then, from time to time she would say incredible things such as: 'You take too much morphine. It's not good for you.' She would simply forget he was already at death's door. And when she remembered, she would burst out laughing with him and kiss him on the cheek. She didn't bother with sympathy or compassion, which was exactly what he wanted. As for the rest, he had everything he needed against the day he found it too indecent to go on living.

In the meantime, however, he refused to put up with pain and, the moment it began, he seized the syringe and liberated its marvellous contents for the chase. He'd even succeeded in timing the speed at which the morphine – which he referred to as his Diana – worked, and he knew that the day the prey became stronger or the huntress less efficient, he would simply put an end to the hunt altogether. Indeed, Béatrice had often come upon him in a state of intense concentration, watch in one hand, an empty syringe in the other. 'It took death to make me into a finicky accountant,' he'd told her, laughing. 'Of course, death does sometimes make heroes out of accountants, but then, I've never quite been able to see myself as the hero!'

It was easier during the day, of course, despite his heavy cough. And there was always the image of those ten lethal little sentinels lying in his drawer to reassure him. It was the night he worried about. Sometimes, in the solitude of the night, he panicked. He became a child again; he wanted to see his mother, he even wished he were married or had a child. Anything so as not to be alone. He had no friends of either sex on whom he felt he had the right to inflict the spectacle of his wasted body, his heavy perspirations, his terrors. When he'd returned from his holiday – if his brief *adieu* to the sea could be called a holiday – he'd tried asking a few of his regular whores to play nurse. Ever gallant, he would pay them the top price for a night, give them dinner with his usual courteousness, explain the situation in his precise voice, and then lie down next to them. He felt no desire, of course; it was only for warmth. Unfortunately, they all became depressed at the sight of their old comrade in such dire straits and, since his chastity doubtless seemed to them more indecent than any conceivable sort of lewdness, they all began drinking too much at dinner. Jolyet would often emerge from his nightmares to find no calm and fraternal body next to his, no soft and even breathing, but rather a restless, snoring, drunken bedmate. In his exasperation, he returned to his solitude, and soon only Béatrice was left. He waited eagerly for her visits. She would come in and find him lying on his bed or in the living-room, immobile and peaceful in a haze of drugs. His indifference and apathy astonished her, as she felt that in such circumstances, she would want to devour everything life could possibly offer.

'I thought the same myself once,' Jolyet said one day when she asked him about it. 'After all, I love music and painting and there are books I swore I'd reread before I died. Except that, contrary to my self-image, I found that all that meant nothing to me. There are no books, no music. They bore me, you see. It tires me, deprives me of time. And anyway,' he added, with just a suspicion of anger, 'no one has any true nature left in the face of death. There's only an assembly of cells that keep refusing to be separated. There's only the void, and my beating heart. It's the only sound I can tolerate, the beating of my heart, and the only thing I need to look at any more is this blue vein still throbbing away in this old man's hand. And the only contact I want is the touch of my own skin. Do you know, Béatrice, that even for someone like me who's never refused his whole life long to try anything once – anything except onanism, of course – it sometimes happens that I put my hand on my own cheek and marvel at it, and keep marvelling at it ... in a way I've never marvelled at any other body. I sometimes wonder how I ever managed to desire all those other bodies and faces. I can't even bear looking at them any more.'

'And me?' Béatrice had asked. 'Why me, then?'

'Because you don't take me any more seriously now that I'm dying than you did when I was alive,' he'd replied. 'Because unlike everyone else, you have no respect for my condition. And no compassion either. Which means you respect the only Jolyet I respect myself, the one who's gay and witty and light-hearted. And which means you're as capable now as you were twenty years ago of standing me up, even on the day of my death. That reassures me. But don't worry,' he'd added. 'I'll arrange things so that you'll be present. I'll kill myself during the afternoon, because I'm too afraid at night and too tired in the morning. We'll talk about something else altogether, you'll watch me fall asleep, and you'll know why I'm being so impolite. Impolite for the first time in my life, I might add.'

'You'll let me know when the day comes?' Béatrice had asked quickly.

'It's up to you. What would you prefer me to do?'

She had hesitated for a moment, then reached out and placed her hand against his cheek.

'I'd prefer you to let me know,' she had said. 'At least then you'll know that I know, and you'll feel less alone.'

Jolyet had glanced at her before his eyes clouded over.

'I thank you, my dear Béatrice. Because you're the only person I know primitive enough – or compassionate enough – not to call the police or the fire brigade or an ambulance or God only knows what other horror.'

To her surprise, Béatrice was not in the least depressed when she emerged from these conversations. On the contrary, she felt oddly refreshed, for neither the precision nor the cold ineluctability of the situation allowed her to forget the petty quarrels and indeterminate tempests of her own life. She never told herself that in comparison with Jolyet's, her own crises were ridiculous. In fact, that was precisely where she felt life really was; in all those small and violent disturbances, in that fundament of vanity and base ambition. She was sure Jolyet himself bitterly regretted no longer being able to participate in just such disturbances. No, in no way did his imminent death make her own life seem absurd; on the contrary, it gave it colour. And even the contempt she felt for certain typically Parisian manoeuvres had become agreeable. Indeed, when Édouard took her in his arms and kissed her, or when she felt him trembling against her in the night from weariness or desire, she often thought of the desperate and solitary trembling of another man just a few streets away who was trying not to spill the contents of a certain phial on to his pillow. Yes, it was just as the soap operas said : love was truly the opposite of death. Of course, one day she too would have to take her first step on that deserted and colourless beach that led to the sea, to death, to oblivion. But at the moment, such certainties did not concern her in the least. She'd always assumed that either she'd die on stage, be killed by a jealous lover, or be smashed against a plane tree in a sports car. But while she was waiting, she never answered Édouard's questions about Jolyet, for Jolyet had forbidden her to do so.

'Édouard's too sensitive,' he'd said. 'He's too much like me perhaps. Too human. He would rush right over and he'd depress me. I prefer your company a thousand times more.'

And Béatrice, smiling, had taken that statement for precisely what it was – a sincere compliment.

'But what do you think I should do about him?' she'd asked Jolyet later on.

'Oh, there's no reason to feel sorry for him,' Jolyet had replied, raising a fatalistic hand. 'He loves you. And he has you for the time being.'

'Yes, he's very attached to me,' Béatrice had said, surprised to feel herself blushing at this somewhat affected expression.

'He's going to take his chances,' Jolyet had gone on. 'And to tell the truth, everything about that young man seems enviable to me. I'd give my right arm to have had just once his kind of great and unhappy love affair.'

With a wave of his hand, he had refused the telephone call his impassive butler had announced, and had turned to Béatrice, a glint of real curiosity in his eyes.

'And you?' he'd asked. 'Have you decided whether you really love him or not?'

The question had caught her off guard and she'd remained silent, even indignant, for a long moment.

'For goodness' sake,' Jolyet had laughed. 'It's not as if I've said anything vulgar, you know. I only asked if you loved your lover.'

'It may strike you as incredible,' Béatrice had finally replied. 'But I've never asked myself that question.'

'Good for you. I've always thought it ridiculous when people ask themselves if someone loves them, but it's even more absurd when they start asking whether they're really in love or not.'

And they'd changed the subject.

As she'd walked back to her flat, however, the question had continued to plague her. Did she love Édouard? Yes, in a way she did, more than any other man she'd ever known. Was she in love with him? Yes, at night, when she said 'I love you', it wasn't just her body speaking. But would she be miserable without him? That was the question, the real one, the one she'd never asked. Édouard gone. Édouard not in love with her any more? It was unimaginable. But why? Because she lacked imagination? Or because he himself had made that particular image inconceivable? By abandoning himself to her the way he had, body and soul, hadn't he imprisoned her in a net that was every bit as dangerous as the more conventional lovers' doubts and anxieties? By accepting her betrayals and yet suffering over them, hadn't he forced her to imagine her future escapades as completely lacking in charm, not to mention good taste? By declaring himself both fatally in love with her and fatally sure she would leave him one day, hadn't he offered her a long and cruel challenge? Hadn't he inspired in her the temptation to hang on to him? And to hang on to him just the way he was – exposed, vulnerable, terrified? Never in all her life had a man thrown down his arms before her so completely, so quickly, so ostentatiously, and with so much pleasure in his surrender. *He's playing Machiavelli*, she thought, not without a smile. After all, the idea that anything Édouard did might be the result of shrewdness or calculation seemed the height of absurdity. Yet she did feel a certain suspicion, something almost like mistrust ... or fear. A wholly unexpected and perfectly exquisite fear.

19

Tony d'Albret sat on the big sofa in Béatrice's living-room, her face composed in what she considered an expression of total devastation. She'd placed her feet side by side in their ankle-boots, folded her hands in her lap, and forgotten to redo her make-up. Unfortunately, since vivaciousness was her only charm, she looked more like some sort of worn out broken-down pack horse than the world-weary and subtle advisor she wanted to appear. For the hundredth time that day, she went back over her sad story. It seemed that Walkers, the man who'd bought the theatre rights to Édouard's play, had also taken an option on the film at the same time. Foreseeing a success, he was now pushing Tony to get a definite agreement. In vain, Tony had tried everything she could think of to get Édouard interested in the project, but the offer had come during a particularly tense period – just as Raoul had begun shooting – and Édouard, preoccupied with Béatrice's moods, hadn't even listened to the wonders and glories his agent had painted for him. Seeing her ten per cent in jeopardy and believing herself a clever psychologist, Tony had hinted that Béatrice was a prime candidate for the starring rôle in this projected Franco-American production. Whereupon Édouard, clutching at whatever straw he could find, had seized on this final argument and immediately agreed. *At least if she leaves me now,* he'd said to himself, *I'll have a pretext to see her again. And perhaps the chance to get her back.*

So Walkers had renewed his final and very generous offer and a delighted Tony had trotted over like a good hunting dog with the contract in her teeth and laid it at Édouard's feet. In the meantime, however, not only had things taken a turn for the better between the two lovers but Walkers had signed an American actress to play the lead. Forced to renounce her expected, albeit imaginary, percentage on Béatrice, Tony took everything she had left and bet on Édouard's preoccupation. The casting change was thus presented as a double sacrifice, one which would be compensated for, however, by an impressive number of dollars. To her stupefaction, Édouard had flown into a rage, thrown the contract in her face, and even threatened to kick her out bodily if she dared renew the offer.

'But really, Édouard,' Tony was saying, huddled on the sofa and for once genuinely frightened. 'There's no guarantee that the play will be successful and, if it's a disaster, the film rights won't be worth a *sou*. What's more, when you think about it, Glenda Johns will be just perfect in the rôle. It doesn't matter about Béatrice; neither of us ever breathed a word about it to her.'

It was true. Édouard had been afraid it would look like blackmail and had forbidden Tony to mention the project in Béatrice's presence.

'So what?' he replied curtly. 'What difference does that make?'

'Simply that her feelings won't be hurt. You have to put yourself in Walkers' shoes, Édouard. Béatrice has just had two consecutive flops and, contrary to what you seem to think, New York isn't as far away as all that. They know everything over there.'

Édouard raised his arm and Tony shrank back further into the cushions.

'And you mustn't forget,' she went on plaintively, 'you mustn't forget I know exactly what will happen. Béatrice is part of my stable, after all. I can tell you it'll all blow over in no time. Her career doesn't hang on any one part, even if it is the best part in your play. And especially,' she added, her voice dropping, 'especially since I don't understand a thing about that part and if you want my opinion, neither does she. But all this money is just the security you need, Édouard. It's the chance to write more plays without having to sponge off anyone.'

Édouard went white and Tony began waving her arms convulsively again.

'Please Édouard, I'm not suggesting you're sponging off

advise you ...'

She stopped short. The front door had just slammed shut and Béatrice walked in smiling, her cheeks rosy from the first touch of winter. Tony's spirits rose. Béatrice had her faults but she was, thank God, a practical woman. After all, she'd benefit from the money as much as Édouard. Tony was quite sure of that.

'Béatrice,' she said, 'Walkers has offered three hundred thousand dollars for the film rights to *Un Orage Immobile*. And Glenda Johns is playing the lead. What do you think?'

Béatrice let out a low whistle of admiration.

'Congratulations,' she said. 'Congratulations, Tony. Three hundred thousand dollars! Even before the dress rehearsal! Not bad. You have to accept it, Édouard.'

'Never!' he cried, looking from one to the other. He spun around and stalked out of the room, slamming the door behind him. Flabbergasted, Béatrice burst out laughing and sat down.

'Whatever's been going on?' she asked.

Tony launched into a long and confused explanation that became clearer as it went on. Night fell, but Béatrice forgot to turn on the lights. She listened thoughtfully, an odd little smile playing about her lips.

'Would you please explain to me what is going on between you two?' Tony demanded finally, thoroughly exasperated. 'That you're pleased with yourself at having such a good grip on him I can understand, but that doesn't make him any less of a fool, don't you see? You *do* see he's being foolish, don't you?'

'Oh yes,' Béatrice replied pensively. 'Oh yes, completely foolish.'

She lit a cigarette and stared out at the garden, showing Tony a thoughtful and tender profile she'd never seen before.

'The more so,' she added, 'the more so since the rôle of Penelope doesn't really tempt me in the slightest ...'

Tony sighed with relief. She'd found an ally just where she'd feared an enemy. *These artists are hopeless*, she said to herself. *They're just not like other people*.

'Don't worry about it any more,' Béatrice went on without

looking at her and in the same preoccupied voice. 'Don't worry about it. I'll bring him round.'

Then, her face still turned towards the garden, she added : 'I'll let you go off now, Tony. You know the way.'

It was only when she found herself on the street that Tony d'Albret realized she'd been quite definitely kicked out, for the first time in her life.

Alone at the window, Béatrice continued to stare out at the now darkened garden, letting one cigarette after another burn down between her fingers. The smell of the city, of cold, of dying mignonette came to her. *I must cover the plants for winter*, she thought, and called Cathy to help her light the lamps. When Édouard came back to apologize for his outburst, his arms laden with flowers, he found her sitting there, perfectly tranquil and inscrutable. Perhaps she knew nothing after all? (Édouard couldn't know, of course, that when women like Tony find themselves in a tight corner, they invariably attack. He couldn't imagine Tony would dare tell Béatrice about her betrayal, nor could he imagine the fact that their friendship – that famous female camaraderie – was based on a fierce and mutual contempt. And so he wasn't surprised when Béatrice suggested, offhandedly, that he would sign the contract.)

'You know,' she murmured later as she got undressed, 'Glenda Johns is perfect as Penelope. She's got those cat-like eyes and just the right intellectual look. It's not an easy part, you know.'

'You really think so?'

'Definitely. In any case, I know I could never do it.'

'But you can do any kind of part!' Édouard replied, surprised.

'Any part that tempts me, yes. But strangely enough, my darling, I only like the men's parts in your plays.'

Édouard was puzzled. She was right, though. His heroines were bland. He'd always been more interested in his heroes, and for a very simple reason : he hoped that one day, one of them – out of madness or idiosyncrasy or just because that was his nature – would be able to seduce Béatrice in Édouard's place. That was why he gave them all the best lines, all the things he didn't dare tell Béatrice himself. And opposite such emissaries, it was only natural that his female characters seemed pale and almost immaterial. And yet he'd never really tried confronting this ideal hero he kept creating and recreating in his mind – the one who was so casual, so courageous, so irresistible – with a real flesh and blood heroine like Béatrice. Because to do so, he would have had to know her, understand her, be sure of her, all of which were patently impossible. In any case, Béatrice's opinions in this particular area were infallible. She knew her trade well, she loved it, and she worked like a dog without any complaints. He was moved, and looked at her.

She was lying on the bed reading, one arm thrown back over her head. He put their record on and lay down next to her. The soprano's voice rose, joined the tenor's, and the great sailing ships of love and death were launched into the air around them. He listened. Béatrice put down her book and listened, too. But when he turned towards her, she put her hand on his forehead and gently pushed him away.

'Not tonight, if you don't mind,' she said. 'I'm a little tired.'

Édouard lowered his head to her shoulder, surprised to find his feelings unhurt. She had refused him so tenderly this time, almost as if she were apologizing. Yes, she really did seem tender and contrite for the moment but, remembering the wild mornings-after that usually followed these brief respites, he hesitated to congratulate himself. The scene with Tony had exhausted him and he fell asleep almost immediately.

At daybreak, in the whiteness and terror of the dawn, he was awakened abruptly by someone shaking him and talking out loud. Frightened, he wondered what new hell was being prepared for him. What was happening? What was she shouting at him? Béatrice's voice was imperious now, and she was shaking him brutally.

'I love you,' the voice was repeating in the darkness. 'You win. I really do love you. Only you.'

Stupefied, he sat up and began to stammer, but a firm hand closed his lips.

'I just woke you to announce the good news and I'm exhausted. Don't say anything. Just go back to sleep.'

She rolled over to face the window again and fell asleep with her usual abruptness, as if she'd literally been struck down. His heart pounding, Édouard remained paralysed for a long time. He'd been waiting for these words to be spoken by that voice for five, no six, years, and finally they had come. Those superb and impossible words – 'I love you' – had been spoken at last by his uncompromising lover. But why tonight? Why at that moment? And, more important, why didn't it make him feel happier and more triumphant?

20

Of course, the following morning, Béatrice acted as if nothing had happened. The day was flat and monotonous, and Édouard finally began to wonder if he hadn't simply been dreaming, or if Béatrice might perhaps have been talking in her sleep. The idea both comforted and upset him. Not until midnight, after the show and a pleasant dinner with friends, did they finally find themselves alone. They joked and laughed as they got undressed, but when Édouard stood next to her in the bathroom, Béatrice suddenly stopped what she was doing and looked at him gravely in the mirror. *God, I've got a lot of hair*, Édouard thought, and their twin reflections suddenly seemed incredible to him.

'How does it feel?' Béatrice asked. 'To be loved back?'

Without waiting for an answer, she passed in front of him and went to sit down at the foot of the bed. Humming, she picked up a nail file and attacked one of her toenails. Embarrassed, Édouard sat down next to her and tried to copy her tone of voice.

'It's very pleasant,' he replied smiling. 'But it's so hard to believe.'

He felt stupid and uncomfortable and definitely not up to the situation. And even though he would have been miserable if she had, he was really waiting for her to start laughing at him, as if it had all been some kind of fantastic and malicious joke.

'What made you say such a thing?' he went on, fumbling for words. 'I mean, how can you know ...'

'That I love you?' she interrupted, abandoning the nail file for a moment, beginning to laugh, swinging her foot backwards and forwards. 'It's simple really. I just asked myself the question.'

'You'd never done that before?'

'No. Strange, isn't it? I've been living with you all this time without even thinking about it. I mean without thinking that I loved you. But when I really thought about it, I realized that now, this time, I do.'

But her tone of voice was still playful and she went back to work with the file.

'But what about me?' said Édouard. 'What am *I* going to do?'

He was astonished to hear what he'd just said, and so was Béatrice.

'Nothing's stopping you from loving me back,' she replied, smiling. 'It'll be what's called requited love. Happiness is the word, I believe. Oh for heaven's sake, Édouard, I hate talking about these things! And don't start looking like the young dewy-eyed husband. Why don't you take off your shirt and rape me? Rape me, now,' she repeated, her hand on his thigh. 'Hurry. I want you. I wanted you all through dinner.'

He seized her and there they were, back together again and deliberately violent with one another. They felt they were giving themselves up to some pitiless struggle, a sort of exorcism. Or as if they were partners in a murder and were trying to forget. Finally, exhausted, they lay on the carpet a yard apart, out of breath but their passion sated.

'Tell me, you wretch,' Béatrice murmured, turning towards him with a rueful smile, 'when it's like this, what difference does it make whether I love you or not?'

'I don't know,' he replied sincerely.

'Nor me,' she concluded thoughtfully.

But that was a lie. For once, Béatrice had lied, not only to him but to herself. Lied out of timidity. With a feeling of despair, she rolled over and found herself looking down into Édouard's face.

So, this familiar, reassuring and sometimes irritating face, this was the face of love? She fluttered her eyelashes, leaned down, kissed his eyes, his temples, his neck; chastely, slowly, respectfully, feeling a long way away from herself. For the first time in her life, she was kissing her conqueror and feeling his victory giving birth to her defeat. But she also sensed that her conqueror was overwhelmed by his victory and it frightened her. Of course, she knew perfectly well that her confession the night before had been more for her than for him. What had happened was simply that his passion had overpowered her indifference, his devotion her arrogance, and his tenderness her ferocity. It was only fair that she should love him in return and that she should tell him so. *Except that this is the moment we're supposed to feel sublimely happy*, she said to herself, surprised that her happiness was far more apparent than his; which was strange since she was the one who'd just taken the plunge into all sorts of perils, while he was at long last emerging from them.

All right, she loved Édouard and she knew it. Her friends, of course, refused to believe it. Nicolas reminded her of all her innumerable whims, Cathy's routine was upset, and Tony found it clearly indecent, not to say absurd and superfluous, that she should pride herself so on being in love. Béatrice found their automatic jealousy, their instinctive desire to spy on her every move, their sense of ownership, perfectly normal. It was as difficult for them to adjust to Édouard's new importance as it had been easy to accept his original minor rôle. Merely from a professional point of view, however, Tony was beside herself. She had gone to a great deal of trouble to put over the image of Béatrice's insensitivity, of her glowing good health and her toughness, and this in an age when solitude, incommunicability, and sexual complication were the rule, and when everyone was clamouring for humanity, even from its film stars. It was true that, surrounded by other actors, Béatrice easily assumed an air of the sated wild animal who had wandered into a flock of poor starving sheep; in fact, the absence of all embarrassment on her part was often highly embarrassing. So what had got into her now? What was she doing shouting her beautiful new passion from the rooftops, a passion that had already become a little stale in the eyes of the *Tout-Paris*, even if it seemed brand new to Béatrice. The whole business was ridiculous; it wasn't like her at all. Of course, none of this would have bothered Béatrice in the slightest if it had been only Tony and her friends who'd voiced their scepticism. But there was Édouard as well. He seemed to have become suddenly suspicious, and almost spiteful, as if she'd broken a promise.

They were in the garden one afternoon and, as he kept glancing at her out of the corner of his eye, she finally gave in to her exasperation.

'So the fact that I love you and tell you so seems perverse to you, does it?' she demanded. 'Or just absurd?'

'Perverse?' repeated Édouard. 'No, not at all.'

'All right, absurd then. And useless. You'd become used to your rôle, hadn't you? You were used to being mistreated and it didn't bother you.'

'Yes, it did. I suffered the torments of hell and you know it. I took all I did from you because it was you handing it out. And I'd still take it . . .'

'But for God's sake!' she cried, at the end of her tether. 'Things have changed. I love you now.'

She called for Cathy in such an imperious voice that the maid appeared at once at the kitchen door, obviously terrified.

'It so happens that I love Monsieur,' Béatrice declared 'and I'd like you to witness the fact. You've known me for ten years, haven't you, Cathy?'

'Twelve, Madame,' Cathy corrected mechanically.

'All right, twelve. And you've seen quite a few men pass through here, haven't you?'

A prodigious sequence of charming expressions flashed across Cathy's face by way of response. First there was genuine desolation that such unfortunate errors had indeed occurred, then the stubborn fatalism of someone resolved not to pass judgement on someone else's past, and finally the distressed and total absorption of someone making a long and unforeseen mental calculation. Béatrice hastened to overtake her.

'Now Cathy, have you ever heard me say to any of these men, in broad daylight and stone-cold sober, that I loved him?'

Cathy's expression immediately became the acme of discretion.

'Even if Madame had said such a thing, I would not have heard it,' she replied, obviously pleased with her resolve.

But, as Béatrice seemed to be getting angry, she hurried on.

'But of course, it would have struck me anyway.' And she smiled amiably at Édouard who smiled back automatically and rather stupidly.

'Thank you, Cathy,' said Béatrice.

As soon as the maid had disappeared, she turned to Édouard, clearly annoyed.

'Do you realize what I've been reduced to? Do you realize I've had to go and make Cathy an Oenone? Really, Édouard, the whole thing's extraordinary. I have the feeling I'm offering my heart in the palm of my hand, complete with all of Verlaine's fruit and flowers and branches, and either no one wants it or it's too late.'

'Oh no, it's definitely not too late.'

His voice had become tender, but Béatrice appeared not to notice.

'Perhaps a little too early, then? Listen, for me all this is true. And it's marvellous! Every single move I make has a meaning. If I wash my hair, it's for you; if you're late, I get frightened. And I want to tell you everything I've done all day. I want to please you.'

'You already do.'

'Yes, but now it pleases me to please you, don't you understand?'

He hesitated, then raised his eyes and looked at her.

'And me?' he asked. 'Do I please you?'

'Oh no. No, it's much worse than that. I love you. I want to tie you to the foot of the bed when I go out and rub you all over with sandalwood oil when I come back. I want you to be free and happy but I want to know that something turns over inside you here (and she tapped his stomach with her hand) when you think of me. Doesn't the fact that I love you do anything to you?'

'Do anything to me? But my God, it's all I've ever wanted!' cried Édouard as he collapsed back into his armchair.

Which was true. It was what he'd wanted from the very beginning. He couldn't remember any more when he'd decided, or rather resigned himself, to loving her more than she loved him. So what was it about this so passionately desired reciprocity that made it seem like a kind of betrayal? Or a bad joke? Didn't he believe her? Of course he did. He did believe her. The signs of her surrender, her defeat, were everywhere. Sometimes during the night, he pretended to be asleep so as not to see her propped up on an elbow on the pillow – so incredibly beautiful and with that new look in her eyes – watching over him. He refused to open his eyes. He was afraid. He was even on the verge of asking himself just what this strange and over-attentive woman really wanted from him.

They were both in tremendous demand, but separately at first. Édouard was a successful author, a fact unconfirmed in Paris but which, as a known quantity in America, carried a good deal of weight. As for Béatrice, she had become a 'character'; thanks to television, her aggressiveness, which had been a handicap for so long, had now become a charming asset. Eventually, however, they were sought after together, since the fact that they loved each other always provoked people to curiosity, then jealousy, and ultimately the urge to destroy. They went from bright light to bright light like a pair of moths, but there always seemed to be a sort of mysterious and invisible glimmer that drew them together instinctively no matter how long the rooms nor how chaotic the parties. When they found themselves alone at night, they seemed surprised. The halo of approval that shone around them made them uncomfortable face to face, as if they were being forced to prolong a play that had no text and was being applauded too enthusiastically. At least it bothered Édouard; he was used to following, to occupying the back seat. He was the one who escorted a woman to parties and who had only a fifty-fifty chance of seeing her home. This new, public and official security made him nervous, and he told himself with a sort of horror that it was because he was so accustomed to anxiety and misfortune, and that he was obviously becoming one of those hopeless and desperate characters for whom the mere idea of happiness always strikes a false note.

Instinctively, Béatrice felt his dilemma, but she attributed it to surprise, the more so since she shared it. After all, she actually loved someone; she loved this tall melancholy idiot she'd rejected five years ago and whom she'd almost rejected at least ten more times during the past year. And now, when he entered the room or when she heard him speak, this love forced itself upon her with an uncomfortable clarity. From the first time she'd ever talked about love or heard it talked about, from the first time she'd begun making others fall in love with her and pretending to reciprocate, she'd felt the same discomfort. Now, however, she felt an almost mystical pride. She too was capable of love! But since Édouard's astonishment kept her from celebrating this glorious event, she was determined to make it a preposterous one. Instead of telling him, and herself, how marvellous it was that she loved him, she talked about how incredible it was. And instead of saying 'I've always dreamed of this happening to me,' she said: 'It *would* have to happen to me!' and shrugged her shoulders. Her smile might have been one of complete satisfaction, but this was mostly for Édouard's sake. She didn't want him to feel mistreated because she loved him, and she didn't want to upset him either. She just wanted him to be happy about it.

On the other hand, she talked about her love to Tony and Nicolas and all the others with a wonderful lack of reticence. It gave her the feeling she was taking on great responsibilities and dangers; that she'd acquired a kind of respectability. When she told them that she loved Édouard, she sounded like a young wife announcing she was pregnant. The only problem was that her friends had believed her to be sterile for so long – at least emotionally – that at best they attributed Édouard's success to a kind of phantom pregnancy which had inflated her words out of all proportion. Besides, since Béatrice never took half-measures, her passion seemed as exaggerated as had her former cruelty. She threw down her arms with as much style and publicity as she had once taken them up, but her friends were less impressed with her surrender than they had been with her more habitual ferocity. There was no dearth of women in love, they said, but women who were fierce and independent and proud of it were painfully few and far between. They felt she'd abandoned a brilliant rôle for a more commonplace one, and they held it against her, even if it did give them a certain satisfaction. In any case, if cruelty were allowed to be noisy and destructive, passion was supposed to be discreet, and by publicizing hers, Béatrice made it less credible. (Everyone expects primitives like Béatrice to fall in love secretly, against their better natures, even against their will. They expect them to cover up their feelings like a skin disease. They may be willing to find out afterwards that the Béatrices of this world are in fact capable of love, but only afterwards, when it's too late, when the affair is already coming to an end. At that point, they can say: 'So she really *did* care about her little Édouard. She really *was* much more attached to him than she'd admit. She really did get led down the garden path this time, didn't she?' And they can joke about it, or be indulgent, while the victim either stays well hidden or laughs at herself or weeps in dark corners.)

Béatrice, however, had never played according to the rules. And so, when Édouard disappeared for ten minutes and she panicked, turned pale, searched the room for him or interrogated the head waiters, there were a great many people, nice people even, who found her behaviour artificial and indecent; or at least out of place. But this time Béatrice wasn't acting. She really did imagine Édouard run over by a bus, his long familiar body torn apart, his clear brown eyes clouded over, his immense love for her annihilated. Then she began to tremble in earnest and when he reappeared, she cried: 'But where were you? I was so frightened!' in such a shaky voice that he flinched, astonished that the purchase of a pack of cigarettes could suddenly take on such importance. And it was at moments like these that he felt it impossible to believe in this love. He simply couldn't imagine that Béatrice had suddenly become such a victim of her own primitive and illogical feelings, she could be so totally helpless before them. It was useless to ask her to try to feign indifference; it would be like asking a man dying of thirst to stand next to a stream and wait until someone brought him a glass. Indeed, it was just this sudden absence of affection that made her appear so affected. When she left the dance floor, for instance, made a beeline for Édouard seated at the table, and kissed him passionately on the forehead, she didn't see him close his eyes and freeze, torn between a physical desire as strong as ever and a pure and simple uneasiness. On the contrary, Béatrice thought that all these impulses of hers must be delighting and fulfilling him. How many times had he begged for just such gestures from her? How many times had he pleaded for just this kind of hug or look? Now she was thrilled to be able to offer them instinctively; in fact, nothing in the world could have held her back. For she found the same starving young man at her side every night, the same hungry wolf, the one who, when she said 'I love you', would make her repeat it a thousand times. 'Say it again,' he would beg. 'Say you love me. Swear to it. Say it again.' How many dawns had she watched this way, how many dawns beige with happiness, with weariness, with fatality?

Édouard also thought about fatality when he remembered her confession of two weeks before. In spite of certain insinuaations, he hadn't imagined for a second that Béatrice loved him for his budding fame and glory. No, he held her in great esteem and, objectively, had as much confidence in her as suspicion in himself. He was still convinced he was living on top of a volcano and that this same volcano would one day expel him with great loss of life and property. Now, however, after all her loving words, such an explosion would seem contrived; it would seem banal and treacherous because it wouldn't happen the way he'd always expected – brilliantly and of its own accord. For, in finally deciding to place her bet, Béatrice had broken all the rules; and in laying down her cards, she'd cheated. It wasn't because she was almost certainly lying to him that he was angry with her, but because she was perhaps telling him the truth. *I can't stand truth any more than I can happiness*, he said to himself, a thought that not only doubled his self-contempt but made him twice as suspicious of his regrets. What had happened to his beautiful tormentor? Where had she gone? And where had this woman in love come from? When she leaned over him, as attentive now to his pleasure as to hers, Édouard felt overwhelmed by a strange nostalgia. Despite the fact that he was invariably transported by her unfailing dexterity, he was invaded by a longing for another woman, the same woman really, but one who still possessed an egocentricity as imperious as it was shameful. For Béatrice could be as irresistible in her demands as in her submissions, and she knew it. But she didn't quite know how true this was for Édouard. She didn't quite know how much he loved it when she summoned him to the bedroom at all hours like a queen and, without giving him time to take off his clothes, without even touching him, barked precise and vulgar orders, followed by terrible insults. Or when she forgot all about him, as if he were some kind of object or accident, and threw her head back, away from him, smothering her cries in the pillow. Those were the times she merged with both Édouard's myth and his memory. It was to the ferocious priestess that he had pledged himself. It was she who had initiated him into this burning and sacrilegious cult from their very first night, and who had made of him – the hitherto mediocre practitioner – an ecstatic and fanatical convert.

21

Jolyet was dying, and Béatrice waited every day for him to decide, but during the past week his mind had seemed to wander
more and more, as if he'd totally forgotten his own death. His
doctor, who was also a friend and accomplice, spoke of remis-
sion with a sort of horrified astonishment, and Béatrice
trembled with fear lest Jolyet too tremble at the last minute,
lest she should arrive one day and, instead of finding him on
his back, eyes riveted to the ceiling and a scattering of empty
syringes on the carpet, hear the butler announce in his toneless
voice that Monsieur had left for the hospital. Once there, she
knew his death would be taken away from him. They would let
him suffer a little too long and she wouldn't be able to do anything for him. And neither would he. The thought terrified her,
but who in fact was she really frightened for? Was this really
the same seductive Jolyet, the man who had walked all over the
city and run after all its women, the man so clearly cut out for
jets and capital cities and chance encounters? Was this the man
who was as comfortable backstage as in his box, as at ease with
success as with defeat, the man of culture and erudition whose
insolence hid no meanness, the ladies' man who laughed at love,
the great hunter always in flight? Was this the same man, this
mummy with the staring blue eyes who seemed unable to flee
any more, to take flight, to finish with life altogether? What did
she want from this ruin saturated with morphine who could no
more find the time to die than he had been able to find time to
love? Once he'd accidentally broken a phial in front of her,
then a second, and Béatrice had broken out in a cold sweat before he'd finally managed to fill the syringe. Yes, she was afraid
for him. What if the fatal day arrived and he was no longer able
to execute the three pathetic and ritual gestures required to give
himself the injection? But he'd smiled at her suddenly that

same afternoon with his old familiar smile and, leaning forward, had opened the second drawer of the bedside table. There, already filled and waiting, lay a long syringe. Béatrice had stared at it admiringly, as she would have stared at a gun or a dagger. Only weapons were beautiful, whereas this ... this colourless liquid in its banal glass tube was going to wipe out Jolyet's mind, his soul, his gaze. Their eyes met and they stared at each other with the same respect and bewilderment.

'Odd, wouldn't you say?' he'd remarked, shutting the drawer.

And suddenly he was himself again, his old familiar self. The timing had been perfect; it was the moment just after the morphine had hunted down and destroyed the pain and was taking a moment's rest before frantically setting off again after another victim – Jolyet's lucidity. There had always been this sort of intermission between the suffering or deprivation, and the inevitable deterioration, but these intermissions were becoming more and more rare with every passing day.

'Don't worry,' Jolyet said clearly. 'I'm watching her very closely.'

He always referred to his pain as 'her' now, and he tended to treat her very cavalierly, talking about her as if she were a mistress who was more burdensome or feeble-minded than the others.

'I had some very pleasant dreams again last night,' he went on. 'But I no longer know where to put the needle in. My thighs have become absolute sieves. So, you see, the war will come to an end not for lack of soldiers, but for lack of a battlefield. It doesn't bore you too much, does it? Coming here every afternoon?'

'No,' replied Béatrice. 'No, really, I like it. It's part of my routine, so I'm going to miss you even more.'

'That's the one advantage left to me,' he said. 'The only one, of course. I mean I won't miss you, you see. I won't miss anything, I imagine. Do you believe in a life after death?'

'Me?' she asked. And she hesitated. She'd always considered herself an atheist, but every once in a while, when life seemed particularly unfair, she'd find herself invoking the name of a God whom she tended to see sitting up there with a long white beard, sometimes like a judge who'd decided to deliver a verdict in her favour, sometimes like a hopelessly senile old man. But from there to actually believing . . .

'No,' she said finally. 'But I've often wondered why not, in fact.'

'Precisely. But then one might just as well wonder why. Although buying a one-way ticket does seem rather the height of stinginess.'

'Which isn't like you at all,' Béatrice had laughed, and they'd looked at each other with sincere affection.

'What's so strange,' Jolyet went on, 'is how difficult it is to come to a decision when you know it's the last one you'll make. When you're healthy, you don't stop a minute to think about conceiving a child or killing someone in a war. But then, suddenly, even when you've had it, you can't make up your mind to finally abandon such a useless pack of bones.'

He pointed to himself with an ironical finger and Béatrice was reassured. She'd been worried for a moment but now she knew he'd come out of it all right. *Now I feel happier*, she said to herself. *But why? He's going to die. I must be mad!* And she felt a sudden urge to laugh.

'Would you bring some mimosa tomorrow?' he'd asked. 'If you can find it, that is. I'd like some mimosa; in fact, I'd like a lot of things now, the way pregnant women do, I expect. Do you suppose people really do give birth to their own death?'

But his eyes were already closing. Béatrice got up and went to the door, then turned around. Jolyet had opened his eyes again and was looking at her strangely. Then he raised his fist above his head in a gesture of militant camaraderie, which was not at all his style. Béatrice came back.

'No,' she said. 'Not between us.'

And she leaned down, placed her cool lips against his warm mouth, and thought *Adieu*.

She felt no surprise the following day when she arrived at her usual time to find him already unconscious. She laid the mimosa on his pillow, sat down in her armchair, and waited for him to die. She waited an hour, her mind a blank, and didn't move when he suddenly turned his head towards the window and opened his eyes. Night had already fallen. And when the butler came in a little later to turn on the lights, when she saw him suddenly come to a stop between her and the bed – thus screening an already dead Jolyet – she got up and left the room without a backward glance.

It was difficult finding a taxi and the fact that it was raining annoyed her. An hour later, having changed her clothes, chatted with Cathy and joked with Édouard and Nicolas in the blue room while they sat in front of the fire deciding which restaurant to go to, she suddenly remembered Jolyet's death. When she told them, both men jumped up, as if she'd said something indecent.

'Jolyet dead? André?' cried Nicolas. 'André Jolyet? And you were there?'

'Yes. I watched him die. We'd agreed on it.'

The two men stared at her in silence.

'But why didn't you say something earlier?' Nicolas finally asked in a low voice. 'It's been at least an hour.'

'I'd forgotten,' Béatrice replied, breaking into laughter at the sight of their astonished faces. 'It's true. I swear, I just forgot.'

'Things like that can happen,' Nicolas said quickly. 'There are things that happen; you see, you think, and then you . . .'

He waved his hand vaguely and the movement seemed to jolt Édouard awake. He went over to Béatrice and put his hand on her shoulder.

'Are you grieving?' he asked.

And suddenly she found herself crying hot and bitter tears, tears of rage, of disappointment, of fear, tears filled with tenderness and regret. She remembered the exact blue of Jolyet's eyes, what his voice had sounded like the day before, the scent of the mimosa blossoms in that empty room, empty once and for all of the warm and irreplaceable life of a man named Jolyet for whom there was nothing she could do now but forget.

22

The funeral was magnificent; all the *Tout-Paris* had shown up and the weather was gorgeous. Jolyet had ordered a full-dress funeral service before he died, knowing how everyone in that world loved a good public cry, or loved to pretend one, or both, and not wanting to deny his entourage this last treat.

Later that afternoon, Béatrice and Édouard sat in front of the fire, talking quietly. Édouard was fascinated by the story of Jolyet's agony, lingering death and suicide. Or rather he was fascinated by the flatness of Béatrice's story, by its lack of elaboration and relief. Listening to her, it seemed the most natural thing in the world for someone to choose the hour of his death, and then let himself slip into it in the company of a resigned and discreet witness. And this seemed both logical and reasonable to Béatrice.

'So why doesn't it happen more often?' demanded Édouard. 'Why do we have to have all the tears and lies and cries and surprises?'

'Because morphine's expensive,' Béatrice replied in her practical housewife's voice. 'And because most people don't have discreet friends. Jolyet knew I wouldn't say anything about it.'

And she hadn't, not even to Édouard. She'd hidden her afternoon visits from him instinctively, as instinctively as a hounded Jolyet had gone to her and her alone for refuge and consolation. He knew she was animal enough to be able to keep him company while he waited for death. (Only human beings, and a few species of animal, flee their dying; most animals gather around and keep their companions warm until the end. Animals and Béatrice.) Édouard marvelled at the surprising combination of tenderness and cruelty that had brought this female to the bedside of an old abandoned male every afternoon. He marvelled that two people who had lived their lives in the midst of so much artifice and disguise, who were themselves archetypes of the so-called hypocrisy and pretence of the entertainment world, and who had decided to join forces one fine day out of mutual self-interest, should automatically seek each other out again on a day that was far less fine.

'But you knew?' said Édouard. 'You knew the day before that he'd decided?'

'Yes. I think so.'

She reached out towards the fire, stretched and then laughed.

'I even kissed him before I left. He must have been furious. He always hated people kissing him when he was ill or sleeping. He said that was how women raped men. Would you kiss me if I were sleeping? Or ill?'

'No,' Édouard admitted. 'No, I probably wouldn't. I'd want to, but I wouldn't.'

'I thought not. I suppose it's just we women who do that. We kiss you in spite of yourselves, with the excuse that we're consoling you. It's funny, though. I don't like it either. I don't like kissing men who're asleep or ill in bed. I feel I'm robbing them of something. Or maybe I'm just afraid of catching their germs.'

Now she was laughing openly, shaking the hair back out of her eyes.

'So why did you kiss Jolyet?' Édouard asked, even more disconcerted.

She turned and looked him up and down, then shrugged her shoulders as if to say he wouldn't understand. But she answered anyway.

'I did it to annoy him. And to make him feel good. Because he knew I was doing it just to annoy him, and because it made him feel good that I still wanted to annoy him. Don't you see? He was a man right to the end, you know,' she added admiringly. 'And men love to be annoyed.'

Then she leaned over and kissed Édouard on the neck, nibbling at him a little, as if to remind him that he was a man as well and that she was delighted to annoy him too. He put his arms around her. *What a bizarre funeral oration*, he thought, pulling her down to him in front of the fire. *But perhaps it's the only kind Jolyet could wish for. To say nothing of myself.*

A little while later, the doorbell snapped them out of their torpor, and Tony d'Albret entered the living-room dressed in beige and black, her eyes improbably hidden behind a pair of sunglasses. Tony was always perfect, both during and after funerals. She may have been the agent for only one tenth of the living celebrities in Paris, but she none the less felt responsible for all the dead ones as well. With a long face, she sat down in the armchair, cast a disapproving look at Béatrice who was casually arranging her hair and asked, in a strained voice, for a glass of port.

'I was sure you'd show up,' said Béatrice gaily. 'I could have sworn to it.'

'I know you loved him too,' Tony began, 'And perhaps my presence . . .'

'Ah, no!' Béatrice cried, her gaiety suddenly giving way to anger. 'Not that! But where were you before you came here? Where've you been playing the grieving mourner?'

'For heaven's sake, Béatrice,' said Édouard, sincerely shocked. 'What's the matter with you?'

'The matter with me is that Jolyet could never stand Tony, and the feeling was mutual. So I suggest we all have a drink and talk about something else. If you're counting on me to give you all the juicy details of his death, my dear Tony, you're mistaken.'

Once she'd got over the initial shock, an annoyed and indignant Tony straightened up in her chair, took off her sunglasses – revealing a pair of perfectly undamaged eyes – and went back to her customary stentorian voice.

'You're too much!' she exclaimed. 'It's true I couldn't stand Jolyet. He was a terrible snob. But is that any way to welcome someone who's come to try to be of some comfort to you?'

'There you are,' Béatrice laughed. 'The real Tony's resurfaced! But don't be fooled, Édouard. She may have despised him, but believe me, her grief is genuine. Every time somebody famous gets buried, Tony sees a possible percentage going to the grave with him. In fact, she's the only posthumous agent I know!'

Béatrice got up and started for the door, apparently caught between anger and hilarity, then shrugged and left the room. Édouard and Tony stared at each other.

'You must excuse her,' Tony said quickly, as if Édouard were the one who'd been mistreated. (He couldn't help smiling, for one of Tony's shrewdest reflexes when she'd been a little too accurately insulted was to generalize the insult and plead for a sort of global comprehension and sympathy for her aggressor. In their discomfort, the witnesses usually wound up according both.) 'She's terribly upset, of course. She and Jolyet were so fond of each other and she does owe him a lot. He's the one who really broke her in, you know. If you'll forgive the expression. But what an idiot I am!' she exclaimed suddenly. 'I keep forgetting. You were around then, weren't you? During the Jolyet period, I mean.'

This nasty and unnecessary reminder of his past amused Édouard. A year ago, he would have been thoroughly disgusted, but little by little he'd become used to the idiosyncrasies of Béatrice's friends, and even Tony didn't frighten him any more. That was one of the good things that had come out of Béatrice's declaration. When she'd said she loved him, he'd suddenly acquired a certain calm and assurance *vis-à-vis* all the intermediaries. Not that this protected him from an eventual break-up, of course, but it did protect him from accidents. For, once she'd confessed to loving him, Béatrice would now have to tell him she didn't love him, should such an eventuality occur. Or so Édouard, in his naïvety, assumed. In any case, he smiled these days instead of getting upset or retreating into his shell.

'Have you given any more thought to our contract?' she demanded, exasperated by his smile. 'I know it's not exactly the moment to talk about such things, but we should at least try to change the subject. Personally,' she added, glancing towards Béatrice's bedroom, 'I am not given to morbidity.'

As far as the contract was concerned, Édouard still didn't know what to do. The famous film contract he'd refused to sign was becoming a real problem, the more so since it wasn't really a problem at all. To begin with, Béatrice didn't even want the part; in fact, she was pushing him to sign. Secondly, Lawrence Herner, the crack English director, had already put in his bid to do it, whether Édouard's play was successful or not. He'd even written about it to Édouard, who admired Herner and had been very flattered. Indeed, Herner's perceptions and enthusiasm were even more embarrassing to him than Tony's pretended fervour. He'd written the play five years ago and the characters had become like old childhood friends or like the people you meet on a journey who suddenly become 'everything' to you, and then, when you run into them accidentally at some later date, you're amazed at how detached and distant you feel towards them, and you're filled with guilt. People said to him: 'Ah, that Jeremy of yours!' Or 'Oh, that Penelope!' And he felt as if they were congratulating him on some forgotten cousin, while he was already launched on a frail, perilous, and brand-new passion – his new play.

His current hero, Frédéric, was totally alive, the more so because he was unfinished. And, because Édouard could still not imagine him interpreted, or even interpretable, Frédéric enjoyed all the charms of the fallible, the uncertain, and therefore the desirable. Of course, the play might not be any good. Maybe it was boring or confused because he wanted it to tell the truth? Or maybe it was really just a lot of hot air? But each time he thought about it, he felt all the old fear and concern and wonderment rise up in him, and he thought again of the chaos and anger from which it had sprung. He'd begun it before finding Béatrice again, and had actually finished it despite all their ups-and-downs; in fact he couldn't imagine how it had ever managed not to take a back seat to anything during all this time. Everything he'd written over the past year had been as much wrested from him as submitted to, for the time he spent writing was so much time that had had to be subtracted from the delicate, precious, and irreplaceable time he spent as Béatrice's lover. He really hadn't had the chance to write just for the sake of writing, or to play with words and ideas. He hadn't even had the chance to hesitate about writing. He'd been like a circus ventriloquist with only one dummy who'd forced himself to fulfil his contract even though madly in love with a rider about to leave the show. Indeed, the dizzying happiness or despair he'd felt while writing the play had seemed like so many miracles and curses. But how could he have given a life and a destiny to that ghostly creature called Frédéric when he was really thinking only about Béatrice? And when he'd thought she'd abandoned him again, when he'd felt as if he were well and truly dead, how could he have written a dialogue that everyone claimed was so sharp and gay and brilliant? How could he have written with such naturalness, with such a tacit acceptance of the divorce between his terrified heart and his agile brain? The night Béatrice had been sweet and tender towards him for the first time, the night he'd felt she'd laid down her arms and almost become attached to him, the night they'd stood in front of the french windows opened wide on to the summer garden, how could he – a mere two hours later – have constructed his hero's desperately cold and solitary monologue, that as far as Édouard was concerned was the finest moment in the play?

All these questions filled him with an astonishment close to fear, but also with a kind of childish pride. He'd always known that while the heart was made for blindness, the mind was destined to remember. Or even to forget – it made no difference. Both were irrational, irresponsible, and spongy elements that retained only certain particular impressions, and those at random. While intelligence, on the other hand, was sharp and trenchant, made for slicing and sorting, like a sword. Yet he couldn't say he hadn't devoted every ounce of his intelligence to their affair. Not for a moment had he stopped thrusting and parrying, imagining and hoping, fighting to feed and satisfy his emotional hunger. In fact, true happiness came in just those moments when his intelligence merged with his heart and his sensuality in the same surge of feeling. Or to put it another way, when he'd felt fulfilled, he'd always known why.

But now he didn't need the help of his intelligence any more because Béatrice loved him, a fact that had ironically transformed his great, unhappy passion into a banal affair. The apparent logic of it all made him suspicious. A successful playwright and a film star – what could possibly be more trite? Perhaps he would have preferred to remain unknown, insignificant, colourless? Yet he couldn't say he'd ever really wished for the opposite. All he knew was that either out of the goodness of his heart or in accordance with the demands of his erotic imagination, he wanted Béatrice to remain proud and triumphant. He didn't believe in equality in love; he'd never believed in it and never would. Consequently, he could never believe in those ghastly and savoury reversals where the worshipper suddenly begins to yawn and the idol grow desperate. Those sorts of relay races where lover and beloved exchanged rôles seemed to him to belong to the stage and not to life. He had thrown himself at Béatrice with too much passion and sincerity not to find an exchange of rôles not only improbable, but commonplace and unworthy. Their story had been written and the parts assigned as rigorously as in a Racine tragedy. Who could imagine Hermione suddenly making love to Orestes? So where were he and Béatrice heading? And to what should he apply his cleverness, his presentiments, his instincts until they got there? There seemed to be no other choice except to be happy.

But who was it who'd taught him how to be happy? Who'd given him the opportunity? The only time in his life he remembered being happy was because of Béatrice. That was five years ago, but then she'd snatched that happiness back from him immediately, as if she'd accidentally given too luxurious a toy to a poor child. Now that the toy had been handed back to him, however, what did people expect him to do with it? He hadn't had the time to learn how it worked, but whose fault was that? They should either have given him the toy for keeps five years ago or they shouldn't have given it back to him today. And as far as this particular toy was concerned, he imagined he'd always feel like a poor child who was being punished. Yet it had been this same poor child who'd written that first awkward and touching play everyone was now raving about and wanting to make films of, and who was being showered with dollars as if to thank him for being so nice and well-behaved. The poor child had written the second play too, which had turned out to be more mature, easier to write, and more effective. And it was the same poor child who'd gone on secretly doing his homework even after he'd been given these final spoils of war, who'd gone on secretly writing a play with a hero called

Frédéric who looked enough like him to be his twin brother. And it was the same poor child who'd spent a year in fear and trembling, suffering and despising himself with as much passion as he'd felt when he'd found himself back in Béatrice's arms. So was everyone now seriously waiting for him to pretend that he'd always been rich and would always be sure of remaining so? No, he couldn't do it. He didn't know how to. Neither Herner nor Tony nor Béatrice – no one in the world – could ever give him back what had been stolen from him once and for all five years before.

(Of course, Édouard didn't really say this to himself. He didn't even think it. But even though he didn't realize it now, one day he'd give it to someone to say for him. On stage. He'd show the world the poor, vanquished, and humiliated child, and when that day came, he would doubtless wonder who could possibly have put such an idea into his head.)

'Are you listening to me, Édouard?' came Tony's impatient voice.

She was watching him with real curiosity now. Her condescension had, of course, disappeared the minute the cheques had begun arriving from America, and curiosity had quickly taken its place – just when that fool Béatrice had started shouting her so-called passion from the rooftops. Tony had assumed then that Béatrice was lost to her for ever, together with all Édouard's pretty promises to her. After all, she'd seen her fair share of men who suffered a thousand torments and promised whole worlds to young (or even ageing) girls. And she'd also seen them take to their heels, or at least renege on their promises, the moment the girls began loving them back. She'd even been fearful for her percentages, for she knew perfectly well that Édouard despised her and that Béatrice was their only link. (When all was said and done, however, she didn't give a damn about Édouard's contempt. She was absolutely certain that his success, indeed his entire future, depended on her and her alone. And she was also certain he'd work this out for himself soon enough.) But there was no mistaking the fact that Édouard was still madly in love, and Tony had very ambivalent feelings about this. On the other hand, she was annoyed; being a woman herself, she would have loved to see Béatrice come up empty-handed just once. On the other hand, as an agent, she felt a certain comfort, and was pleased at how tightly her prize client could hang on to a man once she'd got hold of him. In fact, it was just one more proof of her talent that Béatrice could switch so easily into the loving wife after having played the contemptuous woman for so long.

The fact was that since she had no private life, Tony assumed no one else had either. She never imagined Béatrice in bed, except on stage, or Béatrice saying 'I love you' except in front of a microphone. On the other hand, it was undoubtedly just this lack of imagination that made her such a top agent. Otherwise, instead of turning all her handsome and talented clients into loved and applauded slot machines, she could have imagined stomping them to death.

In the meantime, however, Herner was getting impatient and Édouard had to be made to sign. It was ridiculous for him to be so faithful to a vow no one had ever asked him to make.

'I'm really very worried about Béatrice,' said Tony.

'She'll get over it,' Édouard replied in a soft voice that disturbed her ambitious projects.

'I'm not talking about Jolyet, Édouard. I'm talking about far more serious matters. I mean, more current ones . . .'

Suddenly, she was confused; she'd given herself away but an ever-polite Édouard leaped to her rescue.

'Just what do you want to talk about, Tony?'

'You might think it in terrible bad taste on a day like today, but I want to talk about taxes. As you know, I take care of all Béatrice's business. And as you also know, she's always throwing money away. But what you may not know is that I'm not going to be able to pay her taxes this year.'

This was only a half-truth. The fact remained, however, that Béatrice's generosity was as great as her taste for luxury – no common trait for an actress – and she'd never bothered to set up a little snack bar or launderette to fall back on in the event of public disgrace. Indeed, Béatrice was perfectly capable of wreaking havoc in a restaurant over a bill she thought excessive, and just as capable of writing a cheque for the first person who asked. To be fair, she believed she would die on stage in the flower of her youth, but her agent didn't share such charming premonitions. She watched the money slipping through Béatrice's fingers with as much fear as admiration. The state of her finances may not have been quite as critical as Tony claimed, but like a stroke of lightning or a bad case of acne, the tax people had definitely singled her out and, given Béatrice's two recent failures, Tony foresaw a rather complicated immediate future.

'Ah yes,' said Édouard uncomfortably, 'taxes ...'

He was hopelessly negligent when it came to money. He'd had precious little of it when he was young, and was still unused to both its perils and its charms. In fact, Béatrice had often scolded him for his carelessness and generosity, believing that a man should keep an eye on his earnings the way he would over his wife.

'Yes, taxes,' Tony repeated. 'And you? Who takes care of yours?'

'A lawyer friend of my father's. I worked for him when I first came to Paris.'

'When you become a millionaire, I'm afraid you'll have to hire more of a specialist,' Tony said pompously. 'Because making money can be very expensive. It's not really my business, Édouard dear, but I do suggest that in the meantime you sign this contract. And if you leave the rôle Béatrice doesn't want for someone else to worry about, you'll be doing her a great service.'

'But ... But of course,' Édouard stammered, blushing furiously. 'I didn't realize ...'

He was horrified to realize he'd never given the slightest thought to this kind of material question, much less to Béatrice's financial future. He'd always paid the bills for their hotels, restaurants, and trips, but he'd also been living in her flat. He must have looked like the worst kind of gigolo to the rest of the world, the kind that pretended to be completely unconscious of the more practical side of life. Mistaking the reason for this horrified expression, Tony hastened to reassure him.

'Of course you'll be reimbursed in full, my little Édouard. In fact, we can pay you back very quickly.'

'For God's sake!' Édouard exploded. 'Don't be ridiculous. It's not that at all. Béatrice can have whatever she wants, right now, everything I have ...'

Desperately embarrassed, he stammered and stuttered until he saw the small sly smile of triumph on Tony's lips. *So that's it*, he said to himself. *She's just thinking about her percentage. She really had me fooled for a minute ... But then I have acted like an imbecile.*

'You should know that I belong to Béatrice,' he went on coldly, looking her straight in the eye. 'Body and soul. I'll sign the contract tomorrow, wherever you want, and then you can tell me how much you need.'

Tony hesitated, surprised by the change in tone and rhythm. As always, whenever she found herself in a precarious position, she fell back on propriety. Fine feelings were safer and she'd discovered a long time ago that in this particular circle, it was always wiser to appear stupid than clever.

'Béatrice will be very touched,' she replied. 'Really.'

'No,' said Édouard. 'You're not to say a word about it to her. As far as I know, you're not in the habit of discussing this sort of thing with her, so why bother to do so now? It wouldn't be for my sake, would it?'

They glared at each other, and a mutual distrust – a hatred – seemed to rise up between them and become almost palpable. At last, after months of reticence and politeness, the cards were on the table. Tony felt her pulse beat faster; she felt anger and contempt lodge themselves firmly inside her. Not to mention a new and different scorn – for the contempt she inspired in Édouard.

'What a true and charming white knight you are, my dear Édouard,' she said sarcastically.

'Exactly. A white knight I am and intend to remain.'

He smiled suddenly, like a child who'd just played a clever trick on someone. For a second, Tony d'Albret understood that Béatrice might really be in love with him; he seemed at once so resourceful and so weak, so implacable and so alone. He was like some sort of strange and fearless cock bird.

'And if I am going to continue to be the white knight, my dear Tony, it's thanks to the royal contracts you're going to get for me. You must allow me to thank you in advance.'

He broke into laughter and got to his feet, ever courteous,

but impatient now, his posture seeming to suggest that the meeting was over, the business done, and that she'd earned not only her money but the right to get out, and he the right to make her exit an imperious duty. As she headed for the door, it occurred to her that she was no longer welcome in the blue room – a room she'd helped furnish with her ruses, her phone calls, her devotion, her sweat and blood. And thus she left as she ought to have entered, her eyes filled with tears.

23

Béatrice looked out of the window at the garden, now black with winter, then went over to her dressing-table and picked up the ring. She tossed it into the air a few times, then held it up again to the light. Thirty carats at least – her knowledge of such matters was faultless – and definitely a genuine blue-white. Édouard had given it to her, looking every bit a King of the Magi but, for the first time in her life, Béatrice had had to fake her delight as she opened the case. Until now, she'd always loved jewels; they were something due to her, a sort of tax she levied on those of her lovers who'd been rich. And now, because of this American contract, Édouard had suddenly become a spend-thrift. He was following in the footsteps of his wealthy pre-decessors. He'd never acted like one of 'the others' before, and she was both saddened and disturbed. He'd given her something she could keep after he'd gone – if there was an afterwards – something only she could enjoy. It was the typical man's gift to a woman, extravagant and sumptuous, and she wondered why she would have preferred a weekend in the pretty little Paris suburb of Saint-Germain-en-Laye. Or an opera record. Or even a sweater. No matter what, as long as she could share it with him. For a woman with a past like hers, jewels were like footprints. They were what was left, afterwards, on all those deserted beaches from which even time itself had fled. The trouble was that she just couldn't imagine life without Édouard any more.

Maybe it's just because it's my worst time of day, she thought, putting the ring back on the table. It was the end of the afternoon, the time she'd usually spent at Jolyet's bedside. For over two months, in the midst of her various useful or use-less appointments, she'd always set aside these couple of hours, and she still did so, automatically. Édouard had gone to see some screen tests with Lawrence Herner, Tony seemed to have abandoned them, Nicolas was away on tour, Cathy sewing in the kitchen. She felt very much alone. That evening, she would perform her unsuccessful play to a half-empty theatre, then go to dinner with Édouard and Herner, then come home. Before going to bed, she would lift the hand with the ring and gaze at it – because of course she'd have worn it all evening – and she'd exclaim: 'Really, Édouard, what madness!' in an artificial voice. And then she'd turn to him and see the face of sincerity and love gazing back at her. How was it possible that just now, just when she missed Édouard even while she was on stage and when all she wanted was to tell him the truth, she had to say instead: 'Really, Édouard, what madness!', a line she'd delivered at least twenty times before and in the same voice to men she hadn't loved. Something was terribly and cruelly wrong, but she didn't know who to blame. Not Édouard, of course. He loved her and had given her the ring just to please her. Nor was it her fault if she'd had rich lovers before. It was precisely because she had had so many lovers before him, both rich and not so rich, that Édouard had fallen in love with her. He could never have loved a woman without a past. But perhaps he couldn't love one with a future either? He'd given her the ring with such eagerness, and with such happiness at the thought of hers, that perhaps it was some kind of prelude to his departure?

She returned to the window, leaned her forehead against the cold glass, and shook her head. Was she going mad? Since when was the fact of a man ruining or not ruining himself for her any proof of his not loving her? Poor Édouard. How could he know that all these beautiful stones that had once been so precious to her had now become so many pebbles? How could he know that she'd changed, and that certain words which had always made her laugh, words like 'constancy', 'fidelity', and 'trust' now seemed as sharp and searing as words like 'frenzy' and 'ambition'? How could he know that she was playing the adagio of a strange and foreign rhapsody in a major key, instead of confining herself, as she always had, to the counter-melody and paying no attention whatsoever to the main theme? In short, she couldn't expect him to accept the fact that she loved him so quickly, even though that was what he'd always wanted.

When she thought about it, Édouard's reaction to her

confession had been very odd indeed. She'd thought he would be delirious with joy, that he'd get drunk, that he'd roll about on the floor crying 'Halleluja!' or 'At last!', and offer up thanks to God, to life, to her. But instead of being transfigured, he'd been paralysed with astonishment; he'd even looked upset, disturbed somehow. She'd heard him breathing heavily and unevenly in the darkness next to her for a long time, and his pauses had sounded remarkably like sighs. Of course, she knew he loved only her: he'd spent night after night repeating it, proving it. But when she'd declared her love in the same tone of voice he always used, and with the same passionate words, he seemed almost not to hear her. Their exchanges sounded nothing like the usual dialogue between happy and satisfied lovers; it was more like the monologue of a lover betrayed. And when this happened, the other Béatrice would wake up and take over, silencing the awkward lover with her over-simplified vocabulary. The other Béatrice would give her back the skilful gestures, the silences, and the cries that now seemed so foreign to her. And when *that* woman resurfaced, Édouard was clearly reassured; he could abandon himself to that woman, exhaust himself. For even if Béatrice had been unfaithful to him, her body had always been faithful. It was only natural that Édouard, alternately mistreated and transported by her fluctuating moods, should seek refuge in that other woman, the familiar one. After all these years, she could hardly reproach him for his instincts.

She wandered back to the bed and lay down exhausted, her eyes closed. Introspection was not exactly a habit of hers; after all, her feelings had never been anything but ephemeral, and had always vanished as quickly as they had appeared. She was tired of all this unexpected mental activity. She reached out and turned on the lamp. The light reassured her immediately and she sat up on the edge of the bed.

'It would really be too much,' she said aloud with sudden gaiety, although her voice was harsh with what seemed to be a completely independent irony (an irony she'd always had, of course, but that she'd never allowed herself to hear, doubtless fearing it would keep her from getting to the top of the ladder);

'it would really be too much if the one time I love someone, it doesn't make him happy!'

The words were no sooner out than Édouard appeared at the door, rushed over to her and, hugging her tightly, started chattering about the mechanical models he'd watched filing past him on the screen. He insisted that none of them could hold a candle to her and that he'd spent the entire afternoon dreaming of her. He made her laugh. He told her stories of the serious playwright tackling the cinema, but there was so much self-mockery in his voice that she wound up finding it very disconcerting. To hear him, you'd think that every complication and disaster was invariably a result of his stupidity or naïvety or lack of authority. But she was so used to hearing the men in her harem rambling on about their successes, their intelligence, and their unfailing irony that she found Édouard's masochism charming. So why had she been so depressed all afternoon? What did she have to complain about? Édouard hugged her, begged her to stay where she was and eat dinner alone with him in the bedroom. He told her he loved her and urged her to make love with her usual passionate and insatiable desire.

And then, much later, stretched out next to each other, they exchanged sweet and silky words, the smooth flat dialogue of satisfied lovers unconsciously thanking each other for having achieved this happy, albeit temporary, physical respite. Édouard had put a record on and now he hummed with Frank Sinatra, his head buried in Béatrice's hair.

'And your old opera?' she asked. 'It's been a long time since we've heard it.'

The old opera tune was their song. It was the song through which they'd wordlessly alerted each other to their desire, the song to which they'd made love all spring and summer, the song that had led them to the heights of pleasure, that had so long been both a fire alarm and a reward.

'I'll buy another one if you like,' Édouard replied, half-asleep. 'The record's all scratched.'

'It doesn't matter. I think we were getting tired of it anyway. Don't you think so?'

'Yes,' he replied vaguely, sinking deeper and deeper into her warmth and her scent. 'Yes, you're right. We've heard it too many times.'

And then he fell asleep, perfectly content, his face buried in her neck. He couldn't know that she had opened her eyes again suddenly, and that the question she'd asked had been a real one.

24

Édouard had gone through passport control and stepped on to the escalator. Béatrice had watched him disappear little by little down the escalator's plexiglass corridor, a setting far more disturbing than romantic. He'd turned around, pale, waved his hand, and in order to see her longer, had even bent his knees and crouched down, leaning towards her against the flow. In that line of travellers who seemed so blasé and so used to airports, he looked like a child who'd been torn from its mother. It was obvious he was desperate to run back down the sinister escalator, past the astonished customs officials, and fall into her arms, safe from America, the trip, the hotels, safe from the separation. Béatrice had put on a good face, ironic and amused, but as she watched him leave she felt her eyes fill with tears and her throat tighten. Then Édouard's shoes had disappeared altogether and Tony d'Albret began to laugh.

'It's too much, really! A man of his age, going off like that! When you think he's never been to New York before ... Do you think he intends to make the whole journey backwards?'

Béatrice didn't answer. They were in the car heading back to Paris, to the empty flat and the blue bedroom and a bed that would be too big because it had been shared for so long. It was one o'clock in the afternoon and pouring with rain, and she knew that, although he'd be staggering from boredom and exhaustion and loneliness, Édouard would ring her at about nine o'clock from some skyscraper or other. In the meantime, however, he'd be strapped in his seat in a giant plane, surrounded by strangers, and definitely not trembling with apprehension or excitement at the idea of the flash-bulbs, the Sardis, and the throngs of mythomaniacs waiting for him. On the contrary, if he were trembling at all, it would be from regret; he would be thinking of the blue bedroom, the french windows, the winter garden. In fact, she was sure he was profoundly unhappy.

It had taken the combined efforts of both Tony and Nicolas to convince him to go. They'd told him it was out of the question that the play should open without him or that he should be so rude as to refuse to attend the première to congratulate or console the actors. All three had delivered the same speech, although for different reasons: Béatrice, just to see if he'd go, Tony because it was her job, and Nicolas because, if he'd been Édouard, he would long since have departed for the States. 'It'll be good for you,' they'd said. 'It'll get you out of your rut.' And even if not one of them believed what they were saying, it didn't show.

Once the crisis of parting was over, however, Béatrice began to feel better; happily she watched the Parisian landscape sliding by outside the car window and she was content to imagine her lover flying towards an almost certain success. Of course he'd be bored without her and would come back even more in love than before. But she'd be able to spend a few days thinking about her love, remembering it, waiting for it to return. The pleasure of dreaming about someone who was dreaming of her at the same time was a new one for her. The whole idea put her in an excellent mood and when Tony suggested that they have lunch with Nicolas and some friends, Béatrice suddenly felt young, free, and very sociable.

They arrived at the restaurant late and she was greeted by a crowd of old friends and ex-lovers, all celebrating her return. When a delighted Nicolas threw his arms around her, she realized to her surprise that she'd seen absolutely no one for the past six months. *Of course none of them can hold a candle to Édouard*, she said to herself; but unlike Édouard they were *there*, they were merry, and there were certain stares that reminded her deliciously that she was, in fact, a woman. Not that Édouard had ever let her forget it, but in his eyes she was clearly a woman loved, and not a woman to fall in love with. Now, however, secure in her knowledge that she was desired by a lover who was moving farther away from her every second, she felt even more desirable to all these vaguely familiar men who were suddenly so close. She smiled, she laughed, she flirted, the tension mounted. Her voice rang out clearly and she became once again the whimsical, insolent, and beautiful Béatrice Valmont. Nicolas watched her euphoria and despite his affection for Édouard, was thoroughly delighted. For, as her exiled lover slowly dropped out of sight, so did ten, even twenty, years of her life – and of Nicolas's. Both found themselves young and whole again, and something almost tangible, albeit unconscious, passed between them. Or at least it must have because Tony d'Albret couldn't resist crying: 'Ah, there they are again, the two accomplices! What a handsome couple you make, you two!'

Béatrice and Nicolas looked at each other, then into the mirror, and smiled with satisfaction. It was true. With his blond hair, blue eyes, and carefree look, Nicolas went very well indeed with Béatrice's more distant and leonine darkness. They nodded into the mirror at each other's reflection in a sign of mutual admiration, and congratulated themselves on being as merry and as good friends as they had been fifteen years before.

Tony left for one of her eternal appointments straight after coffee, and they drank a few brandies to her health, although continuing to talk about her with their usual mixture of sarcasm and affection. When they left the restaurant, it was five o'clock and already dark. They tried a couple of nearby cinemas but the publicity stills outside discouraged them, as did the write-ups. Both were reluctant to break the spell of closeness and good cheer, not to mention availability, that hovered between them.

'Let's go to your place,' Nicolas said finally. 'We can have some tea and I'll tell you about my tour.'

The flat was empty. Béatrice had taken advantage of Édouard's absence by giving Cathy a few days off. And so she was relieved that Nicolas was accompanying her into the dark rooms, helping her turn on the lights, light the fire, take the ice cubes out. She went into the bedroom, took off her wet coat, put on a warm dry sweater, a pair of slacks, and some flat shoes, then returned to Nicolas who'd settled himself in front of the fire and was purring like a big cat. It was one of his charms, this ease he had in entering strange or forgotten houses and immediately making himself at home in the best spot with a simplicity equal only to his gratitude. In fact, Nicolas was very comfortable in other people's houses; he felt not only content but useful, and was always happy to be there and never reluctant to show it. He looked at Béatrice, her face washed and freshened by the rain, her eyes sparkling from the warm brandies, and he told himself that he'd been a fool. He would happily have lived the life of the contented pasha with the dangerous woman next to him, and he was sure that in the long run they would have understood each other quite well. It was too bad he hadn't realized that ten years earlier.

'So how was the tour?' Béatrice asked. 'Or should I say, who seduced you? The little Beaufour?'

'No. I mean ... Well, not much ... It seems I was far more attractive to the gorgeous Hermione.'

'For God's sake! How old is she now?'

'There was no way of knowing until I climbed into her bed,' Nicolas laughed. 'And afterwards ... Well, how do you expect me to know? It doesn't matter though. She's exquisite.'

'I'm sure she is,' replied Béatrice, shivering suddenly. 'It was so cold outside. Poor Édouard. He's going to freeze in New York. Do you think it's very cold there?'

'Definitely not,' Nicolas replied, rather annoyed but not knowing quite why. 'You *did* put a scarf in his suitcase, didn't you? And his nose drops?'

'Bastard!' laughed Béatrice. 'Why don't we go dancing tonight? I feel like dancing. It's been so long.'

She got to her feet and stretched.

'Don't you feel like dancing?'

Nicolas turned away from the fire and looked at her. The firelight had given her face a devilish expression. And the lady felt like dancing!

'You have a record player, don't you?' he asked, a little thickly.

With a vague feeling of fatality, he unwound himself, stood up, walked past her and placed a record on the machine. It was a slow number, just right for dancing. 'Very nice, that,' he murmured before turning around and offering her a bow that suggested challenge as much as a kind of ceremonial respect. She smiled, slipped into his arms, then suddenly stopped smiling. They missed a few beats, as if surprised to find themselves back in each other's arms then began to dance. The record player had an automatic arm and the same song played over and over again. They danced once, twice, wordlessly, not thinking about anything specific, not even remembering just what they meant to each other apart from the fact that he was a man who desired this particular woman and she was a woman greatly troubled by her desire for this particular man. *How strange*, Béatrice thought, *How strange that it should be Nicolas*, but feeling at the same time such happiness, such a wish to live, such delight in being alive.

It never occurred to her that she might be repudiating Édouard, or deceiving him, or forgetting him. Instead, she felt in a confused way that she owed her good fortune – or rather the happy appetite of her body for the pleasure this man was about to give her – to the faithfulness and completeness of Édouard's love. If he hadn't loved her so completely, or if she'd been less sure of his love, she would have been sad or uneasy, and then all she could have asked of Nicolas was a strong shoulder to cry on and some words of sympathy to calm her down. She would have been reduced to herb tea and lukewarm platonic infusions. Whereas now the strong hot drink of desire was coursing through her body, bending it to its yoke, making the blood pound in her wrists, her legs, at the very centre of her being. The pulse throbbed in her lips as Nicolas kissed her, and an hour later, the same record found them on the carpet in front of a cold fire.

At the very moment Nicolas was reaching out wearily to turn off the record player, Édouard's plane was landing at Kennedy Airport in the midst of a terrific wind. Dazed, he let himself be led along with the rest through the ritual formalities of customs and passport control, then the yellow taxi, the rain glancing off the road, a bridge, and finally the phantom city itself looking so unreal in the grey light. Then there was the hotel with its welcoming voices, the suitcases, the hordes of people, even some messages. Until finally, stunned and exhausted, the survivor was allowed to pick up his phone and ring Paris.

He heard Béatrice's low tender voice straight away, as if from the other end of the world, and he felt reborn. Despite the nightmare of the journey, he was suddenly reassured; he thought he might now be able to really see the city at his feet, even to find it astonishing and beautiful. Thanks to her warm voice, New York was being offered to him. Yes, she already missed him, and yes she loved him, and yes she was waiting for him. And so he fell asleep, calm and carefree. And he had every reason to be in fact, for Béatrice was not lying to him.

She was in bed, prostrate with weariness and euphoria, delighted to be alone at last. And as she lay smoking a cigarette in the darkness, she was thinking lovingly of her Édouard.

25

The Americans were delighted with Édouard, while he was completely bowled over by New York. Indeed, he showed his dazzlement so willingly that journalists as well as theatre people were enchanted. He was a sort of miracle, this thirty-six-year-old man who admitted in all innocence that he'd never been to America before! Or anywhere else outside France for that matter. And what a novelty, this not-so-young young man from the provinces who didn't bother either to hide or to brag about his origins. It was only logical that Édouard's naturalness should seduce other children of his age, and fortunately New York was teeming with them. The expression on his face – enthusiastic but not delirious – and his painstaking English made him the talk of the town (with a little help from Tony's New York associate). Both men and women threw themselves at him and only his unvarying politeness and his poor English got him out of a wide variety of embraces. The star of his play, who had immediately settled herself in his arms two evenings in a row for publicity and then decided to stay there, was amazed to learn he wasn't a homosexual. He was just in love. And very faithful. When the word got around, Édouard's charm moved into the realms of eccentricity. The actress talked about her failure everywhere, as well as the reason for it, and the new Candide suddenly became the subject of numerous bets. The bet was won one drunken evening by a gorgeous starlet; or rather lost since, when Édouard woke up, miserable, furious, and with a raging migraine, all he could think about was getting back to his hotel and ringing Béatrice. *My God*, he said to himself as he pulled on his clothes, *What's the matter with me? Why was I so bored? It was a miracle I could manage it; it was like sleeping with a doll! And it's Béatrice's fault, she's alienated me from the whole human race!* In fact, Édouard was acting very much like a heroin addict to whom someone had slipped some hashish. Drunk on Béatrice, his body felt as if it had suddenly been forced to kick the habit, as if it had been expelled overnight from that zone of sensuality in which it had been bathing for a year. He must have been roaring drunk, or his body must have picked up some awfully tyrannical habits, for him to have paid no attention to his heart – for once a bit more clear-sighted than usual – while in bed. There was obviously no connection at all between the ridiculous pantomime he'd just performed on the fiftieth floor, and his devastating memories of other movements in a blue bedroom with its doors open wide on to a winter garden.

Surrounded on all sides, pushed, petted, and photographed, Édouard derived his only real moral support from the hotel's night porter, an elderly and melancholy Italian who would talk to him when he came back at night. The old man's gentleness and nostalgia, not to mention his fatalism, helped Édouard cope each morning with the terrifying energy and efficiency of his colleagues. Since the final dress rehearsal had been put off, he decided to do some sightseeing. He fled Manhattan proper and on his way out, discovered strange dirty areas packed with foreigners, then the suburbs and finally the port. Fascinated, he told Béatrice over the phone about all these incredible places, the bars, the lost little corners of the city that she'd never seen herself despite her frequent visits to New York.

Finally, however, the play opened to an ear-splitting fanfare. Later that same night, some critics shouted, 'ingenious' and others 'esoteric', but either way, Édouard was no longer an unknown quantity when he went back to the hotel at two in the morning. He couldn't have cared less, of course; all he dreamed of still was getting back to Béatrice. But he did feel a certain pride at finding himself not only intact and independent, but also heaped with laurels. And he knew too that once he'd placed these laurels at her feet, he'd forget all about them. Tony was the only one who would watch over them, to make sure they didn't wilt too quickly. He dodged a variety of vague but sensational offers that would have taken him to spectral cities like Los Angeles and San Francisco because, despite the fascination of New York, there was only one city he thought of as inhabited, and that was Paris. With the sound of triumph in his voice, he telephoned Béatrice to announce his return and spent the night before his departure eating dinner in a luxurious Italian restaurant with the old night porter.

'Édouard's coming back tomorrow,' Béatrice announced in a neutral voice.

Seated on the floor as usual, Nicolas didn't move at first; then he came to and looked at her.

'Is he pleased? According to the grapevine, everything seems to have gone very well.'

'Yes, he seems very pleased. Pleased to be coming back, in particular.'

Since their first slow dance, they'd had a sort of tacit agreement, and both had scrupulously avoided any mention of Édouard. Nicolas had come back to her flat the following morning, as if it were the most natural thing in the world, and since then they'd spent almost all their afternoons together, caressing and making love, or just talking like old friends. From time to time, they went out dancing, but with such style and bravado that no one imagined there was anything between them except friendship. People openly asked Béatrice for news of Édouard, as if he were her husband, and she replied just as openly. The expression of delight on Nicolas's face was more than enough to stop any suspicious comments.

'Are you going to tell him?' asked Nicolas.

'Are you out of your mind? What's the point of hurting him?' Nicolas turned back to the fire.

'You think it really would hurt him? I mean, is it really a question of hurt?'

'What do you mean?' Béatrice said curtly, her irritation quickly turning to anger. He may have been her oldest and best friend, but what gave him the right to interfere in what was literally the cornerstone of her whole existence? Yet, even in her anger, she wished she were more surprised by his question. Or more indignant.

'I told him once,' she went on. 'And believe me, he didn't take it terribly well.'

'He couldn't have taken it very well,' said Nicolas. 'He loves you. But I wonder whether he might not love you at least in part for just that reason?'

'You mean you wonder if he's not a bit of a masochist?'

'Not at all,' Nicolas replied. 'That'd be too simple. When things are going well, he's perfectly happy with you. But when things go badly ... well, he's still happy. I think Édouard feels alive only when he's afraid of losing everything.'

'Well, there's no risk of that,' said Béatrice coldly. 'I love him and he knows it.'

'I'm sure he does. Just as he knows you left him five years ago, and just as he knows you slept with someone else six months ago. And just as he knows you can lie when you want to.'

Béatrice stood up abruptly and went to sit a little further off in an armchair.

'I think you should try minding your own business, Nicolas. All this has nothing to do with you.'

She was instinctively avoiding the question. She felt she'd been backed up against a wall that hid some horrible truth, some troubling and sombre secret that didn't really interest her but that she knew was there.

'True,' said Nicolas, stretching. 'Quite true. But if he ever finds out about it – about us, that is – what do you suppose he'd do? Leave you? Beat you? Go out and sleep with someone himself? No, I don't think he'd do any of those things, do you?'

'I can't imagine how he'd ever find out,' Béatrice said finally.

'Oh, not through me, my sweet,' Nicolas smiled. 'And you know that. Now that I've discovered it, I find this rôle of interim lover perfectly charming. Really.'

He went over to her and put his arm around her shoulders. Forgetting her anger and fear, she leaned against him automatically. It *was* Nicolas, after all. He stroked her hair, then stepped back.

'I think I'll be off now,' he said. 'I doubt if you want me around today. Why don't you tidy up the flat and buy some flowers for the homecoming? Believe me, he's worth it.'

He waved his hand and went out quickly, leaving her open-mouthed. An instant later, however, it hit her with full force.

Édouard was really coming back! She'd see his brown eyes again, hear his voice, his laugh; everything would make sense and be marvellous once more. It struck her that she was going to be happy. *Me happy?* she said to herself. *What a ridiculous word!*

Béatrice had an instinctive lucidity and she'd always had nothing but contempt for the frenzy with which her era advertised everyone's obligatory desire for happiness. Until now, it had never mattered to her whether she was happy or not; all that mattered was being on stage, giving shape and content to the air around her. But the thought of Édouard's arrival forced her to admit that this frothy impatience she felt, this desire — all the keener since it was about to be satisfied — was indeed commonly known as happiness. It was impossible to start dissecting the word, or even to doubt its concept, just as it would be impossible for anyone to get over the shock if the word were to disappear from the language. She had told Édouard she loved him and it had been the truth. But now, thanks to his absence and the imminence of his return, she'd suddenly discovered this public meeting ground, this shining thing called happiness. She began to tremble at the thought of seeing him again, of holding him in her arms. It felt like some kind of second-rate novel. And it wasn't just physical desire that was making her tremble. Never, never had she waited for Nicolas this past week the way she was waiting today for Édouard. It wasn't the same kind of waiting, a distinction she sensed clearly even if neither her innate sensitivity nor her life in general had accustomed her to these sorts of subtleties. It seemed to her that with Nicolas, she'd been parallel, so to speak — parallel in the broadest sense of the term — but that now, thanks to the convention people referred to pompously as love, she was going to find herself once more caught, tangled up, and finally dissolved in Édouard.

She stretched out in bed happily. Tomorrow there would be a foot on hers, a weight across her body, a human being next to her all night long. He might be as cumbersome as he was reassuring, but she couldn't, and wouldn't, kick him out of her bed even if he did disturb those activities of sleeping and forgetting that were so vital to her equilibrium. The point was that she could for once stand the fact that Édouard represented discomfort; indeed, she even demanded that he do so.

Her happiness arrived at Roissy-Charles de Gaulle Airport on time, glowing and refreshed by the sharp New York wind and looking as if he'd just come back from the seaside. Unconsciously, he'd acquired that air of ease, well-being and success that America invariably seems to bestow on its visitors. After all, New York is not exactly famous for its subtleties; it isn't a city where you can play games with success or failure. Whichever it is, it is both fast and clear-cut and whether they are aware of it or not, even the most indifferent come out as stamped by the experience as their passports. It was obvious, however, that the brown-eyed young man in the tweed suit coming down the steps and rushing madly towards the exit had not been defeated. Whereas Béatrice, always pleased at her lovers' triumphs – for their success tended to confirm her own – was more than surprised at her disappointment. He disappointed her, this traveller who seemed in such a hurry and who was casually hailing porters, picking up his luggage, and not bothering with customs. She was too used to the childish and self-centred efficiency of the men she hadn't loved not to find this efficiency altogether vulgar and misplaced in the man she did. Although she hadn't admitted it to herself, she really had expected an immigrant without baggage or laurels to arrive in this futuristic airport, a hurt and childlike Édouard whom she could console. And so she was disappointed, even depressed, by the young and triumphant author she seemed to be taking home with her. Édouard opened his suitcases as soon as they arrived, and there were countless packages – for her, for Cathy, for Nicolas. (The name of the latter had no effect whatsoever on Béatrice, for, thanks to her notoriously selective memory, she'd half-forgotten their belated but delicious reunion. And so the look she gave a loquacious, dishevelled, but visibly pleased Édouard contained no shame, but instead was severe.)

She couldn't know, of course, that what made Édouard look so proud and happy was simply the fact that he'd been able to live through all that time without her, that he'd actually survived the cruel and meaningless trip, that he'd come home again. Instead, she interpreted his look of relief as so much self-satisfied vanity, assuming he'd got along perfectly well without her. *It's awful*, she said to herself with scandalous honesty for once. *After all I feared and imagined and suffered for this man, it's awful to find him so happy!* In fact, Béatrice wasn't far from feeling that taking the discreet and familiar Nicolas for a lover had been tantamount to remaining faithful. After all, this wasn't the first time such a thing had happened. No one knew about it and not only had it restored her general equilibrium, but it had also offered her a pleasant way to pass the time, without risks and particularly without daydreams – other than of Édouard. (One of the things she'd learned from her various escapades was that in love, the greatest treason was to imagine or dream about someone else. She knew – because he'd told her so – that Édouard had never dreamed or fantasized about anyone except her. And in any case, she'd spent too much real time on Nicolas to have had any left over for daydreaming.)

At first glance, then, Édouard and Béatrice had been equally treacherous during their two-week separation. Édouard had made love to a strange woman – an act that always left the door open for a real betrayal – and Béatrice had let herself slip into the arms of an old friend. (She was over thirty and at that age, old habits, particularly sensual ones, are every bit as attractive as new ones.) As far as their intentions were concerned, then, they were even. At least that's what Jolyet would have said, had he not been nourishing the green plants, insects, and other mysterious elements found in Parisian cemeteries for the past two months. Yet if this famous happiness everyone was so busy praising were a real criterion, and if the morality of an action did indeed derive from its success or failure, then Béatrice had definitely come out on top. Whichever way you looked at it, there was no comparison between an exasperated Édouard wandering down the corridors of an overheated skyscraper-hotel and a fully satisfied Béatrice watching a contented Nicolas take his leave. It wasn't fair, of course, but there was nothing to be done about it. Just as there had been nothing to be done five years earlier when a younger, charming, and sensitive Édouard was being tormented and rejected by a younger and beautiful Béatrice Valmont in the interests of the seductive fifty-year-old André Jolyet. (That was, after all, the rickety merry-go-round of life.)

Tony d'Albret, on the other hand, was infinitely reassured. Since advertising and publicity demanded that the reunion of her two clients be absolutely sensational and their liaison consolidated in some definitive way, she had made a point of ignoring Nicolas's constant presence in the blue room. Indeed, she was in the midst of preparing a celebration in Édouard's honour when a certain Bacillus K672 (unknown to the Chinese, feared by the Germans, and scorned by the Spanish) had had the effrontery to attack Béatrice. And so, barely resettled in Paris, Édouard found himself at his mistress's bedside.

She lay in an elegant chiaroscuro of varying shades of blue – her nightdress, the walls of the bedroom, the shadows under her eyes. She felt terrible. Édouard knew all too well that, where Béatrice was concerned, any illness or drop in tension was an outrage and he had no desire to confront this outrage with his own good health and his happiness at being back home. Given this insight, he spent the better part of his time lurking about the garden, the dining-room, the living-room, the kitchen, like some undesirable or criminal. Unfortunately, however, Béatrice interpreted these courtesies as evidence of his indifference. *A year ago he would have been beside me trembling, laden down with thermometers, bottles, doctors, books, chocolates,* she told herself. *It's obvious he doesn't love me anymore.*

The misunderstanding was mutual. He didn't want to disturb her, she thought he'd gone out. He whispered in the kitchen, she thought he was in a café bragging about his triumphs.

All this wandering malaise was totally beyond Cathy, and as their only intermediary, the best she could do was limit herself to whispering, 'Hush now' whenever one asked about the other. In the end, Édouard's uneasiness became contagious and to reassure herself as well as Béatrice, she said Édouard was fine whenever Béatrice asked for information. So Béatrice coughed harder and asked by what terrible error a man who was so devoted and so obviously made to be her bed-partner – as either lover or nurse – should disappear from sight? In spite of themselves, they finally reached the extremities of the absurd: in a ridiculous choreography, Édouard would take three steps into the bedroom, kiss Béatrice's hand, assure her of his passion in a neutral voice, and then rush out. While Béatrice, her imagination inflamed by *La Traviata*, which she listened to nonstop, ended up confusing Édouard with Armand Duval and herself with Violetta. All that kept her from feigning agony and prolonging her cough were her pride, her outrage, and her ambition – the last rekindled by the offer of a new part which for once seemed fascinating. Tony and Nicolas scurried backwards and forwards between the two, totally lost, understanding nothing of what was going on. And like a great ship off course, snagged in the seaweed above intolerable depths, Béatrice and Édouard's love began to flounder. *In the final analysis*, Édouard thought after a few days, *my coming home cramps her style. In the final analysis, he obviously didn't want to come back at all*, Béatrice thought with exasperation, and the very idea seemed to slow up her convalescence.

Her fever went at last, however, and one evening she asked for him. She was exhausted and depressed. It wasn't only the thousand chemical poisons running through her blood-stream, but also Édouard's absence, and the absence of love, that had sapped her strength. Unfortunately, Édouard, who was at the very limit of his anxiety and melancholy and who was terrified of disturbing her even through two walls, had decided to go out for the evening. When Cathy told her, Béatrice gave in to the first melodramatic gesture of her life. She got out of bed, picked up the old scratched opera record she'd found the day before, put it on, and despite the doctor's orders, added several brandies to her antibiotics. She saw her bed become a raft and watched as she floated away – feverish, her hair slicked down with sweat – towards a carpeted ocean she'd never known about before. She cried. She felt unloved; while Édouard sat at the corner café, wondering how he could get back to the bedroom and the smooth sleeping profile of his one true love without waking her up. And so it was that he stayed out all night and she didn't sleep a wink.

26

Settled in an armchair with his long legs respectfully crossed, Nicolas contemplated Béatrice. The fever had brought back her slender adolescent figure and given her a fragility that was in marked contrast to her usual look of the arrogant vamp. Buried in the blankets, Béatrice looked back at him, a blank look on her face.

'It's strange,' he said, trying desperately to cheer her up. 'I've never seen you like this before.'

'Like what?'

'I don't know exactly. Vulnerable, I suppose. Disarmed. Without your sword and chain mail.'

'You *have* seen me naked, you know,' she replied with a shrug.

'Which is precisely when you're the most thoroughly armed,' he shot back gallantly. 'And the most explicitly.'

'That's not true!' she cried, furious. 'I'm a very modest person. All sensual people are modest. They don't kiss in public and they don't cry either.'

'You can kiss me – or cry, if you want,' Nicolas laughed. 'We're all alone.'

She laughed back a little too loudly and lowered her head. When she raised it again, her eyes were filled with tears.

'Édouard doesn't love me any more,' she declared simply. 'I mean, not like before. That's why I feel so awful.'

'Ah, I see.'

Nicolas's little world had suddenly and unpleasantly been turned upside down. That Béatrice had feelings was already a lot to swallow, but that she should openly confess to failure was beyond him. At the same time, he was surprised at how concerned he felt, given how recently he'd wished that Édouard's reign would come to an end and he be the fortunate successor.

Béatrice's sudden surrender seemed even more terrifying because he didn't understand the reasons for it. What was happening to her? Was this unexpected weakness a sign of age? What an atrocious thought! Because if Béatrice was getting on, then so was he, and it wouldn't be long before he found himself driven to confront an antiquated image of himself, one that would be reflected not only in his mirror but in the looks of others – the image of the failed actor. No, there was no time to lose. He would have to pull out all the stops to prevent such an outrage, both for himself and for her. For they were tied together not only by mutual attraction, but by all their years of schemes and struggles, panic and pleasure. They'd been friends a long time.

'You're wrong,' he told her firmly. 'Édouard does love you. He's loved you for six years and he'll never change his mind. What could he possibly have said to you?'

'Nothing. That's just it. He hasn't said anything. Since he's been back, he talks only about America and Broadway and all his little deals. He just struts around ...'

'That's unfair,' Nicolas interrupted. 'Édouard's not a strutter. You have to remember he's never been sure of you. Except in bed, that is. And when he came back, you already had 'flu, didn't you? You were tired and grumpy.'

It was true that Béatrice found it both exhausting and inappropriate to make love when she was ill, but forgetting her beliefs – or perhaps remembering one of them – she blurted out:

'But all he had to do was rape me!'

Nicolas burst out laughing, while Béatrice, seeing she'd gone too far and disappointed at having lost her audience's concern, burst into tears.

That's twice in two weeks I've used tissues for something besides taking off my make-up, she thought. Nicolas, meanwhile, fought to keep a straight face, for the mere idea of Édouard attacking Béatrice for any reason whatsoever seemed the height of comedy.

'What does Tony think?' he asked.

'You know Tony doesn't think. She sees nothing and understands even less. Her brain's an adding machine. Édouard brings in so much, I bring in so much, and between the two of us, that's a lot. So we have to love each other, and we have to be happy. What a bitch,' she added, her voice suddenly returning to its naturally clear and ascerbic self. She blew her nose.

Relieved, Nicolas sighed. He'd known a fair number of unhappy women and they didn't exactly have a wide range of feelings to offer, only the most monotonous and elementary reflexes: desolation, doubt, and hope. Their feelings were painted in naïve primary colours beside which irony and reflection became so many stylized pastels.

Meanwhile Béatrice, for once sensitive to someone else's mood, saw Nicolas return to his usual gaiety and brightened up.

'Anyway, I'm fed up,' she declared. 'If it goes on like this, I'm going to show the creep the door and send him back to wherever he came from.'

That was sheer bravado and Nicolas knew it, but it obviously wasn't the moment to say so. So he took poor Édouard's defence while, a few feet away in the empty living-room, the defendant himself sat waiting to interrogate his old friend Nicolas on the subject of Béatrice's feelings.

'You'd be making a terrible mistake,' replied Nicolas, raising his hand. 'I read Édouard's play this summer and I can tell you it's the work of a sensitive and intelligent and tender soul. Now what's the matter?'

Until now, Béatrice had been only vaguely annoyed that Édouard had chosen Nicolas as a reader instead of her. But her eyes suddenly filled with tears. What more proof did she need of her impotence? What more proof that she meant nothing to Édouard beyond an exciting mistress or a seductive executioner? It wasn't self-pity, however. No, she was crying over the efforts she hadn't made, the cruelties she hadn't avoided, the solitude she hadn't known how to break through.

Nicolas sat in another armchair now, his legs stretched out in front of him. Édouard had intercepted him on his way out and was now sitting opposite him. Resigned and just a little put out, Nicolas suddenly crossed his legs and lit a cigarette.

How kind-hearted he was, he thought, to be sailing like some sweet Iago or gentle Oenone between two such complicated lovers. Listening to tales of woe, patting backs, and binding up wounds was not really his speciality. If he hadn't kept reminding himself that he'd spent the week before pushing Béatrice's consenting body backwards on to this very carpet at his feet, he might well have felt that irreparable damage was being done to his rôle as seducer. With a sort of listless good will, he took the glass Édouard held out, but when he raised his head he was struck by the pallor and the worried expression on his face. Regretfully, he put aside the theatrical aspects of the situation and admitted that he really did love these two morons a great deal and that they were probably his best – and only – friends.

Édouard's hair was too long, an infallible sign of depression. He was even sporting a fake hail-fellow-well-met smile that didn't suit him at all. *What a fool*, Nicolas thought again, tenderly. *What a complete and total fool*. But when he saw that fake and foolish grin, he thought better of it.

'So?' he began. 'How was America? Were you pleased?'

'Oh yes,' Édouard replied with a start. 'Yes, yes. It went off pretty well, you know. I mean, I think Tony's very pleased.'

'If Tony's pleased, then everybody's pleased.'

Béatrice's tears had completely confused him and a sort of nervous reaction had now set in; he felt a terrific desire to make jokes and it took a great effort to control himself.

'And you?' he went on. 'How were the women over there? Were they nice to you?'

To his great surprise, Édouard blushed. Nicolas was enchanted. He'd been to New York a few times himself, usually at the heels of some woman, and he remembered the ease with which he'd navigated more or less at will from cocktail party to bed and from bed to cocktail party. Poor Édouard must have played the Frenchman one drunken night and must now be kicking himself in shame and guilt.

'I don't know,' Édouard replied. 'It was a quick trip. Tell me, how do you find Béatrice?'

'Very well. Apart from her 'flu.'

'I have the feeling something happened while I was away,'

Édouard went on. 'Something or someone.' (For a moment, Nicolas lamented the fact that all so-called traditional rôles always wound up sounding like vulgar accusations, no matter who was playing the part of accuser.) 'She's not the same. I make her nervous, she can't stand having me around. I can't decide whether I came back too soon or too late. Did she say anything to you?'

He watched Nicolas anxiously, and Nicolas marvelled at the idea of this young, talented, devoted, and utterly transparent man begging him – the traitor – for an answer. Was it possible that Édouard was ageing less graciously than he? Surely he would never dream of doing callisthenics or keeping his distance where emotions were concerned or putting up a fight against the burden of passing time, as Nicolas himself had been doing for years. Perhaps the slender Édouard would be clumsy, bald, and bloated twenty years from now? Perhaps his physical charms would have disappeared, leaving room for that last unprofitable and contemptible one known as virtue? Except that no matter how old he was, whenever Édouard looked lovingly at a woman, she would feel she was really loved, and with no strings attached. And when people spoke of Édouard, they would say how passionately he'd been loved, whereas they would talk about what a likeable fellow Nicolas still was. And when she sat by the fire in the evening talking to someone about love, Béatrice would always see the same face emerging from the past – Édouard's face, and not Nicolas's.

'If I were you,' Nicolas said, suddenly resentful and getting to his feet, 'I wouldn't ask so many questions. I'd wait until Béatrice felt better and then I'd make love to her. And in the meantime, bring her some flowers, a box of chocolates and your manuscript.'

Édouard's voice stopped him at the door.

'But do you think ... I mean, are you sure she didn't sleep with anyone else?'

There was something in his tone, something so visibly akin to hope, that made Nicolas speechless. Suddenly he felt he had to defend Béatrice against some unknown and highly ambiguous danger.

'I have no idea,' he replied sharply, more as the protector of

a fierce proud woman than the friend of a sensitive young man.
'I certainly haven't heard anything.'

Then he turned round and left so as not to have his suspicions confirmed. Or have to see the transparent shadow of disappointment fall across the face of the ecstatic lover.

27

They lay next to each other, Édouard half on the rug, his head on Béatrice's shoulder. There was only one lamp lit in the blue bedroom, and it formed a big round halo of light, calm and peaceful like a sleeping animal, and warmed them. Édouard allowed himself to sink into his happiness. How could he have dreamed a year ago that he'd be here now, that Béatrice would still love him, that she would refuse to have anyone else around and would be content to stay just as she was, lying against him and not saying much. He thought how incredibly lucky they'd been, and he kissed her hand gently.

'You know,' she murmured, 'I'd like to read your play very much.'

Édouard smiled. Nicolas must have given her a talking-to, and now, despite her fever, she was ready to plunge into a text that bored her and that, by her own admission, she didn't understand. He'd never really said as much to himself but, although he suffered cruelly from Béatrice's coolness to literature, he never thought of reproaching her for it. He had two passions in life: literature and Béatrice, and he considered it normal, or rather healthy, that they did not mix. This state of affairs put neither his work nor his mistress at a disadvantage. He'd known from the beginning that they were two different worlds, and had never dreamed of a spiritual communion with Béatrice. His desire for her was blind and possessive; it was an obsession far removed from any idea of judgement.

'No,' he replied. 'You're not to tire yourself out reading. In the first place, it's not finished, and in the second, you know it would bore you.'

All he'd wanted to convey was that his text was obscure in parts. He hoped it was a poetic one, but felt it might not be suitable for a quick and earthy mind like hers. In other words, he was criticizing himself, but of course she didn't see that. She heard only condescension, even scorn.

'But Nicolas has read it,' she protested. 'I don't see that he's any better a judge than I am, and he told me it was superb.'

Nicolas's name completed the scenario already begun in Édouard's imagination. He was sure Nicolas had suggested the reading to her, since he'd just finished complaining to him about her indifference. He looked at her and was sincerely touched. His afternoon had been filled with doubt and depression but now, seeing her stretched out in the soft shadows of dusk and convalescence, he knew he was happy and that she had nothing to feel guilty about.

'That's true,' he replied cheerfully, already anxious to change the subject, to talk once more about his love for her. 'Nicolas did read it, but you know it was only by accident. Anyway, I've sent it out to be photocopied, but I'll have a copy for you in a week or so ... if you still want it.'

This was meant as proof of his tenderness, but, to Béatrice it sounded like nothing more than an excuse. She was deeply hurt and astonished at feeling so attacked. It was like being bitten by a thousand piranhas of humiliation and grief. The blue bedroom seemed to go grey; the truce had been all too brief. She knew she couldn't stand that sort of scorn for long. In fact, given her basically indestructible good health, she had already, despite her exhaustion, begun imagining what diabolical forms her revenge might take. Men were creatures of habit; they always suffered more than women when it came to a separation. It was time she remembered the old maxims. They might be banal, but they were accurate. Suddenly, however, she grew sentimental. After all, she did love him. She thought of the inevitable suffering this boy with the soft hair would go through, and she turned towards him and smiled. They looked at each other for a long time, wholly in tune with each other's feelings, yet as far apart as it was possible to imagine.

'What a charming picture! What an absolutely delicious picture!' a voice rang out.

It was Tony d'Albret, her handbag slung over her shoulder and hair plastered to her skull.

'I took the liberty of walking in since Cathy told me you were alone,' she declared.

'It's when people are alone,' replied Béatrice, 'that other people shouldn't barge in.'

'My poor darling,' murmured Tony. 'In your condition and with your fever ... I do hope you're being reasonable.'

Édouard laughed, bowed, and put his hand over his heart.

'But of course we are!' he replied gaily, much to Béatrice's consternation.

Tony looked at him. Here at least was a gentleman. Having already forgotten that, before his great success, Édouard had seemed hopelessly antiquated and old-fashioned, Tony was now delighted to find him so refined. Yes, he and Béatrice were definitely an extraordinary couple, a type of lover that had become remarkably rare since the war. She may have spent a year lamenting over how Édouard diminished Béatrice, but now she decided that in fact he complemented her.

'Ah, yes, Édouard,' she began funereally. 'One thing I do know and that's our Béatrice. How many years has it been? Fifteen? Twelve? I can't remember any more.'

'Six,' said Béatrice curtly.

'Perhaps, but I feel we've known each other all our lives. I remember the first time I saw her; it was at poor Jolyet's, and I said to myself right then, I said: Hard head but a good heart.'

The speech was obviously addressed to Édouard, who lowered his eyes while Béatrice yawned ostentatiously.

'For years I've watched her struggle,' Tony continued. 'I've watched her fight and work ...'

'Tell me,' Béatrice interrupted, 'haven't you had a few too many?'

Tony smiled fondly, then turned back wearily to Édouard.

'Well, do you want me to tell you, Édouard?'

'No, he doesn't. He doesn't want you to tell him anything. He just wants you to shut up.'

'Too bad. I'll tell him anyway. Édouard ... Béatrice is a faithful woman.'

The words were scarcely out of her mouth than you could almost see their pulses beating, the tension rising, and the billions of chemical, biological, and mental reflexes start racing through them. Neither knew why, but Tony's declaration rang with catastrophic reverberations. Happily, however, she'd already continued.

'I'm not just talking about friendship, of course. She's proved that already. No, I'm talking about love. You were away for two weeks, my dear, and with whom do you think we saw Béatrice all that time? With which single person during those whole two weeks? Why, with Nicolas, dear Édouard, with good old Nicolas.'

For an instant, Béatrice thought she was dreaming. If not, was it possible that for six whole years, she hadn't known that Tony had a sense of humour? One glance was enough, however; Tony, awash in port and the sound of her own voice, was obviously sincere.

'There they were every night, laughing together just like children. And when Béatrice began looking thoughtful – because of you, of course – Nicolas knew how to keep his mouth shut. What an exquisite person he is, that Nicolas.'

Édouard nodded. For once he agreed with her.

'I was a little nervous,' Tony admitted, delighted to have found a kindred soul at last. 'People can be so stupid and Béatrice so rash. I mean, she could have gone out with anyone, even some horror, like that poor Cyril, and everyone would have had a field day. But Nicolas, the faithful Nicolas; that shut them up in no time. It's so futile, really, all that viciousness.'

'Of course,' Édouard nodded. 'Of course.'

He was a little nonplussed. And a little disappointed. When he'd left Paris, he'd been resigned not to Béatrice's being unfaithful to him – that was something he couldn't even begin to think about without wanting to shoot himself – but to her taking advantage of his absence, after all the months of togetherness, to make sure her seductiveness was still in good working condition. As far as Nicolas was concerned, Édouard knew he'd been exposed to her seductiveness before, and escaped. So, he had to be immune. No, it was the Ginos he feared, the new blood. (He didn't remember how unprovocative that new and pretty girl in New York had seemed next to Béatrice.) Of course, he'd suffered the torments of hell during those five years in his solitary bed remembering certain gestures of hers, but he'd never imagined that those particular memories would be the most durable, nor that their persistence frequently forced even the most distracted lovers to fidelity.

Tony was already bored, however, unused as she was to praising virtue, and she soon reverted to her natural ferocity.

'So it seems the handsome womanized Nicolas is finally slowing down,' she said laughing. 'Maybe he did a lot of bed-hopping when he was twenty, but now when he gets into them, believe me it's to sleep.'

'Do you really think so?'

Béatrice's voice was soft and even, clearly the calm before the storm. She didn't really know why she'd said that, but she did know that none of this had anything to do with her love for Édouard, or with his jealousy or contempt. Those feelings were as natural to him as gossip was to Tony. Nor did it have anything to do with her. What she'd said had to do with something else altogether: with the fact that she'd slept with someone called Nicolas a week ago, that she'd enjoyed it immensely, and that she wasn't about to repudiate any of it. Most of the time, she felt a woman's obligation stopped there, but now she was obeying a sort of moral law that might have been considered bizarre, but that was fundamental with her. The law of recognition. It was intolerable that someone should talk about the muscular body and gentle hands and agile mouth of a man as devoted to his own pleasure as she was to hers, as if he were a puppet, or a eunuch. She may have entertained a lot of ridiculous ideas about sentimental love, but never about the physical. No, there was a debt of honour between a man and a woman if the debt had been contracted in bed. It didn't matter that she'd always paid her interest in cries, tears, and a rather savage reckoning of accounts. All she knew was that it was dishonourable to deny all those superb moments spent mouth to mouth, those urgent questions and obvious responses, that need they'd each felt for one another. And this was true even if that gaze and that mouth and that body were no longer desirable, even if her honouring that debt in her memory, her refusing to deny or disguise it, meant the worst punishment she could imagine – the loss of another body, another mouth, another gaze.

212

But this noble sentiment was so unfamiliar to Béatrice that she immediately began to minimize it. After all, perhaps it was less a question of honour than of precision. What right did these two pathetic creatures have to accuse Nicolas of impotence or candour or loyalty when they'd always known him to be a profligate and unscrupulous womanizer? She could feel her irritation mounting towards this muddle-headed intellectual lover she couldn't understand and the greedy agent who'd suddenly begun playing the fool. What right did they have to cast doubt on Nicolas's virility? Or on her own perversity? How could they know that in this world of stage sets and special effects and *trompes l'oeil*, these very things were the only real cries and talents at an actor's disposal; that is, if he had any sensuality left at all? They weren't like her, Édouard and Tony; they weren't actors. There was a different kind of blood in their veins.

'What? Do I think what?' Tony replied, startled. 'What do you mean? I don't think anything.'

'Yes, you do,' said Béatrice patiently. 'You just said so. You think Nicolas and I went out together for two weeks and that we reminisced about old times and that he left me every night at the front door, isn't that right?'

'Well, yes, I suppose so,' replied Tony, disconcerted and already refusing to imagine anything else.

'Well it's true, up to the part about the front door, which he opened for me every night, you see. But then he came inside with me and we went to bed together.'

There was a moment of silence while Tony and Édouard prayed to everything imaginable – to Béatrice herself, to God, to the heavens in general, to the thunderbolt of Zeus, or simply to an error in hearing – that what they'd just heard wasn't true. Tony's prayers were a bit more precise; she merely prayed that Béatrice simply hadn't said what she'd just said, for she knew that certain betrayals which seem so banal as long as they are kept secret become permanent and catastrophic once confessed. She looked at Édouard. Paralysed, he slowly turned an astonished face in her direction. Oddly enough, however, he seemed almost amused. Béatrice, on the other hand, was clearly exasperated. And so the woman Béatrice had never really known and had never particularly respected, the inflexible and blood-thirsty woman who always demanded the truth, the whole truth, and nothing but the truth, the woman who didn't really belong to the same race as herself, the 'other' Béatrice got to her feet and held forth.

'It was the day you left, Édouard,' she heard herself say in a strange and unfamiliar voice. 'I was depressed. We'd had lunch at *Lipp* and Nicolas brought me home. And as Cathy was on holiday, he helped me turn on the lights.'

She addressed herself only to him, in that distinct, distant, and rather worldly voice she hadn't used for ages. But Édouard recognized the voice, finally understood what she was saying, and believed her. The vision of their street on the day he'd left flashed through his mind. He saw what the weather had been like. He saw the familiar, bustling, and brightly-lit *brasserie*. And in devastating clarity, he saw the handsome Nicolas lying naked on top of another body, one he knew only too well. The imagine was so clear he panicked and flailing for help took Béatrice's hand, forgetting who she was.

'You're joking!' came Tony's plaintive nasal voice, as if from a great distance. 'Really, Béatrice, your humour is in very bad taste.'

But Béatrice sat immobile, a study in stark black and white. The room hadn't moved. Édouard half-rose to his feet, then sat down again and bent over slowly, as if executing a particularly difficult yoga posture. For once, Tony d'Albret felt herself definitely unwanted. She sat up, gathered up her handbag, which had spilled its contents all over the carpet, and got to her feet, red-faced, dishevelled, and ashamed. Before backing out silently, she flashed Béatrice a look of what she hoped was reproach, but Béatrice didn't notice. She was staring at the curve of the back, at the shoulder blades, the neck, and the fine soft hair of a man bent double by a pain she herself had deliberately inflicted. She listened to her heartbeat, marvelling at how slow and steady it was, and suddenly she yearned desperately to be alone, for ever.

Édouard was on his tenth bar, which was a lot for someone usually so sober. Alcohol made him garrulous, as well as sorry for himself, and if he'd been brought up differently, he would certainly have confided his tale of woe to the sympathetic barman who was pouring him this particular series of drinks – he'd lost track of how many a long time before. He would have talked about Béatrice, the woman he'd loved so passionately and for so long, and whom he still loved. The woman he'd trusted so unconditionally, and who had thrown herself into the arms of his best friend the minute he was out of sight. The woman who this very afternoon had pretended to be interested in his life and his play, but who was only following the hypocritical advice of her other lover. He knew the barman would take his side. All men would take his side, and all of them would condemn her. She should have known – after all, hadn't he? – that respect, trust, and fidelity were as necessary between two people who loved each other as physical attraction. He had thought it better to forget about this sort of thing, but now she'd forced him to remember. She'd proved beyond a shadow of a doubt that he'd been right from the beginning. Love consisted of sharing life the way you shared a loaf of bread. In no way did it demand that life be turned into a pendulum between caresses and whiplashes, into something that was inflicted, or had to be endured. Béatrice had taken advantage of his blindness. She'd camouflaged her weapons with great care. She'd even led him to believe they were too blunt to hurt a fly. And she'd told him she loved him. She'd tested his weaknesses very carefully before chopping him to pieces. And just because he'd confessed that he was sick with love for her, she'd been bent on destroying him from the start.

How could he have believed her? How could he have believed she loved him? Loved the ridiculous Édouard, the ridiculous lover, ridiculous successful author, ridiculous traveller, ridiculous friend! He saw his long dark-brown reflection in the mirror going fuzzy as the whisky took effect. She'd been right to prefer that clown, that bright amusing brilliant Nicolas. They must have had a good laugh while he was telephoning from the depths of his depression on the fiftieth floor. She must have loved forcing him into the puppet's rôle, the rôle he felt he'd always played and had even been resigned to playing opposite her and her *Tout-Paris* paid applauders. Oh how she must have loved insulting him! And loved seducing little Gino. How many other atrocities had she committed that he didn't know about? How many other foul deeds had she got away with because of his blindness and his all-consuming love – his, Édouard's, the little scribe from the provinces, the imbecile, the unloved?

But even now in this absurd bar, dense with the smoke of countless cigarettes, it never occurred to him to consider revenge, or to forget all about her. Or even to wait around cynically until she got old and frightened and came looking for him. All he thought of was getting out, fleeing to his native Dordogne, to the stone steps in front of his house, the noisy pigeons, the bad childhood poems, the single bed. Except that the minute his imagination got to this stage, it was the more immediate memories, and not those of his childhood, that twisted his heart. Instead of a narrow bed with two wooden panels on each side and a pair of shutters opened as far as the eye could see on to sweet-smelling fields, he saw an over-sized bed, a bed limitless and forever unmade sprawling on a blue carpet and cradled by the city's soot and pollution that blew in from a garden the size of a handkerchief. There was a woman on the bed with her hair loose and her eyes closed. She was begging softly for all sorts of unmentionable things. Once again he heard the well-worn music of an old opera and then, his head whirling, the woman crying out in pleasure at the precise moment he – a banal unknown fellow with dark-brown hair – was used to giving it to her. There were the same paintings on the wall, the same carpet, the same curtains, and there was the ever-unflustered Cathy excusing herself for not having thought to knock. And the same king-sized bathroom, and the man's bathrobe whose owner he'd never discovered and that had always seemed a good deal more solidly anchored on its hook than all its temporary, and future, occupants. There was Béatrice yawning, Béatrice curling up to sleep, Béatrice saying *tu*, calling imperiously for love, Béatrice acting, talking, lying, Béatrice everything ...

When he returned at dawn, unshaven, with rumpled clothes and a no less rumpled soul, there she was, lying on her stomach, one arm over her head in one of those deep brutal sleeps he'd seen her devastated by so often during the past year. He gazed at her profile, at the hand dangling from the side of the bed, at the long eyelids, and then lay down fully dressed next to her. It didn't occur to him to wake her. His fate – the fate of their love – was obviously beyond his control. In fact, it was as obvious as the happiness that flooded Béatrice when she woke up three hours later.

28

Édouard slept. He'd come back to ask for an explanation, to add to his misery, to beat her up or to forgive her. He'd come back with the firm intention of having it out, as lovers who've been betrayed are so fond of putting it. But whisky was treacherous, and he slept on. Béatrice watched him. He looked so different from when he was awake. He looked happy. She'd always been troubled by the sight of Édouard sleeping. The hungry, complicated, agitated man slept like a contented child. Even his dreams seemed happy, as happy as he seemed to be as he slid into them. He was so relaxed, stretched out like that with one hand over his heart, that his mind and body seemed in perfect harmony for once. She watched him grope for another body in the bed, then abandon the search and curl up again, a smile on his lips. It was like watching a sort of symbolical re-enactment of his entire life as a man. Whether awake or dreaming, he seemed so different from her other lovers who'd clenched their teeth or complained or cried out soundlessly with grimaces of horror on their faces. Édouard slept the sleep of the innocent. And he *was* innocent, which was what she loved. He must love her too, she thought, since he had come back. He'd thought it over, had understood that the episode with Nicolas had been a case of mountains out of molehills, and had forgiven her. She looked at him – haggard, unshaven and so trusting – and she wondered what perversity had made her mention Nicolas. Why she had felt she had to tell the truth to someone who couldn't stand it. But that was precisely why she loved him, wasn't it?

Humming softly to herself, she went into the next room where Édouard kept all his papers and where he'd slept when she was ill. *I must buy some new curtains*, she said to herself, *and a new carpet and some new furniture*, thinking how ironical it was that just when you decided to keep a lover permanently in your bed and bedroom, you always rushed to set up bachelor quarters for him where he'd be safe from your love. Whereas there were never any retreats or safe places for someone you no longer liked. The most he could do was retrace his steps (preferably at a gallop) down the short path that had led him in the first place from the front door to your bedroom. Édouard's blue notebook lay on the bedside table. She opened it, surprised at how neat and clean and carefully written it was. She thought she might just skim through the first few pages and then go and make herself a cup of coffee.

Two hours later she'd forgotten all about the coffee. And all about Édouard. She was waiting for Frédéric to come home. He had his strengths and his weaknesses, this Frédéric; in fact, he was a little like a faithful dog. But he didn't mince words. And neither did his women. They said ghastly and very amusing things to each other. Some of the passages were superb, and in others the starkness of the lines was very moving. Béatrice suddenly felt as if a new weight had been placed on her shoulders. It was heavy, yet somehow easy to bear, and she could neither ignore nor reject it. It was the weight of Édouard's talent. She'd read his other plays and knew he had talent, but he'd obviously made enormous progress. He'd tightened up the lines, purified the dialogue, slipped in some blood and tenderness. In short, he'd become a great playwright. And it had happened right beside her – and without her, since he'd never talked to her about it. It didn't matter, though; there was no room for wounded egos in the presence of this polished, or even unpolished, beauty. Far from feeling excluded, Béatrice sensed a certain fulfilment. The play had been written right beside her and, although she herself hadn't had anything to do with it, her cruelty and the warmth of her bed clearly had. She felt proud of his accomplishment, proud of herself, proud of both of them.

Édouard sprawled across the bed, still sound asleep. She put her hand on his forehead and he opened his eyes, then shut them immediately, surprised to find himself there and already worried that she'd be angry.

'You got in very late,' she said. 'Do you want some coffee?'

He remembered everything then, and the same wave of love and despair washed over him. He thought he'd lost it all – the blue walls, the french windows, the furniture, the modern painting, and the dark seductive woman in her Russian dressing gown. He'd seen all of them pass before him in the bar, and he would have liked to have seen all of them again, but in the past tense, like the heartbreaking memories they were. Even now they had a cruel and obscure beauty in the morning light. He caught hold of Béatrice, laid his head on her shoulder, and kissed her neck. He was sure he reeked of stale tobacco and despair. He remembered all the bars, all the strangers, the regrets, and his eyes stung. But Cathy was already bringing in the coffee and delivering her 'Bonjour' in the usual nasal voice. Somewhere the phone was ringing, and the whole universe was galvanizing itself to prove that it had all been a terrible nightmare. And so he surrendered to his happiness, took the coffeepot from Béatrice's hands, kissed her arms, her eyelashes, her breasts, her cheeks. He was the lost, delirious, and defenceless lover once again, the lover who had conquered Béatrice.

'You know,' she said, smoothing his hair. 'I read your play this morning, while you were sleeping.'

He flinched, as if expecting a blow, and she felt it.

'It's wonderful, you know,' she went on quickly. 'It's really wonderful. You're a great writer, Édouard.'

He raised his eyes to hers and knew she was telling the truth. Tears of triumph and exhaustion poured down his cheeks and they both knew then that whatever he might say, her rather barbarous and instinctive reaction was the only one that mattered to him. He loved her. This tender, complicated, dark-brown young man, this great sufferer who blossomed under her talents and secrets, this foolish, jealous and irresistible creature belonged to her. Leaning forward, she laid her head against his forehead and felt their tears mingling, as in some sentimental novel. They both cried softly, and when the forgotten and incongruous February sun entered the bedroom and bathed them in its pale light, she almost had to believe in God, in the human race, in the irrefutable logic of this rotating earth.

Édouard had opened his eyes and was basking in her scent, the feel of her skin, the miraculous ray of sunshine. It was for her he'd written the play, for her he'd created Frédéric and charged him to speak in his name. He'd done it secretly, of course, but in the very differences he'd established between the ages, characters, contexts, and ambitions of his heroes, he'd put all his respect for her. Nothing in the play really resembled Béatrice; there was nothing to enable her to identify with the heroine. He'd wanted to make her happy by the sheer force of his prose. He hadn't wanted any other point of reference save that of beauty, because she was perhaps the only one who could appreciate the discipline that decision had required, the sublime and maniacal obsessiveness he'd had to feel in order to maintain that objectivity. He'd hoped she would understand, but he'd never dreamed she would. Yet, given the tears and the eyes and the voice in front of him now, he had his proof and was overwhelmed with happiness. She loved him, understood him, admired him. He was sure of everything now – of her, of himself, and even of all the Nicolases to come. They'd been joined together by happy tears, the first they'd shared since those Béatrice had shed for Jolyet and he for her. They'd made each other suffer and they'd suffered because of it, and still, after a year, they could say 'I love you' with the same awe and terror. When he said it to her now, she merely replied 'Me, too,' in a small frightened voice. At the same instant, the sun vanished from the bedroom, clawing the carpet as it went. They watched it linger a moment on the window sill, sardonic and theatrical, as if delighted with the impudence of its brief appearance.

'Jonas could play Frédéric,' said Béatrice. 'And Zelda the heroine, don't you think?'

'It's funny,' he replied. 'I had them in mind from the very beginning.'

'They'd be marvellous,' she said.

They eyed each other warily. There was a new complicity now, as if they'd finally recognized the passion they shared for all the charms of the theatre, for the smell of polished wood, the rehearsals in darkness, the orchestration of the voices, the fear, the luck, the unconscious gracefulness of a look.

'But you?' he said. 'Would you do one of my plays?'

'If you could imagine me in one, yes. Of course I would.

Only . . .' She stopped suddenly, then straightened up. 'Only the day you take me apart and put me back together again for the public, like that woman in the play, it'll mean you don't love me any more.'

'So people don't write for those they love?' Édouard asked, smiling.

'Yes they do. They write to give them pleasure. But they don't describe them; they describe themselves in relation to them. You, for example, you're Frédéric.'

As Jolyet once pointed out, Édouard thought, *you don't love others; you only love your love for them. In the theatre, that is.*

She slid over next to him and kissed his prickly cheek.

'We must look like a licentious print again,' she said. 'You in your jacket and me in a nightdress. You look like a thug,' she added, in the voice she used for love.

The voice enveloped Édouard and thrust him against her. *Like a drunken sailor,* Béatrice thought, surprised and delighted by his unexpected savagery after the softness of their conversation. But she'd always had a thing about drunken sailors, especially this particular one. And when she cried 'Édouard!' before plunging into her ecstasy, she knew she'd be saying that name and no other her whole life long.

Afterwards, they rested side by side while the sounds from the city filled the bedroom, reminding them that it was the middle of the afternoon and that they were mad and exhausted and very pleased about both. They were incapable of getting up, incapable of leaving each other. Propped up on her elbow, Béatrice drew Édouard's face with her finger.

'And if I told you it wasn't true about Nicolas?' she asked pensively. 'If I told you for instance that I'd made it all up to make you jealous? What would you think?'

'I'd be disappointed,' Édouard replied calmly.

She made a movement of surprise and he smiled.

'I wouldn't have been disappointed if you'd stayed faithful. I'm not really a masochist, you know. At least not yet. But what would have disappointed me is that you'd hurt me deliberately, that you'd made me suffer all night for nothing. All night long, like an idiot, in all those bars.'

'Yes of course, that would have been awful,' she murmured ironically, but so low he didn't hear.

'It doesn't matter, though,' Édouard went on. 'Because I wouldn't have believed you. You don't have to invent things like that. It's not worth it. Your natural cruelty is quite enough.'

'But what if I hadn't slept with anyone else,' she asked, not without an effort. 'What if I didn't want to any more? If I'd changed?'

Édouard gave a small sad smile and without looking at her, placed a reassuring hand on her thigh.

'You'll never change,' he replied. 'Believe me, I know. But you mustn't worry about it. I love you just the way you are. In fact, I suppose it's because you're the way you are that I love you.'

Reassured, Béatrice knew she'd met her match, she who'd thought for a minute that she should, and could, change, even in her naïvety that she had changed. She laid her head on his shoulder. He was right: at her age, Béatrice Valmont the actress was definitely not about to change.

Nevertheless, a week later, Édouard seemed preoccupied and Béatrice decided to test her confused and cruel intuition about their relationship. When Édouard came back at eight o'clock, he found the door locked. There was a note saying: *Don't be angry. I just want to be alone tonight. See you tomorrow.* He spent the night in the café across the street, telephoning regularly and watching the front door. And because she truly loved him, Béatrice waited until seven in the morning before answering the grating jangle.

'What time is it?' she mumbled into the receiver. 'Hello? I've just woken up ...' and various other absurdities. She didn't dare tell him she'd spent the night counting the rings of the telephone and listening to him suffer.

He arrived fifteen minutes later, his arms filled with roses of every colour, real garden roses he'd found at the corner. He scattered them around the bedroom, then on the bed and across Béatrice who was pretending to stretch as if she were just emerging from a dream. *He doesn't look so distracted any more,* she thought as she watched him take off his clothes and listened to him whistling their old opera tune a little breathlessly.

And when she opened her eyes and saw herself in the mirror, a sombre and fatal woman surrounded by dead morning roses misted with dew, she couldn't help thinking that he was offering her not only a great love, but the most magnificent rôle of her career.